WHAT
REMAINS

BOOKS BY WENDY WALKER

All Is Not Forgotten

Emma in the Night

The Night Before

Don't Look for Me

Hold Your Breath

American Girl

What Remains

WHAT REMAINS

Wendy Walker

ORION

This edition first published in Great Britain in 2023 by Orion Fiction,
an imprint of The Orion Publishing Group Ltd.,
Carmelite House, 50 Victoria Embankment
London EC4Y 0DZ

A Hachette UK Company

A CIP catalogue record for this book
is available from the British Library.

ISBN (Paperback) 978 1 3987 1683 4
ISBN (eBook) 978 1 3987 1682 7

The Orion Publishing Group Ltd
Carmelite House
50 Victoria Embankment
London, EC4Y 0DZ

An Hachette UK company

Printed and bound in Great Britain by Clays Ltd, Elcograf S.p.A.

www.orionbooks.co.uk

To my late aunt, Arthea Kempf,
who found her greatest peace reading books.

CHAPTER ONE

I'm in the towel aisle at Nichols Depot when I hear the shots. Two *pops* followed by a chorus of screams.

I think the sounds might be distant, from outside the store. But this place is enormous, a vast warehouse of goods stacked floor to ceiling, wall to wall. The screams echo, then stop. Elevator music fills the void.

I stand frozen in these seconds, my eyes taking in several brands of towels in two dozen shades of pink. I'd pulled one from the middle shelf and brushed it against my cheek, wondering if it was soft enough for my girls. It's still pressed to the side of my face when the sounds come and go.

There is a place inside me that knows this is gunfire even as I think instead of balloons from Amy's ninth birthday party and then Fran jumping on a piece of Bubble Wrap and then the generator backfiring after the last power outage, which caused Mitch to haul it from the garage. None of those were followed by screams.

I don't move because fear has reached my body before conscious thought catches up. Racing heart. Shallow breath. Narrowed vision.

They come again, two shots.

Pop. Pop. Bright balls of color tied to folding chairs in the backyard as I carried a cake from the house. Corkscrew curls flying around the gleeful smile of a five-year-old in the kitchen. The smell of gasoline.

That is where my mind goes, and I feel a fleeting rush of warmth as I see the faces of my children and husband, even as I drop the towel to the floor and reach for my gun.

I am suddenly aware that, after twelve years in the department, this is the first time I have drawn my weapon in the outside world. My four years on active patrol had been quiet, and for the last eight, I've worked cold cases. It's difficult enough for me to face the anguish of the ones left behind, the loved ones of the missing and the dead. That has been my battlefield—balancing the empathy and the implications of horrific crime with an otherwise normal life. I had never sought the thrill of a chase or a crime unfolding before my eyes. And now, as a crime does unfold, I feel as much a civilian as anyone else in this store.

It is an old reflex, a relic from my training, that causes my hand to grip the handle, though it shakes through to my arm and down the back of my spine.

I am ill-equipped for what I now know for certain is happening. I was just here to get towels—soft pink towels for my daughters.

My partner, Rowan, is circling the parking lot because I said I wouldn't be long. Megastores unnerve me—the height of the shelves, the length of each aisle, the endless choices in every department from produce to video games to home goods. Towels. Pink towels. Two dozen shades. All of it wreaks havoc with my anxiety, which Rowan has had to endure these eight years. There are small things, like checking twice that we've locked the car, and bigger things, like never letting anything go—a piece of evidence, an unlikely suspect, a witness who lies. Things that are out of my control have no place to live inside my head, and Rowan gets that. He never complains. He has his own demons.

Mere moments ago we were driving back to the station after an interview when I spotted Nichols. My girls needed new towels, having worn the old ones down to bare threads. I saw the store and thought, *Yes, I'll get them.* I'd surprise everyone when I got home later. Fran would shriek with excitement. Amy would seem indifferent but be secretly pleased. Mitch would whisper something sweet in my ear—something like "Thanks, babe"—because I'd spared him the chore.

"*There's this thing called the internet—you can order stuff like towels there . . .*" Rowan had said. He knew what was really going on with me. The interview had been unsettling. A missing woman. A grieving husband and child. I was frustrated that we hadn't made progress on the case, the frustration leading to anger, the anger fueling my anxiety. I couldn't do a damned thing to help them, but I could face my fear of department stores to help my family. It was an absurd deflection, but he knew he couldn't stop me.

"*At least the wardens will be happy,*" he'd said. That was the term he used to tease my girls. They had names for him too. Their affection for him ran deep.

I'd gotten out, closed the door, watched the car pull away from the curb, then marched through the entrance. My phone had rung just after I found home goods. I'd turned on my earpiece and heard Rowan's voice.

"*Hey, can you get me some laundry detergent?*"

I'd answered with a sarcastic quip about "this thing called the internet."

He was distracting me, pulling me away from the sorrow of that family and then the sea of shelves and the thousands of things piled upon them. That's what happens when you spend every day with someone, thinking out loud about unsolved crimes and lingering tragedies. In between, you kill the time talking about other things. Your likes and dislikes. Your personality defects. They're impossible to hide, even as you construct boundaries that honor the relationship between the two of you and the ones at home.

I was the boring, married lady with the little girls, and he was the former Marine who wore a badge and carried a gun, all of which got him a date any night he wanted one. Anxiety led me down rabbit holes, while worries rolled off his back and into pints of beer. We were different in countless ways. But Rowan had become one of my own. Like kin.

I think now, as I scale the side of the aisle, gun drawn and clutched with both hands, that I want him to be here, pulling me behind him, taking the lead. Rowan is a soldier. Rowan has fired all kinds of weapons. He would give his life for mine, but I would give mine for his, so I swallow the need.

The screams that follow the second round of shots stop, their echoes bouncing off the walls and the sky-high ceiling before yielding to silence. I hear movement at the far end, the one that leads to a door with a sign: Employees Only. A young woman is on her hands and knees, her face taut, hair spilling over her eyes. She wears a brown-and-white uniform. She crawls across the floor, sees me, and stops, leaning back on her heels. She puts her hands in the air and whimpers. I realize then that I am in plain clothes. That I'm holding a gun. That it's pointed in her direction.

I release my left hand and pull the edge of my jacket away from my waist so she can see my ID, and she seems to understand. She slowly rises, pointing to the place where the gun fired and the screams echoed, and I nod. Then she swipes a keycard and opens the door.

I expect her to slip inside and lock it behind her, but she waits, waving to people I don't see until they emerge from hiding in the aisles on either side of mine. She waits for them to follow, leading them to safety. She waits until there are no more. Not one left behind.

I stare at the empty hallway as I make a move. The silence breaks with isolated cries. And then I hear the voice in my ear. It reaches so deep inside me I choke back tears.

"What's happening? Elise? Elise!"

I'd forgotten about the phone and the earpiece. Rowan is still out-side in the car.

Thank God, I think.

I should run. I should hide. But I don't. A switch has flipped, and the fear retreats. I think about the woman with the brown-and-white uniform, fighting her own terror to help strangers. I look back at the pink towel on the floor. The flashes of balloons and Bubble Wrap are gone. The faces of my girls, my babies, fade away. I'm not a mother. I'm not a wife. I'm not a sister or a friend. I'm not a partner.

I'm a cop, and I'm alone.

Rowan says we don't know what's inside us until we're tested. He said this after Mitch's affair four years ago. I'd gone to him for advice and comfort while we were fighting to save our marriage, and to confess what I'd done to gather enough evidence to believe it was happening.

He hadn't judged me for that, and he didn't persuade me one way or another. He said I would know what to do. That it would come from inside. This is a different test now. I am about to find out what else has been hiding in my heart and in my mind. Perhaps even in my soul.

"Elise!"

My vision is sharp and focused as I walk out of the aisle and down the hall toward the cries. I disregard the vacuum cleaners and toilet paper, the floor tiles and the faces of people—so many people frozen in place, crouched into little balls, trying to disappear—as I move through the vast space. I am again surrounded by human suffering, by people who will never be the same, even if they come out alive. But I can't think about this now.

Hearing honed, drowning out the elevator music, the heating vents blowing overhead, the whimpering, and yes, even the screaming. Listening only for the shots so they can guide me to the source. In the moments between them, I hear the beats of my heart and the whirring of my breath as my body settles in for the fight.

Rowan is in my ear. *"Don't move! I'm coming! Help is coming!"*

"Stay in the car," I whisper back.

He doesn't listen. I hear muffled sounds—his car door slamming shut, then the world outside, the vastness of the air reaching up to the sky, broken by human chaos and distant sirens and his feet racing across the concrete sidewalk. "*Clear the area!*" he yells to those who have made it out.

"I'm going to find the shooter," I tell him.

"Elise, no!"

At the end of home goods, the aisles open up to a large circular area with racks of clothing. A sign hangs from the ceiling on long silver chains: Men's Department. I take in the scene, then retreat to find cover in the last aisle. I close my eyes and bring the picture into sharper focus.

There was a man turned away from me, facing the entrance to a rectangular structure—the dressing room. Jeans. A gray hoodie. White sneakers. Long, stringy hair. A gun in his hands, aimed.

Someone else was moving, running toward that same structure. A woman in a dress. I think that her shape was round or maybe the dress was loose. I did not see her face.

And a second man, standing still. Exposed. Tall and thin, in khakis and a button-down shirt. His hands were in the air, as if surrendering or pleading for his life.

A new wave of fear unleashes. I feel the chemicals surge in my blood, and I draw a deep breath to make them settle. This is the part that can't be simulated in training. This is the part I'm not prepared for. I rely on knowledge, lines from a textbook, words from an instructor. It's not the same. Not even close.

The instinct returns. I could find my way outside through a back exit or fire door. I could get to safety. There is still time for flight. I've never been a fighter. Not like this. Not in combat.

I studied forensics because I was drawn to the order it created. The solving of mysteries and puzzles. I'd taught at the local college—classes on evidence and crime scenes. All of it pulled from past cases or hypothetical situations. Everything known or under my control. The survivors we encounter are not in danger. They suffer from their loss. Grief. Despair. Sorrow. They are not devoid of emotion, and that emotion torments me. But the terror has faded. Terror has a short shelf life.

Yet that is what electrifies the air. What races through every person in this store. That man standing, the next target, is paralyzed from it.

Run! The thought, the urge, is powerful.

And yet my body responds to a different call. To the tall man pleading for his life. To the others in the back of the store who might be next.

My head clears. My fingers close around my gun and release the safety.

"Elise, stop! Help is coming . . ."

The tall man sees me as I step out of the aisle and move quickly toward the suspect. His face changes with a wash of desperate hope, and the suspect turns his head. He's so young. Maybe twenty. His expression is calm, but his eyes grow wild when he realizes he's not the only one who is armed.

I call out. "Police officer! Drop your weapon!"

My hands are raised just below my chest. I peer over the end of the barrel, taking aim. The shaking is gone. My finger teases the trigger.

Then, suddenly, the tall man moves toward the dressing room, passing through the peripheral vision of the suspect, who turns his head back and then his torso. The gun is aimed and moves with him, and I think, *This is it . . . he's going to fire, he's going to kill that man . . .*

Suddenly, I know what's inside me—what has been revealed by these mere minutes, crashing over the order I've created, the family I've fought for and loved with every cell in my body.

I take aim at the back of his head, and I feel my finger squeeze, and God help me, I pull the trigger and watch him fall.

And my life is forever changed.

CHAPTER TWO

THE KILL ROOM

Thirty-six miles from Nichols Depot, a body is found.

The location is rural and has a large backcountry—thousands of acres of woodland in a state preservation. Over the years, the backcountry has been a place to find solitude for campers and people living off the grid. There are no public utilities. Spotty cell phone coverage. One trail weaves to a modest peak with a lookout, but it's hardly worth the effort for an experienced hiker.

In the 1970s a small group of hippies settled there. Aerial photos revealed several shelters scattered throughout the woods. Some were barely visible beneath the canopy of leaves. They were occasionally raided and cleared, but the occupants always returned a few at a time.

Complicating matters, the entire preserve is available to licensed hunters for two weeks during the fall to reduce the deer population, which would otherwise starve, die, or become a nuisance in the winter months. It is a problem that runs up and down the entire Eastern Seaboard—deer have no natural predators and an unnatural food supply in the lush gardens of its residents.

Local law enforcement from the surrounding towns asked the state to tear down what used to be the hippie shelters, but the hunters now use them to store their gear and seek refuge during heavy rainfalls. Some even camp there overnight if they've traveled far. The hunters who like to hunt and the wealthy residents who like their gardens outranked those enlisted to serve and protect.

And now there's a body.

Two hunters discover the remains. They'd stopped by the largest shelter to reload, take a piss. They knew not to leave their scent in the field. Some of the shelters have outhouses. Others just have areas where the hunters do their business, then cover it with garden lime. The serious hunters don't mess around. They know the rules; they have a code. They operate on an honor system, keeping their hands off other hunters' gear and guns, closing the doors, taking their shits correctly. They don't allow smoking of any kind. Smoke scares the game.

Three years back a man was murdered in this same shelter. Beaten and shot in the back of the head in the smaller of the two rooms inside— the one across from the stairs to the basement, the one where the hunters take their kill to clean and dress and do whatever it is they do to the dead animals.

The press dubbed it the Kill Room, and the name stuck. It was a big story then, the first one to draw attention to the backcountry and how it was being used by more than hunters and squatters and people wanting to disappear from the world.

Traces of drugs were found all over the place. The police dogs went crazy, even though it had been wiped clean. The dead guy was a lowlife dealer, wanted in New York City, just fifty miles away, for failure to appear on a possession charge. Two priors for assault and petty theft. Working his way up the ladder. Taking shortcuts that cost him his life.

The state agreed to put up game cameras, hiding them in trees and small boxes under thick brush. But they had no way to send a signal, no internet, so they recorded onto memory cards, which were collected and replaced, then analyzed. Not only did this attenuate the evidence from the criminal activity that was recorded, but once the cameras were found and the cards destroyed, so was the footage. And finding them was the first thing the squatters and dealers learned to do.

This particular shelter had a wood-burning stove in the main room to generate heat, and a well and hand pump providing access to water in the Kill Room. No plumbing for a toilet, but more amenities than the others that had just four walls of wood with flat rubber roofs.

It also had a large animal cremation oven in the basement, which had been the most lurid piece of information that circulated through the media when the body was found three years ago. No one could trace the oven to a buyer, but the hunters who were questioned back then all believed it had been installed by "some rich guy" who didn't like the idea of leaving a carcass to rot. The hunters could take whatever they wanted from the animals—meat, hides, etc.—and burn the rest. It operated on power from a generator outside the back door. Engineers opined that it had been installed during a renovation because there was "no way" it was carried down the narrow stairs.

The hunters who found the body heard the oven when they arrived at the shelter to gear up. It rumbles when it's burning, so they went down to the basement, turned it off, then left to kill things. As they settled into the spot they'd chosen for the task and waited and waited and waited for an animal to appear, it occurred to them that the oven being on was strange. Technically, the hunting season had ended two weeks ago, and even if a hunter had turned it on to burn a carcass, where had he gone? So when they returned, they raked it out. That's when they found the bones. The remains of a femur and pelvis. Some teeth that looked human. More were later found by the state forensics team.

Most people are unaware that bones survive cremation, even in a professional crematory. The bones are removed and put through a machine that grinds them down into dust so the family can have the entire body. Otherwise, they would have a pile of ash but also gruesome, charred chunks of their beloved.

It only takes a few hours to burn a body in this type of oven. First, soft tissue—skin, muscle, fat, tendons, internal organs, hair—is turned to ash. Everything but teeth and bone is destroyed. Second, it changes the chemical composition of the bone, causing it to shrink, contort, discolor. Bones become disfigured under extreme heat for extended periods. Third, it damages the DNA found inside the teeth and bone—sometimes completely, sometimes just enough to make it impossible to match in the CODIS database.

The science is constantly progressing. But without the DNA, the most common method of identifying a burned body is with dental records or other X-rays taken when the person was still alive. And that requires having a possible victim. It begins with a missing person and works backward.

The time of death, cause of death, and even gender of the victim cannot be ascertained with any reasonable degree of certainty from the bone fragments and teeth.

The state takes over the investigation from the local police, who were called to the scene by the hunters. The land is under their jurisdiction, and no one argues because anything having to do with the shelters will stir the pot of disquiet over tearing them down or leaving them up and the local chief is an elected official. *Good riddance.*

The state investigators begin with the most likely scenario—another drug deal gone wrong. They plan to work the case from two angles— missing persons and forensics around the shelter. Maybe the victim was killed inside or nearby. There will be blood, tire marks, footprints, fingerprints. Surely an abundance of evidence. They brace themselves for the work, which can be tedious and time consuming. They also have to contend with the falling leaves, which continue to alter the crime scene outside the shelter minute by minute.

They assume that the oven had been turned on to cremate this body and not a subsequent animal carcass because no animal remains are found among the ashes. They put the time of death inside forty-eight hours. The generator runs on gasoline. It is small and hand-filled and was near empty when the investigators arrived. Taking into account the burn rate of that particular generator and the energy required to run the oven, two days is the longest it could have been left running.

The forensics team begins their work both inside and outside the shelter. The investigators interview the hunters who found the body and prepare to follow up on any leads that develop.

A piece of clothing is discovered later that first day, hanging on a hook attached to the back of the door. The forensics team only notices it once they are assembled inside and the door is closed. The investigators ask the hunters, but it doesn't belong to either of them.

One of the men remarks that it wouldn't belong to any experienced hunter. They know to wear brown-and-green camouflage. Most use orange safety vests.

The jacket hanging on the back of the door is bright red, and he insists that no hunter would wear that in the field.

This is all the evidence they have on the first day: teeth, twisted bones, and a red jacket.

CHAPTER THREE

I wake slowly on the sofa in the small study downstairs, confused and disoriented. *How did I get here? When did I leave our bed?*

After Mitch's affair four years ago, I didn't sleep in our bed for two months. Even then, when we were through the worst of it, I would fall asleep beside Mitch but wind up here by morning. That lasted for another year.

Mitch is a contractor. He builds and renovates large houses for our wealthier neighbors. He works with the wives because they're more likely to be home all day. The affair had been brief but devastating. Fran was barely a year old. Amy just starting preschool. I'd been immersed in motherhood. Endless demands on my body and emotions in every possible way. Mitch's father had just passed, and he'd fallen into the arms of a woman who could give him what he needed. Time. Attention. Physical comfort. Her name is Briana. Mitch was renovating their kitchen.

I'd felt tired then. Even in our bed at night, there was work to be done. Emotions to either feel or sweep under the rug. Talking. Thinking. Negotiating. Fucking. And loving. That was the hardest thing. The most exhausting.

I was drawn to Mitch from the first time I saw him when I was still in grad school. He was on the construction crew building a new wing to the science building. It was physical. Chemical. Not just the way he looked, but the way he moved and carried himself. I walked past the site every morning and every afternoon. I watched him from the window in the lounge on the fifth floor. Months passed with this man in my thoughts, the possibility of who he might be and what it might feel like to be in his arms easing the unrest that was always stirring.

Mitch is an intelligent man, but I was surrounded by intelligent men in my classes. The attraction grew more from his physical presence and the calm that lived inside him and soothed everyone he folded into his life. His smile, his walk, the gentle touch of his hands, and the kindness of his words, which I came to know after a carefully planned "accidental" meeting. The crew took their lunch break whenever the food trucks arrived. It wasn't hard to be walking by one day, catch his eye, drop my bag. I knew he would get out of the line to help me gather my things. Maybe it was an absurdly banal scene from a formulaic rom-com, but it wasn't beneath me. I'd been desperate to meet him.

There is a look that passes between people destined to become lovers. It is indescribable. Raw, primal attraction in my case, fueled by many nights of intimate imaginings. I sometimes wonder if I was the sole cause of this look that passed between us and the conversation that followed and Mitch's request for my number. The date that came next and the ones after that and the first kiss, which was a runaway train and didn't end until we fell asleep wrapped in each other's arms.

He became home to me. The place where I could lay down my sword and shield and close my eyes, knowing I was safe. That didn't just disappear when he found solace with another woman. Something that integral to living, surviving, doesn't leave so easily. Yet the struggle between the places of the mind and body where love resides was brutal.

I feel tired now as I open my eyes and sit up. Sunlight pours in through the window, rousing conscious thought.

What comes at me first are moments from the night before. Walking from Rowan's car to the house. Leaning against Mitch for support. The girls racing into my arms. They'd been told only what was needed.

What was appropriate. The department shrink, Dr. Landyn, had talked Mitch through it on the phone.

Shower, change. Sit with the family for dinner. Rowan stayed for a bit, comforting Mitch more than me. Telling him everything they knew. There was a dark energy in the house. The relief that I left Nichols in one piece didn't last long. What came quickly on its heels was the knowledge that I had been in danger and a sense of foreboding about what it had done to me. Even Fran had been wary, watching me with caution to see who I was now.

I took one of the pills the hospital prescribed and chased it with a glass of wine until my brain shut down and my eyes closed. I had been settled in my bed, tucked beneath the covers. Mitch curled up behind me, telling me the things he was supposed to. That I was safe now. That it will be better in the morning, in the light of day. But some things should be left in the dark.

I feel a heavy breath in my chest. In and out, as though preparing me for these things that are also beginning to wake and swim to the surface. They're coming now, and they want to be seen.

They arrive like bursts of vibrant colors, exploding in my mind, bringing a wave of nausea.

A young man dead, lying on the ground twelve feet away. Blood pooling in a halo around his head. Then movement from the racks of clothing as the people who'd been hiding inside them slowly emerge. It was surreal at the time, how the clothing seemed to be coming alive. A pair of jeans. A bathrobe. A dress shirt. Some ran, screaming. Others stood, frozen, hand to mouth, eyes wide. Staring at the man and at me, also frozen, the gun still clutched in both hands.

A television hung on the wall outside the dressing room. Whatever had been on before had been interrupted by news coverage of the scene outside, the scene I could hear in the distance.

I don't know how long I watched it. Customers running from the store. Police, firefighters, paramedics scrambling to corral them before they could leave. A team was assembled and ready, and I wondered if any of them knew what I'd done.

Then Rowan's voice in my ear, calling my name. *"Elise!"*

"He's dead," I whispered back. "The shooter's dead."

The sickness in my gut grows as I struggle to recall each moment. There is no internal rule book for the behavior that follows in the aftermath of a trauma. Reason and common sense are the first things to disappear as the stages begin to cycle. I taught this in one of my classes. It's important to our work in law enforcement. Understanding what's happening inside the mind of a suspect or a witness, especially the victim, helps us get to the truth, even years later when a case remains unsolved. The first stage is shock and disbelief. Then confusion.

I went to the body and checked for a pulse. I held my hand to his neck long after I knew he was gone. Rowan said he heard me scream then—*"Come on! Come on!"*—as if I could will him back to life and spare myself what was sure to follow and what now pulses through me. A witness said that I laid my jacket over the body, covering his face. Another said that I bent down at his feet and straightened one of his legs that had twisted beneath him when he fell. I don't recall either of these things.

I picked up the semiautomatic weapon that lay beside the man. It had been altered in a way I didn't recognize so I didn't try to disarm it.

It was right then, in that moment, that the tall man began to consume my thoughts—as he does now, in the aftermath. I knew, even with the shock and disbelief, and the confusion that was setting in, that I had to find him—the last person in the line of fire before I killed the man who lay at my feet.

I walked into the dressing room like a zombie, someone said. Holding two guns. In a daze, a trance, another described. What I recall now is the ceiling lined with panels of fluorescent lights. The mustard yellow paint on the walls. The white doors swung open on their hinges. Clothing hung from hooks on the outside and littered the floor. A large rack leaned against the back wall, overloaded with items that had been tried on and rejected. I heard whimpering from behind the one door that remained closed—the last door at the end of the long, narrow room.

I took a step toward it but felt a hand on my shoulder, spinning me around, then a second hand, strong and firm. One of them moved to my face, pulling it upward until my eyes followed.

"Elise!" It was Rowan.

I did not fall into his arms. I did not rattle off the series of events that had just occurred. My mind was on the task at hand, the one closed door.

"There's a man," I told him. "He came in here."

Rowan took both guns from my hands and dislodged the ammunition cartridges. He asked me if I was hit because I was covered in blood from the shooter. He tried to reason with me to come outside. This man could wait. He was safe now, somewhere in the dressing room, and Rowan promised to go back and find him as soon as he took care of me.

The first responders reached us. Units came from miles away to assist, and I was handed off to a female officer I didn't recognize.

I knew the protocol. That part was clear in my mind. First, a medical check at the hospital. Then a meeting with a union rep. Then an interview at the station. They would draw blood, check for drugs and alcohol, anything that might have impaired my judgment. I'm a cop, and I'd killed a civilian.

The tall man is before me now as I sit up on the sofa. I can see him standing in the men's department, hands above his head. Trembling, pleading for his life. And then the move toward the dressing room. I search for the missing piece of the memory—the one I couldn't find yesterday and the one that haunts me this morning.

Was he still in the open when I fired? Or had he cleared the doorway to safety?

No one tells you about this part. How desperate you become to believe you were justified.

As the officer walked me through the departments—electronics, toys, school supplies—I searched for the tall man as we passed the survivors. A woman on the floor, her body engulfing a child, his one blue sneaker poking out from beneath her right thigh. A health-care worker comforting an old man in a wheelchair. A young employee speaking to a responder, trembling like a weed in a windstorm. Parents squeezed the life from their children, tears streaming, mouths gaping open with screams. Some of them loud like thunder, others silent, muted by the onslaught of emotions that strangled their voices.

Bodies were lying and sitting on the ground, paramedics tending to them. I could not tell which of them were physically injured and which were in shock, too afraid to move. I don't remember seeing blood beyond what was on my hands and clothing. And, of course, an army of responders now searched the store for other possible shooters or accomplices, corralling shoppers into clusters who were then wrangled outside for questioning.

We passed the bathroom, and I asked to go inside. There were ten stalls, with the same number of sinks on the other side, each with a mirror. I counted them twice, my mind desperate for a calming task.

I was not alone. Women washed their hands and the faces of their children, then dried off with wads of toilet paper because there were just two air dryers mounted on the walls. One woman ripped open a package of paper towels from her cart and offered it to the others. Crying, nervous laughter, heavy sighs as I found a stall, fell to my knees, and vomited into the bowl. The woman with the paper towels slid three sheets under the door, and I sat on the cold tile, leaned against the wall, and wiped my mouth. Two officers entered then, ordering everyone into a line. The cop assigned to me moved us past them, through the remaining aisles to the exit.

All of this I recall, but what followed starts to blur. The chaos outside, the hospital, the interview. It fast-forwards to the moment I was finally alone with Rowan. No one would tell me what they'd found. How many dead. How many wounded. There had been many shots fired, and yet somehow the urgency of the medics at the scene had not felt commensurate with mass casualties. No one would tell me about the tall man. What he said. What he remembered.

God, how it crashes down now. I close my eyes and cover my face with my hands but I can't stop it.

"How many?" I asked Rowan.

He took me by the arms, beaming. "None, Elise. No one was killed!"

I was confused, but only for a second. "But I heard the shots . . ."

Rowan told me that the shooter was firing as he marched through the store but didn't hit a single person. No one was dead; no one was wounded. "It's a fucking miracle," he said.

I was relieved—of course I was—but there was no escaping what I had to ask next. "Did he come there to die?"

He rambled on then, as he had to, about how it was a justified kill. The gun was semiautomatic with live rounds. "He wasn't shooting blanks. Even if he'd come there to draw fire upon himself, suicide by cop, he was still a danger. He was shooting that gun in a crowded store, Elise. And not at the ceiling."

Thoughts began to spin. Wild and frenzied. It didn't matter what the department would say. How they would cast me as a hero, redirect the narrative to the difficulty of handling that gun and the man's lack of training and how we got lucky, as a community, that he didn't hit a target. That's how it would play. But it was just a story without proof to back it up.

I asked Rowan who he was, this man I'd killed. I was desperate to learn that he was a hardened criminal. That he was a sociopath. That he was destined to be violent, to hurt people. That he was beyond rehabilitation. That he had, in fact, come to Nichols to kill people.

None of that was true.

Rowan hesitated but then told me. "His name is Clay Lucas," he began.

Reports came in all morning, on the news and internally. Each piece of information was more devastating than the one before it. The news carried anecdotes from friends of the family and former classmates of Clay and his siblings. Most of the facts came from the department's investigation.

Clay Lucas was twenty-two years old. He was five foot ten and weighed 172 pounds. Hazel eyes. Brown hair. His face was narrow and long with well-defined cheekbones and thin eyebrows. He had big ears, which his parents said had drawn some teasing in grade school.

They thought that was the cause of his antisocial behavior. It started in fifth grade. Kids can be brutal. The other signs started to appear when he was thirteen. Delusions, depression, mania. They didn't get an official

diagnosis until he was sixteen. Schizoaffective disorder—the hardest of
the four types of schizophrenia to diagnose. Clay presented with symp-
toms of a mood disorder, which made it even harder.

He had lived with his family until he ran away a few weeks ago.
Their house is located on the other side of our small city, close to the
downtown, which is really just a small cluster of office buildings and an
indoor mall. From there, streets lined with businesses and apartment
buildings fan out like the legs of a spider until they become hospitals
and churches and community centers, then strip malls and side roads
with modest houses like my own, and, finally, bigger houses with lawns
between them and wooded areas behind. I couldn't tell you where the
neighborhood lines are drawn, whether it's at the supermarket or the
Dunkin' Donuts. We are all part of the same community.

Nichols Depot is in one of the strip malls. The station we work at
is farther downtown. Beyond that, on the side that ends at the river, is
where they believe Clay found shelter when he ran away from home.
There's a bridge over the river, and beneath the bridge is a refuge for
drug dealers, sex workers, the homeless. An older woman living there
recognized Clay's picture early this morning. She couldn't recall how
long ago she'd seen him. Recent enough to remember his face.

He was in and out of hospitals. On and off different meds. The hospital costs overwhelmed the family. The behavior was impossible to live with.
The older brother moved out. The sister went away to college. His mother
is a nurse. When they couldn't afford help anymore, she worked nights. His
father is an electrician. He works days. They did their best to watch him.

The morning he disappeared, he beat his mother with a shovel, calling
her names for the devil—Gorgo, Loki, etc. She said he called out a different one with each strike. She was beaten unconscious, suffering broken
ribs and internal bleeding, requiring nearly ten days in the hospital.

Rowan knew only some of this yesterday, but the picture was formed
the second he told me the diagnosis. I cried, and Rowan held me as if
he could wring the anguish from my bones.

"It gets easier," he said.

Rowan had killed in combat. He'd fired thousands of rounds.

Soldiers died, but also civilians, even children. But I'm not a soldier. I haven't had to make life-and-death decisions over and over until callouses formed around the consequences. I had no protection from the pain that was only just beginning.

Alone now with these memories of the day before, I pull my hands from my face and open my eyes. A gust of cool air rushes in through an open window. It's the one with the ripped screen, and I think that I must have been the one to open it, but I never open that window because the bugs get in, and now I can't remember doing it or how I ended up on the sofa.

This is just the confusion, I tell myself. *The brain adjusting to what's happened.* I want it to stop. I don't want this to be real. But what I want slips right through my fingers.

Fran is the first to wake. She carries her baby blanket in one hand and her iPad in the other—the big and little girl pieces of her struggling to coexist.

"Good morning, my sweet," I tell her, wiping my eyes. She climbs onto the sofa and slips beneath the quilt, her body pressed into mine, and for a brief moment, I feel like myself. Like this is any other day.

Restlessness soon creeps in, and she sits up. She finds a cartoon streaming on her iPad and leans against me like I'm a part of her. Like we are just one body sneaking in a show before the day begins.

Amy and Mitch stir upstairs, and Fran runs off to get dressed.

"Are you coming?" she asks me because that's what we would normally do. The two early birds hearing the call and getting on with things.

I pull in a breath. My head spins, but I shake it off.

"Beat you up the stairs," I say. I move from the sofa and pretend to give chase. Her laughter steals the breath I've drawn because I can feel it now. I can feel the new version of myself finding her way around inside my body and my mind and the walls of this house.

Mitch doesn't go to work. He drives the girls to school to shield them from any kids who might know about the shooting and what I've done. We don't yet know how this will play out. While he's gone, Rowan comes by. We sit at the small table in the kitchen at the back of the house. He's brought me coffee and a blueberry scone from the place we always stop when we have a morning interview with a witness. The normalcy of this is unsettling. Nothing feels normal to me today.

"You never told me what happened after I left the dressing room," I say. "What you found in the last stall."

The back door opens, and Mitch is here now, returned from the drop-off. "What's happened?"

I hear his car keys slide across the kitchen counter. I don't have it in me to explain. I am laser focused on my partner and getting the answers I need. I take hold of Rowan's arms, one in each hand.

"Did you find the tall man?" I ask him. I've been drowning all morning, and the answer to this question is what might save me.

It was in my statement, how I saw him, how he was in the line of fire, how he tried to make it to the dressing room after he saw me and the shooter turned, and then turned back to him, his weapon still aimed.

"Was he there?"

"Yeah," Rowan says. "He was there."

I ask more because I need more. His name, at least. What he saw and did it match what I saw? Was he in the line of fire? Was his life in danger when I pulled the trigger? I can't see it anymore. The memory is blurred and contorted and I know it will never straighten out.

"Don't worry about that now," he tells me. He says the tall man left the dressing room while Rowan tended to a pregnant woman. The one I'd seen wearing the dress. The one whose shape was round. The man left before Rowan had a chance to speak with him.

"What man is this?" Mitch asks, standing over Rowan, looking at me.

Rowan answers. "There was a man in the line of fire when Elise took out the shooter. He was trying to find shelter in the dressing room."

Mitch is confused but he lets us continue.

"Did he give a statement?" I ask.

Rowan shifts his focus to Mitch, then back to me, and I guess the answer.

"We don't know," he says. "But they haven't finished going through the witness lists, or the surveillance footage from the store."

He tells Mitch how the man left the dressing room, then the men's department. How he must have been stopped at the entrance to the store, made to give a statement. How they would have him on the security footage, but they needed time to go over it all.

I rattle off questions which come across as accusations. How is it possible that this has not been done? Why is this man not a priority? He saw me fire my weapon. He saw me kill the shooter. I try to explain but neither of them understands my fixation.

"I need to know if I had to kill that boy."

Mitch reaches down and takes my face in the palm of his hand.

"What are you talking about? Of course you had to! You saved countless lives in that store. Over a hundred people were shopping at Nichols when it happened. Isn't that true?" He looks to Rowan, who nods as he puts together the fact that I haven't told Mitch more. That Clay Lucas may have come there to draw fire. To die at my hand.

I feel the fixation grab hold. This could give me the answer I need. Did I kill this young man to save the life of another? They've found bullets in the walls just past where the tall man stood, hands over his head, pleading. Clay Lucas had fired, but when? And where was his aim?

There is nothing to be done now, here in my kitchen. Rowan leaves and heads back to the office where he can help with the investigation. He promises to look for the tall man's statement himself. He promises to make this his priority. It will be all hands on deck. All hands—except for mine. The union rep negotiated two weeks of paid leave plus four sessions with Dr. Landyn before my return to active duty. We begin tomorrow.

Mitch sits at the table and reaches for my face. I want his touch to heal me, but I can't feel him.

There was a time when Mitch's touch reached every part of me. When it put my mind to rest. Set my body on fire. Filled my heart with contentment. I would take any of those. I would take something new, even something painful. I feel his skin on my skin, but it is nothing more than a physical sensation. I am a million miles away, running after the answer to my question about the tall man.

And it terrifies me.

CHAPTER FOUR

I was right to be worried.

Twelve days after the shooting, I'm in Dr. Landyn's office for the last of my mandated sessions. I'm careful with my words when I meet with him. Everything I say will be a factor in his decision to clear me for work tomorrow. And I need to work. I need distractions. I need to not be at home.

I haven't been myself. The woman who was content. Happy at times. Who felt moments of joy and love and irritation and amusement and tension and release—countless feelings every day. She was gone. The woman I have become in these two weeks feels nothing.

Thirty-two minutes are left on the clock.

"Tell me more about the gifts and flowers," he says. "And the commendation from the mayor yesterday. I saw it on the news. You looked—apprehensive."

Dr. Landyn is sharply focused. His notepad sits on his lap, the pen gripped in his hand, the hand that dangles off his knee, the leg that's crossed on top of the other. And he stares at me with concern. I have not been hiding well enough.

"No," I lie. "I wasn't apprehensive."

"And the gifts—are you still giving them away unopened? Not reading the notes on the flowers?"

Did I tell him that? *Stupid.* Small wrapped gifts and flowers had been arriving every single day since the shooting. I opened the note on the first bouquet. It read simply, *With gratitude to a true hero.*

I couldn't see those words again. I was not worthy of gratitude. This was not a cause for hanging a piece of metal around my neck at the town hall.

I drove the flowers to the hospital and the gifts to a local thrift store. I wanted to put the award in the basement, but Mitch had already set it on the mantel and given a speech to the girls about how their mother was a hero. I didn't have the heart to take it down and make them wonder why.

I think of something to tell Landyn.

"I was worried after what you told me in our first session," I say. "About being careful with the others from the shooting."

A spark of recognition lights up his face. "How so?"

"You said that sometimes people who come close to death transfer their feelings onto rescue workers. That they need a way of understanding why they survived."

He nods, so I continue, "You said they can sometimes believe the rescuer was destined to save them and that they were meant to be there."

Dr. Landyn draws a long breath and taps his pen on the notepad. "Okay," he says. "But opening a thank-you note is not the kind of interaction I was concerned about. I'm more interested in the possibility that you still have doubts about what you did and whether it had to be done, and if your ambivalence is what has made these gestures difficult to accept."

Yes, of course. This is his job—both to heal and study me. If I have doubts, I might hesitate next time. And that could be detrimental to others. Rowan, for one. What if he'd been in Nichols, standing beside me? What if I'd had the shot and hesitated? And the tall man? What about him? He might be dead.

The question still lingers and now, it seems, is destined to remain unanswered. There was no reason for this man to be the subject of an ongoing investigation. Many witnesses left the scene amid the chaos from media trucks, responders, and relatives who'd flooded the parking lot to search for their loved ones. I had pleaded with Rowan to look for the tall man for my own sanity, and despite his efforts, all he could find was one glimpse from the camera surveillance outside the store that showed him getting into a blue pickup truck and driving off. The plates were not visible.

"Elise?" Dr. Landyn waits for my response. He wants me to tell him that I've come to terms with my decision to kill a man.

"He was going to keep shooting," Dr. Landyn says. It's not the first time he's said this, and I imagine he's watching my expression and my movements to gauge my reaction. I remain perfectly still. "Every forensic report. Every psychological report. Every image captured on the security cameras. It all points to that conclusion. Clay Lucas was not going to stop shooting, and eventually he was going to hurt someone. The rounds they recovered were in the walls, not the ceiling. Witness accounts all say he was shooting to kill. It doesn't matter that he missed his targets before you shot him. And it doesn't matter where this other man was or what he was doing."

I manage a nod and nothing more because I can feel the heat build inside my head. It has become a separate entity—an unruly toddler that demands an answer and won't stop screaming until it gets one. It is unbearable to live with.

"I'm afraid you will never have what you want, Elise. And not just in this more significant life event. Uncertainty is inherent in the human experience."

Dr. Landyn is frustrated with me. I can hear it in his voice. Most of his patients can accept this degree of closure. Most of them live with this "inherent uncertainty" as they muddle through their "human experience."

Dr. Landyn and I have discussed my need for certainty. It has impacted my life for as long as I can remember. My marriage. My parenting. My career. I downplay just how much because they don't let people with these types of conditions on the force. He pries and probes to see what's there but finds nothing. There is no childhood trauma to indicate pathology, which disappoints him. That's an easy line to draw. Early childhood trauma, especially in the years before we have memories, can hardwire our brains for all kinds of emotional damage. The question had come the second after he detected the anxious brain that makes it hard for me to buy towels at Nichols, decide what to order at restaurants, and believe my husband when he tells me he's working late.

But my childhood was fine. Normal. My parents stayed together until they passed, two years apart. My mother first, and my father just after Amy was born. My brother lives in Boston, and we speak once a week. He's married with three children. There was nothing to see here. I was born this way. Genetics. Nature over nurture.

In our first session, Dr. Landyn homed in on my teaching. "I understand you created your own textbook for your class. That's unusual, isn't it?"

He was right. I had wanted to engage my students, not put them to sleep. Forensics was fascinating if you looked at it the way we did—thinking like a criminal who doesn't want to get caught. Thinking backward from the inception of a crime.

"It wasn't an actual textbook," I told him. "It was all online, anecdotes drawn from cases, written from the perspective of a criminal."

He nodded. "Right. What was it called again?"

"Leave No Trace—How to Plan the Perfect Murder."

"Can you give me an example?"

I gave him one from an actual case I worked with Rowan. A husband who claimed to have walked into his apartment and found his wife murdered. He was ruled out as a suspect because the bloody footprints in the stairwell were from a size eleven shoe and he wore size nine.

"When his alibi seemed shaky, we canvassed every shoe store in a twenty-mile radius looking for the purchase of a size eleven dress shoe with cash. Showed the picture of the husband. And, sure enough, he'd bought the bigger shoes to kill his wife so he could leave exculpatory evidence."

Landyn circled right back to my need for certainty. "That must have been very satisfying." He was a dog with a bone.

There was something soothing about this field. How every action left a mark. A hair. A fiber. A tire track. A fingerprint. How every crime had a criminal. Every missing person was somewhere, dead or alive. I work this job because it's where I belong. Rowan is here because it's where he needs to be after the PTSD set in.

We work cases that are more than a year old. It takes days, weeks sometimes, to organize the contents, read through the notes, and listen to the taped interviews. Some are so old they exist only in dusty boxes with nothing even logged into a computer. We run physical evidence through new databases—DNA, genetic tracing, even fingerprinting. We check back with witnesses, look into new leads, collect new samples—sometimes without a suspect even knowing. We've grabbed a wine glass from a restaurant table. Pulled a hair out of a vacuum bag we took from a garbage can. DNA is everywhere if you know where to look. Even in the bones buried in a grave. You have to burn a body to get rid of it for good.

It's slow, methodical work. But when it pays off, it feels like we've righted the universe.

I liked sharing this with my students. If there was even one person I reached who could understand the satisfaction, feel the passion for the work and maybe pursue it as a career, then it was worth it. I kept teaching until Fran was born, but even now I update the materials from my class with interesting cases I come across. The school has a portal where teachers can post things for students, past and present. I have no idea if anyone ever reads what I post, but I do it anyway. For them. And maybe for me.

Dr. Landyn presses on as the clock ticks down to the end of our relationship. "How are things at home? Do you have the support you need when you start back tomorrow?"

"They're good. Really good," I lie again. "I just want to get back to work. Back to normal."

I don't tell him about the sleep that won't come. Or how I sometimes stand in the kitchen and watch my family move through a morning, breakfast on the table, coffee in the pot, cupboards opening and closing. Or how I sit on the couch in the living room, a little girl on either side, both giggling at the TV, and how I find a way to laugh and give them each a squeeze or a kiss on the forehead but that I feel nothing as I do it. I don't tell him that I am chronically numb, head to toe, inside and out. Numb to my beautiful girls. Numb to my husband, so desperate to help me and safeguard our marriage, which may not be what we had before, but still worth keeping. A broken teacup glued back together. Fragile, but capable of holding water.

I don't tell him, but he still knows somehow.

"We talked about this," he says. "There is no 'back to normal' after a trauma. You can't escape it. No one can. You have to go through the stages and get to a *new* normal, which you will come to accept."

Fuck. I feel the emotions swell.

He looks at his notes from our first session. "Do you still feel lonely?"

I nod and breathe and get ahold of myself. "I'm trying to spend more time with people," I tell him.

He's not buying it.

"There is a kind of loneliness that is more painful than being alone," he says. "I think that's what you were describing—when you're with the people you love and they can't understand who you are now, what you think and feel. That kind of loneliness can seem hopeless."

"I feel that sometimes," I say. I can't get around this one. I'm not the same person I was before I killed a man. Mitch can't understand. Certainly not my children. Even Rowan—it's different for him. His "new normal" happened years ago.

"It's getting better," I assure him. Though it's not.

"Even with Mitch? It can be difficult for the spouse. They can't help you through this, and that makes them question the relationship and even how well they really know you. Because, you see, you are in many ways a different person."

I respond with a quip that feels like a premonition as it leaves my mouth. "Does anyone really know anyone else? We reveal what we choose, don't we? Even if the decisions are made moment to moment, subconsciously?"

Landyn smiles. "That may be true, and it's an interesting philosophical question. But I'd rather you focus on your relationship with Mitch. Talk to him, Elise. Fight in those moments to make a different choice and expose yourself—so he can come to know the ways this has changed you."

Dr. Landyn gives me homework. Things like sharing my feelings, even if I fear they'll disappoint people.

"We all need to be seen for who we are. That's what connects us."

I make promises, nod my head, find an expression that conveys optimism.

And by some miracle, the time ends, and I am officially cleared to resume my duties.

We stand. We shake hands. Dr. Landyn smiles, though I can feel his apprehension at releasing me into the world.

"Good luck, Elise. And come back anytime you need to talk. Anytime at all."

I thank him and leave.

I walk from his office out to the parking lot next door. He's in the building next to the police station, and I have my own space there.

I should go home. I should start dinner. I should take a nap. I should do laundry or organize the girls' closets. I should keep fighting to find my way back to the life that I loved and that I know I still love, to get out of this maze of rabbit holes I've taken myself into. I need to call out to that life, through the twisty tunnels, to come and take my hand and lead me there. I want it back. I want the feel of Amy in my arms and the smell of Fran's strawberry kisses and the comfort as I rest my cheek against my husband's strong shoulder, to reach beyond the surface and into my heart. I want the joy to return.

Fuck new normal. I want my life back.

Anguish grips my chest as I get to my car. A cry escapes after I close the door. The pain from being numb is indescribable. It's strange to be numb and still feel pain. To be numb and still cry. But numbness is not a feeling. It's a wall that holds them at bay. And all walls have their cracks.

I sit for a while, sobbing into my hands until I've exhausted myself. I open my eyes and stare at the sign marking my space that says Officer Sutton, and then I notice, on the far right, a flash of blue. It moves past me, then stops parallel to the row of cars in front of mine, facing away, toward the exit.

Something ignites as I turn fully to see it. The flash of blue. A blue pickup truck. I can see through the back window. I make out one figure. It appears to be a man in the driver's seat.

In the side mirror, I see a face and I swear I know it. I know that face. I've been seeing it in my mind for two weeks.

The truck moves toward the exit.

This can't be happening. But what if it is? What if it's him? My hot head, the unruly toddler, screams louder, *Don't let him leave!*

I wipe the tears from my eyes and back out of the space just as the truck pulls into the flow of traffic on the adjacent street. I swing around, move into drive.

Shit! Where is he going?

I step on the gas and follow the blue truck. I stay two cars behind, change lanes twice as we drive away from the station. The street narrows, winds through neighborhoods. The other cars turn off, so I stay as far behind as I can without losing sight of him.

I don't ask myself what he was doing at the station. I don't call Rowan or Mitch or anyone. I don't want them to stop me, and I know they would try.

I follow the tall man until we are miles from the station, on the outskirts of town. My hot head is suddenly cool and focused, holding at bay the instinct to turn around that churns in my gut and the alarm bells that sound in the distance.

CHAPTER FIVE

THE KILL ROOM

When the forensics team first arrives in the late afternoon, they drive an ATV through a clearing to the edge of a makeshift road. It is seven feet wide, give or take, and leads them on a thirty degree incline for a quarter mile until it abruptly stops. From there, they follow a short path through trees and brush to the large shelter where the body has been found.

The team of four travels by foot in their booties and plastic suits so they don't disrupt any evidence or leave any evidence from their clothing and shoe prints.

One of them notices the absence of any tire tracks beyond their own and the first team of investigators, even though interviews of local hunters revealed the use of the road by those who knew how to find it. Especially when they were bringing supplies for the two-week season. And, they assume, gasoline for the generator.

The clearing has low brush, packed leaves from last year, and new leaves that have just fallen. Some dirt and rocks. But no felled trees or branches that obstruct passage. There are multiple parallel lines in the dirt, and after further inspection, they determine that the entire road has been raked by something pulled from a vehicle. The lines are even and continuous, which would not be the case if the raking had been done by hand and with a smaller tool.

The game cameras are useless. The memory cards, which were last rotated three months before, have been removed, the cameras turned to face the ground. They do not assume this is connected to the body. Everyone who uses the shelters knows about the cameras—even the local teenagers who want their privacy. Spotting the cameras is no different than finding pieces of broken glass on the floor. Wait until dark and shine a flashlight.

Then, of course, there are chat rooms and social media posts that share information about the backcountry, the location of the shelters, the dates of the hunting season, the informal rules about storing guns and taking shits, and, also, where to find the cameras.

All of this is common knowledge, and it boggles the mind that the state hasn't bothered to upgrade the equipment or at least move the damn things so people would have a harder time finding them.

So there is no surveillance, and someone has raked away the tire tracks. All they find on the road are the two sets of footprints left by the hunters who discovered the body. They find this interesting and make a plan to investigate who might do this and how and why.

They find more footprints around the perimeter of the shelter, heading in and out of the woods. And inside, as would be expected. The season just ended two weeks ago. The hunters who found the body were technically in violation of the park rules. They shouldn't have been there. Regardless, all of the footprints are from boots. All of them men's sizes, from nine to twelve. Nothing distinguishing.

The main shelter has just one window facing the front. It opens with shutters and is wide enough to climb through, if need be, or to let in cool air at night during the summer months. It is shut and locked now.

There is no furniture, just benches that line the walls and racks for guns. There is no kitchen, no way to prepare food or store food. Where the kitchen might be is a counter about four feet tall and eight feet long with an overhang that allows for the storage of three barstools. A place to sit and have coffee or a beer or play cards. The small wood stove is nestled in the corner.

Beneath the counter is a gun mount. They find a rifle there and learn from one of the park rangers that a hunter from upstate leaves it during the off-season because his wife won't allow guns in their home. It is not visible except from the floor looking up.

The rifle has been wiped clean and becomes a possible murder weapon, assuming the person whose body has been found was shot. Murdered. They search for a bullet or casing and find nothing. The hunter who owns the rifle has an airtight alibi. He was at a work conference, a plane ride away.

There are prints all over the surfaces inside. Hundreds of them. Except on the latch to the front door, the gun and rack mounted under the counter, the countertop, the knob for the basement door—the list includes every surface someone might have touched had they come here to kill someone and burn a body. Someone tried, and maybe succeeded, to not leave their prints.

The red jacket is found hanging behind the door and sent to the lab for testing. There might be hairs, skin cells, and from those, DNA. It could belong to the victim. It could belong to the killer.

The smaller room across from the basement stairs is normally covered in plastic sheeting, according to the hunters. The plastic keeps the blood from soaking into the wood floor, though it has done a piss-poor job. The plastic sheeting is not there when the body is found, and the exposed floor is stained with blood—some of it is old and some of it is new—and there is so much of it that it's unlikely they'll find anything useful. There is a sink against the far wall and the hand pump for the water from the well. The sink, too, has a burnt orange color where the blood has been absorbed into the white porcelain.

They assume the killing took place here or outside, but either way it is likely the body was wrapped in the plastic sheeting that normally covers the floor of this room, the Kill Room, dragged down the basement stairs, shoved into the cremation oven, and burned. There were chemicals released from the plastic found inside the oven and no bloodstains on the inside walls, which would occur if a body was burned without first being exsanguinated—unless it was wrapped in plastic.

They consider their initial findings as they stand in the Kill Room.

The raked path—no evidence.

The footprints and fingerprints—too much evidence, except on the places likely involved in the killing or, if it wasn't a killing, the cremation.

The plastic pulled from the floor and burned—no evidence.

And the body—cremated.

Aside from the red jacket, which could be nothing or, possibly, the sole error in an otherwise well-executed crime, there is either no evidence or too much to be useful.

The report will note that the crime was "textbook." The best way to destroy evidence on a body was to burn it. And the best way to fuck with forensics was to leave them too much and too little.

Of course, they were far more eloquent than that.

CHAPTER SIX

I follow the blue truck for six miles. It stops on a back road near a wooded park. The leaves have turned but have yet to fall, so we are shielded from sight.

I shouldn't be here. I should have stopped before the traffic thinned out and the stores became houses and the houses became woods.

There is no plate on the truck. A temporary paper license is taped to the back of the window from inside the cab, but it's undecipherable from this far away. It could be newly registered. Or he could be evading detection without technically violating traffic laws.

This, too, should give me pause.

But I don't let it. Not the plates or why he was at the station and has kept driving when he appears to be heading nowhere. Surely he knows by now that a gray Subaru is following him.

I have tried to tell myself that this obsession is mixed up with the stages of trauma recovery. The pain and guilt that follow shock and confusion. The anger and bargaining that follow those.

The waters have been muddied by the role I played in the trauma. By the killing of Clay Lucas followed by flowers and gifts. The award at town hall. And the not knowing about the tall man and whether my shot saved his life.

The people I love watch me with dismay and frustration, so I've taken to hiding. I show them what they need to see. That I'm adjusting, moving through the stages at a steady clip. Marching toward acceptance.

I think about what Landyn said. The loneliness of not being seen. How I've gone numb from the pain of it and how the numbness causes more pain.

So I don't think about the license plates or the odd behavior of this man in the blue truck, luring me out of town. Instead, I steady my gut and get out of my car. This all has to stop, and maybe now it will. I feel dizzy with anticipation. With hope.

The man gets out to greet me. He's taller than I had guessed. Maybe six foot five. He wears a suit and tie like he's come from work. Dark hair. Handsome features. He's thin but not scrawny the way I remember him, though I already know my memories from that day can't be trusted.

He smiles and walks toward me. We meet by the bed of his truck, stopping a few feet apart.

The suit he wears is gray. Beneath it is a striped shirt and a yellow tie with red checks. He smells clean, of soap and deodorant as if he's just taken a shower. I am suddenly self-conscious in my jeans and sweatshirt. I lost track of the time after the girls went to school, reading the notes Rowan had dropped off on the case he'd been working alone. No breakfast. No shower. I flew out of the house for my appointment with Dr. Landyn without a minute to spare.

The tables have turned. Now I'm the one who's disheveled and shaking. He is the picture of confidence.

"Officer Sutton," he says. It's not a question. He knows who I am.

He holds out his hand. I take it, and he squeezes firmly. His palm is sweaty, or maybe it's mine. Either way there is something unnerved between us.

"Thank you for following me here. I wasn't sure if it was appropriate to meet in public. I didn't want to get you in any trouble."

I nod and look at my feet, which shuffle on the pavement. "No—it's okay. I . . ."

He senses my apprehension and charges in with an introduction. "I'm Wade Austin. Sorry, I should have started with that."

I get my shit together. Enough to ask more questions. "How did you find me? I mean, how did you know where I'd be?"

He looks away, embarrassed. "I work downtown. Not far from the police station. Shield Insurance?"

I shake my head. I've never heard of it.

"I've been driving by the station to look for your car. The spaces are marked, and yours has been empty since the . . . since that dreadful day. I don't know why I've been checking. I suppose I needed to know you were okay. There's been nothing in the papers beyond the award and all that. I thought if I saw a car in your space, then you were back at work, and all was well."

I stand perfectly still now as I listen. I continue to build the case for why I should be here. The reasoning to justify my impulsive behavior. What he says is not only rational, I tell myself, it feels honest and vulnerable and aligns with a normal psychological response.

"I've wanted to see you. To speak to you. But I didn't know if you would think it was strange. And then today—there it was. The car was in your space, so I waited. Hoping it was you."

I smile softly, though my mind is making calculations as to how odd this is or whether it is odd at all. I have nothing for a measure.

"Are you back at work, then? Investigating the shooting? The papers said you were on leave."

"No," I tell him. "I was just . . . doing some administrative things."

He seems relieved by this, but I don't know why.

I can't hold back one second longer. I need my answer. "You left the scene without giving a statement."

Wade reaches out and touches my arm. It startles me, but I don't pull away.

"I was in such a daze after it happened. I waited for a while outside, but there were so many people crying and yelling and the sirens—I just needed to get out there. I felt this powerful urge to get home and take a shower and be in silence, you know? To see if I could somehow slip back into the Wade Austin I was before I went into that horrible place to buy a new pair of pants."

Yes, I think. *That's exactly right. Shock and disbelief. Confusion.* We hadn't pursued him. There was no plea to the public through the media or otherwise. His statement was not important to the investigation because we had the gun and we had the suspect and we had me and what I saw. No one was questioning my actions. We also had the pregnant woman who ran into the dressing room—Vera Pratt.

"I can come in tomorrow," he offers. "I don't have much time today. I said I was meeting a client."

"I don't either," I tell him. I think about how I promised to meet the girls at the bus. This is my last day home with them before I go back to work.

"I just wanted to speak with you," he says. "I wanted to tell you that I'm so grateful to you and for what you did. I haven't been able to get it out of my mind. Every second that passed after I heard the first shots. They reminded me of balloons popping."

"Yes!" I say, leaning closer to him. "I thought that too! I thought about my daughter's birthday party last month. And Bubble Wrap and—"

"Cars backfiring!" he interrupts.

"Yes! We have a generator that does that as soon as we turn it off—"

"You need to clean the carburetor. Remind me the next time we meet and I'll explain."

The frenetic exchange gives way with this last comment. *The next time we meet . . .*

I ignore the thought that I need this to end. I need to go home and think about this man and his actions that to anyone else would appear bizarre. I am still vulnerable, cycling through the stages.

"I have questions about that day—"

"I'll give you my number." He sounds eager.

I hesitate as he motions to the phone in my hand. I pause, but then unlock the screen and enter his information.

"Try it now so I can capture yours."

I send him a text and hear his phone ping inside the truck.

"There!" he says.

He moves closer, this time squeezing my shoulder. There is an energy about him that feels electric, like a starstruck fan meeting a movie star. He's nervous and excited all at once.

I take a step back and cross my arms at my chest. I should leave. I have no weapon. We're miles from town. I don't know what to make of this. Of him. I wonder if any of us came out of that store unscathed and how our behavior has changed. He needed to meet me here on a secluded road. I sleep on the sofa, wander the house at night in a trance. I talk myself into believing there's nothing wrong.

He needed to see me. But I need something from him too.

"Please—I have to ask you a question." My heart beats faster, and I begin to think the energy is coming from me and not him.

"Anything," he replies.

My head is light as I stumble on the words. I think about Rowan and Mitch and Dr. Landyn telling me again and again that it doesn't matter. It shouldn't matter. I remain unpersuaded, and now I might, finally, know if I was justified in killing that young man.

"Did you see it?" I ask him. "Did you see him fall?"

Both of his hands reach for my face, and he holds it firmly at the jawline. "Oh no! Is this what's been bothering you? Why you haven't returned to work? Why you can't sleep?"

Fuck. How does he know that?

"Are you asking me if you really saved my life?" He stares into my eyes, his hands suddenly stronger as they press all the way to the back of my neck.

"Yes," I say. "That's what I'm asking. No one else was hit. But you . . . I thought you were in a direct line of fire and at close range . . ."

He releases my face and pulls my entire body into his. My forehead presses against his chest. I feel his hips beneath my rib cage. His arms are like metal bars behind my back, locking me to him.

"Of course you saved me," he says. "He had already fired, but the shot went right past me. Then you came out of nowhere. I saw you shoot and watched him go down. I hadn't reached the dressing room."

I swim in a sea of emotion, held captive by the body of this man but set free as well. A weight lifts from my heart as my legs buckle and I begin to cry, sob, in the arms of this stranger.

"Shhh," Wade whispers, stroking my hair. "There, there. It's all right. You're all right now."

I smell the soap, stronger now, and feel the warmth of his body. Intimacies coming from a total stranger. The alarm bells grow louder, but they are quickly muted by the relief that has rushed in.

He tells me then, in a soft, quiet voice, every detail of what happened. He describes the pieces I know, matching them second by second. "When he knew you were behind him, he turned and I saw him aim his gun at you, so I moved, hoping to draw his attention, and I did, didn't I? My eyes never left him. He saw me and turned back, and that's when you fired. I saw it. I saw the shot, but I kept moving into the dressing room to help the pregnant woman."

I begin to calm as the torment eases, and Wade Austin releases me. I take a deep breath, and he tells me he's sorry for not coming forward sooner. "I just assumed you knew. There were so many people there."

I explain how the others had found hiding places and how the cameras didn't cover the area where all of this happened. As we stand beside his truck, leaning against its side, I tell him I've been tormented.

I tell him the things I haven't told anyone because no one else has understood. I've had to be their hero. I've had to be rational and stable to return to work. I've had to be a mother and wife. Here, I don't have to be anything but what I am. What I've become.

"This is why I wanted to see you," he says. "I needed to know what that moment did to you because it changed me too. And no one wants to talk about it. I've tried to reach out to other people who were there, finding them through chat rooms and news reports. They all just want to put it behind them."

Wade looks into the woods across the road and grows reflective. "Every night I see it. I see that creature with dead eyes walking toward me like he had not a care in the world. I see the pregnant woman pushing past me, running for the dressing room. All those people climbing into the racks and hiding like cowards. I've been over it in my head, asking myself why I stood there, why I didn't run or try to hide. I like to believe it was an act of bravery. That something inside me was willing to draw the fire. That I was sacrificing myself so the others could live. It was instinct. Pure and simple. Just like it was for you. Knowing when to shoot. Knowing it was the last chance. I saved their lives by offering my own, but then you saved mine."

I picture the scene, the parts I can remember. His hands in the air. The desperate hope that washed over his face when he saw me. And then he tried to escape. He moved toward the dressing room. But he remembers this part differently. He believes he was trying to draw Clay Lucas's attention away from me. I say nothing. I don't challenge his recollection. The way he's reconstructed his actions. I don't judge him for creating a story he can live with.

I remind myself that every memory from that day is subject to scrutiny—especially my own.

"That day," he says, and now I see the red streaks on his skin and the tears welling in his eyes. "That day changed me the way it changed you. And all these feelings, they don't just stop, do they? But there's no place to put them."

We talk for a long time. Close to an hour. It passes by in an instant. I tell him about the crime that goes on under the bridge where Clay Lucas had taken refuge. How it's likely that's where he got his hands on the gun. How he was having delusions about the devil. I tell him how pervasive the problem is—drugs and guns—how the dealers come from New York. How one of them was even murdered in the town north of ours, a state reserve with hunting shelters, one that had a Kill Room—that's what they call it now.

"We weren't people to him. We were demons or zombies, evil creatures he needed to rid from the world." This is the narrative that comes together now that I have found Wade Austin, the tall man. Now that I have my answer. Clay Lucas did come to that store to kill. And he would have killed Wade had I not stopped him. I am set free, lost in the euphoria.

We talk about who's to blame. And who should be punished. Clay Lucas was dead, but he wasn't the only one responsible. The dealers under the bridge. The medical system that failed him. The conversation weaves and spins around crime and criminals. He tells me he found my course materials online when he was trying to learn more about me. He tells me how clever it was, thinking about evidence like a criminal planning a crime. "Why did you stop teaching?" He asks questions that dig deeper into my life, but they feel natural as the conversation progresses. Or maybe I'm just high as a fucking kite from what he's given me.

I talk about my children, and he asks how old they are, and then about my husband and is he a cop, and then how long have we been married, and he almost got married but had his heart broken, and I tell him I'm sorry, and we talk about how hard life can be. Relationships. Marriage. And then the alarm bells return, and I start to sober up. He senses this the second it begins and returns to the reason I'm standing here with him in the first place.

"I can't believe you doubted yourself," he says as we wind our way back to the shooting. "I feel terrible. My God, what you've been living with." He shakes his head with sincerity.

"You couldn't have known."

Silence creeps in. It's subtle, the shift, and I sense he has more places to lead us, but this has been enough for one day. I am spent. This degree of emotional outpouring can't be sustained for long.

"Well," I say, moving away from the side of his truck. "Thank you for this. All of it. I would have carried this with me forever. It will help close the case if you could come in tomorrow—give a formal statement."

He mirrors my actions, standing now, taking a step closer. "No—thank you. For saving my life." He leans toward me and kisses my cheek. And then he says, "With gratitude to a true hero."

I gasp in a breath and freeze.

I know these words. They are the exact words from the first bouquet of flowers that appeared on my doorstep. Then came more flowers and gifts, every day since the shooting. I didn't read the other notes. I didn't open the gifts. I wonder, but then he tells me.

"They were from me. I didn't sign my name because you wouldn't know who Wade Austin was. But I knew you would understand, you would know who'd sent them."

I can't speak now. I try to hold a steady expression—one that won't alarm him. My head spins. I don't know what this is, but it's not what I thought. Suddenly, I'm that girl who went home with a guy she met at a party. That kid who took a ride from a stranger.

I have to get out of here.

"I should go," I tell him. "I have to be home for my girls."

I turn and walk back toward my car. Wade follows. He stops me just as I get to the driver's side. "When can I see you again, Elise?" he asks. He grabs me by both arms, his strong hands closing around them, holding me against the car.

The fear is full-on now. I try to think, to focus through the panic that surges. "Come to the station tomorrow. I'll be there."

He looks surprised, then disappointed, then something else—angry, perhaps. "So you are working the case. You lied before . . ."

"No—I didn't lie. Tomorrow is my first day. I've been on leave . . ."

His eyes narrow, and his mouth gapes open, like he's just made a disturbing discovery. "You know what happened—don't you?" he asks. "You've been pretending this whole time."

I try to relax my face, my body. "Wade," I say with a smile. "I don't know anything except what you've told me just now. I haven't been working the case."

He takes a moment to study me, and he knows I'm scared. He's good at this. Reading people.

"What have they said about me?" he asks.

Now I study him, but I have no idea what's happening. "Who?"

"The others."

"No one's told me anything about you. I've been on leave. No one even knows who you are."

"You're a liar." His hands dig into my flesh. He waits for an answer to a question I don't understand.

My heart is in my throat as I pull out more words. "I promise—no one has said anything . . . Let's talk more tomorrow. I really need to meet the school bus."

He's turned on a dime. Some delusion he had about me has left him. He can sense my apprehension, my fear, and he doesn't like it.

Fuck. What have I done?

This is how people get themselves killed.

"You're a liar," he says. "You don't want to see me again. You think I'm a coward, don't you? Everything that just happened was bullshit!" He spins me around, slamming me into the door, my hip bones the first to strike against the metal.

I say nothing more. I don't want to provoke him further.

"Do you know what I could do to you right now?" He pulls me away, then slams me back into the car, his face next to mine. His breath on my cheek. "We were meant to be in that store together. It's not a coincidence. I thought you understood that. I thought that's why you followed me out here . . ." His words echo Dr. Landyn's warnings.

I let my body relax into his hold because I know I can't get out of it. My training in hand-to-hand combat is rusty, but I remember enough to realize that he's already taken the advantage. I need to wait for an opening. I feel it will come, that he will let me go. His anger is big, too big to be satisfied by this one moment.

His body presses into me. His chest against my back. His stomach against my twisted arm. His thighs against the flesh of my ass. His face rests against my face, and I feel his breath on my skin.

"But you will, Elise," he says as he pushes into the sides of my neck with his forearms, cutting off the supply of blood. "You will see that we have to be together."

I cling to his words—if I will see something after today, then today is not the day I will die. He's not going to kill me. Everything fades to black.

When I come to, he's gone. I'm in the driver's seat of my car. The door is closed.

He's placed me here. Carefully.

A bouquet of flowers in my lap.

CHAPTER SEVEN

I pull into our driveway moments before the bus. I open the front door and toss my purse inside. I leave the door open as I usually do when I've been home and walk to the mailbox. I stand there as if I've been waiting a while, sifting through the junk mail and bills until I hear the squeaky wheels pulling to a stop three houses down.

My body aches, and this isn't even the start of it. This is before the adrenaline wears off. This is before the shock subsides. Other than this dull ache, I don't let myself feel anything as I move through these tasks. Not one single thing.

I check my phone to make sure I haven't missed a call or message. A forensics team has gone to the road where I've just been assaulted. They've been over my car and my body. A woman from the unit took swabs and photos and asked questions. I was grateful for her discretion—and to have this done at the scene so I could get home to meet the bus—but it felt like a second violation just the same. After the assault.

It was surreal to have that word, *assault*, in my head. To hear Rowan say it out loud.

He wanted me to go to the hospital or the station, but I needed to be here to meet the bus. Mitch was an hour away on a job. These were my children. My babies.

"You've been assaulted, Elise."

That's what he'd said, trying to convince me to let a squad car meet the girls. But I needed to be here. I needed to make it through this afternoon. I couldn't let Wade Austin take that from me. I was the one who'd followed him to that secluded road. I was the one who'd been lured in, who'd ignored the signs. He knew I didn't sleep. He knew where I parked my car. He knew where I lived. I ignored everything for the greater need of easing my conscience.

I was a fucking idiot, and my children were not going to pay the price.

Rowan said he was going to Shield Insurance with a unit to find Wade Austin. A second unit, an unmarked detail, is parked on my street in case he tries to come after me here. He's been coming every day for two weeks, delivering flowers and gifts, unnoticed. Undetected.

I shake it off. I can't think about that now.

I watch five kids climb out of the bus and smile, waving to a mother, a father, a nanny, an older sister as they wait at the stop or the end of their driveways. We don't let our children walk alone, even a hundred feet from the bus to our homes. These are the times we live in, and no one gives it a thought.

Fran bounds down the steps, and I choke back the emotions that are breaking rank. Her hair flies every which way, unruly and wild, just like her spirit. Amy is right behind her, poised and groomed. She straightens her skirt after reaching the sidewalk, worried it wrinkled as she descended.

They fold into me, Fran squeezing with all her might. Amy is more tentative, leaning in just enough for me to give her a quick pat on the back.

"How was school?" I ask.

We walk up levels of flagstone to reach the front door, and they answer with words I don't hear. Still, I manage to say things like "That's great, honey," and hope they don't notice my distraction.

They drop their backpacks, kick off their shoes in the front hall, and follow me into the kitchen. It's still warm for late September, so there are no coats to hang.

"Why is it so dark in here?" Amy notices first.

I haven't been inside to turn on the lights. I say something they believe about it being good for the environment as we walk to the kitchen.

But then, "Where's the snack?" Fran asks.

Every day since I've been on leave, I've had something homemade waiting. Apple cake. Banana bread. Cookies if it's Friday. I have overcompensated for my negligent emotions. For pretending to feel when I've been numb to my precious girls, and the husband who's been so patient with me as I leave our bed every night to be alone on the sofa.

"I've been super busy," I tell them.

They sit at the small oval table in the kitchen, and I heat up something I made yesterday, smother it with butter, and serve it with cold milk. I sit with them and watch them eat and then feel their eyes lift and fall upon me. And I know that they know.

"Mommy?" Fran has stopped eating. She looks at me and then Amy.

Now Amy is looking at me as well. "Mom?"

I smile as wide as I can, and this causes the muscles of my face to move, and I realize tears are falling. I can't believe there are any left.

Maybe they've been waiting for this moment. Maybe I haven't pretended as well as I've thought. Kids are instinctive creatures. They have to be because grown-ups are always hiding and lying.

Santa Claus. The Easter Bunny. Grandma is in heaven, looking down on us. Grandpa is too. They are together. We lie and lie and lie.

We tell them we're just getting dressed when we lock our bedroom door. We tell them we're fine after they hear us yelling in the kitchen. Sometimes about other people. One of Mitch's clients. One of my cases. Sometimes about the past. Her name still rings in my ear. *Briana.*

On and on. We lie to protect them. We lie to protect ourselves.

"What's wrong?" Amy asks.

I construct a new lie. "I was just thinking that this is our last afternoon together. I'm going back to work tomorrow, remember?"

Fran climbs on my lap, nuzzles her face into my neck, and strokes my hair. And then they both rattle things off to comfort me, about how they do remember because I told them last night and Daddy told them again this morning, and I shouldn't be sad because they like Kelly, our sitter, and maybe I can make the snack in the morning and save it for the afternoon and I can still see them all weekend.

They tell me they love me.

They tell me they're proud to have a mom who has such a cool job.

They tell me if I didn't have my job, I wouldn't have been able to save all the people in that store. They are too young to know the truth about that day or what just happened to me on that back road. How the one thing led to the other thing, and now I have gone from being numb to feeling enough to cry.

I squeeze Fran and gaze across the table at Amy, and the pain rises and rises beyond the clouds, and then something breaks loose. It comes barreling down from the heavens to this kitchen table, to my children, my loves, and crashes and explodes and the wall breaks into a million pieces.

"I love you," I say. But I don't just say it. I feel it. For the first time since the numbness crept in, I feel my love for them.

And with the love comes something else. A different pain. In my arms, where large hands held me against my car. And around my neck, where they cut off the supply of blood to my brain. And on my hip bones, where they slammed into the side of my car.

It won't be long before the swelling comes, the bruising.

Whatever emotional path I was on before today, in the aftermath of the shooting—the stages of trauma recovery or maybe not, maybe just profound self-loathing—Wade has now set me on a new course. I am no longer numb. I feel everything. The pain in my body. The love in my heart. But also the fear in my bones.

I breathe my way back to center.

We talk more about new things and scary things, and they offer me their wealth of experience, like maybe I can just take one day at a time and see how it goes and, if it's too hard, I can let Rowan be in charge. Then we talk about Rowan and make jokes about how messy he is and what our shared desk probably looks like after two weeks on his own and how he needs to find a wife to teach him how to be organized because girls do everything better than boys, but then who would marry Rowan, *yuck*, then giggles.

I let myself be in this moment, knowing that I have broken free of something but entered a new reality where I have been assaulted. And in which I will now respond and react in ways I cannot yet imagine. I haven't even begun to deal with the emotions from the shooting, as Dr. Landyn made so painfully clear when I evaded his inquiries. The stages of trauma from that event are now surpassed by this one. I consider the irony. I have gone from the assailant to the victim, the fallout from both now competing inside me.

Mitch arrives just after four. I'm in the shower and don't hear him until I've turned off the water. The girls are on our bed, doing their homework. Fran has to draw a picture of the story that was read to them on their trip to the local library. Amy is writing a short essay. She is meticulous and easily frustrated, especially by English because there's no right or wrong—everything is subjective and therefore uncertain. I can see my anxiety flowing through her, and I have already begun the mitigation. There are coping techniques now, skills she can learn that will serve her throughout her life. Things my parents and teachers didn't understand when I was her age.

My thoughts ricochet between homework and dinner and what happened to me not hours before. For the briefest moment on that back road, I had felt free of the shooting. Wade told me that he saw me fire my weapon and he knew he would be dead if I hadn't killed Clay Lucas. It had washed me clean of the guilt. Now I don't know what I can believe or not believe. The relief can't be trusted, and what has come in its place is fierce. Unruly. The stages of trauma recovery will have to wait.

I'm naked, dripping wet, my skin red from the heat when I hear the high-pitched shrieks and giggles and then my husband's deep voice.

"Why are there monkeys in my bed?"

I can tell from the sounds that he's jumped between them, tickling them on their bellies with his strong hands and on their faces with the beard he's grown since the shooting, and they are filled head to toe with excitement. His love for them is enormous, and he expresses it in enormous ways. Maybe that's what made his affair so shocking. It was such a deviation from everything he stands for. What's at his core. Maybe that's why we pulled through after it ended.

And *thank God*, because right now I'm desperate for him.

I open the shower door, grab a towel, and dry off. I wrap it around my hair and twist it so it stays piled on top of my head. The room is filled with steam. The mirrors are fogged, so I wipe one down with my hand—the one behind the closed door that runs from floor to ceiling. And when I stand back, I observe the damage.

I am walking the walk of a victim for the first time. And now seeing for the first time the marks that have been left on my body as they develop. They are worse than I imagined, and I worry now that the girls noticed.

The giggling stops.

"Babe?" Mitch calls out for me. "I'm home. Are you okay?" His voice is upbeat, but I know he's worried. He wants to see me, to see what this man has done to his wife.

I let out a quick breath to steady my voice. "Give me a second."

I assess the damage in the mirror.

My right arm has the darkest bruises. Below the elbow, above the wrist. There is a thumbprint just beneath my armpit and a set of purple circles that could be some kind of tattoo the way they form a circular pattern. That was the arm he pinned over my head against the car after he spun me around to face away from him.

My left arm has a dark contusion above the wrist—the arm he twisted behind my back to immobilize me. Then he'd used his pelvis to hold it in place, freeing his arms to grab hold of my neck.

There is slight discoloration ear to ear. It hides in the shadows unless I tilt my head back, which I do now, to see how far I can let it go before the injury is exposed. Wade folded his forearms there, on either side. Then he'd jerked my head back into his chest so he could press against my carotid arteries. That's why there is soreness in the muscles. I'd fought against him, but my neck was no match for the strength of his arms.

Finally, my hips—one with a bruise, one with a protruding vein. I think these are the worst of the injuries.

Standing before the mirror, observing myself, naked and exposed, my precious ones just beyond the door, the bruises map out the assault. It happened in an instant. It lasted less than a minute. It was stunning—in the sense that it stunned me. Caught me off guard. Unaware. Unsuspecting.

The miraculous connection, the answer to my question setting me free. He had seemed genuine in every way. Even in the psychological damage that had been done by the trauma we both endured.

And yet, suddenly, he had become violent.

The worst injury might actually be inside my head. I followed a stranger to a secluded road. I let my need drive me and override the danger I knew was there. *I knew it*, and yet I ran right into it. A head-on collision.

Mitch is here now. Knocking softly. "Can I come in?"

I reach for the robe that hangs on a hook and pull it around me, tying it tightly with a sash. When we're alone behind the closed door, he holds me, and I feel myself give in. He doesn't ask for details, which means he's spoken to Rowan. Instead, he asks me why.

"It isn't like you to take that kind of risk. To put yourself in danger."

How do I begin to explain what led me to that back road? I hear Landyn in my head. I need to tell him. I start at the beginning. The shot that killed Clay Lucas, and my doubts about whether I'd had to take it. Then the man who disappeared. How fucked up I've been since that day.

"Why didn't you tell me sooner?"

I give him the only reason I have. "I didn't want you to see me the way I did."

Mitch hangs his head and runs his hands over the beard. I wonder now if the beard is helping him hide what he's been feeling these past two weeks. "I let you go through this alone. I didn't see it." He takes me in his arms again, and I listen to his heart. "Tell me what you need," he whispers. "I'll do anything."

He's said this every day since the shooting, and I've never answered because my needs were beyond his reach, and now I've finally told him. But where is the watershed of feeling? Why do I still not feel him? I hear a scream inside my head—telling him to take it away, to be my protector, to erase what's happened. He managed to do that after the affair, cordoned it off so when we were like this, holding each other, we were skin to skin without a trace of Briana between us. I'm no longer numb, but something new has come between us, and I still can't feel him. Not the way I used to. Before the shooting. Before the assault.

What has Wade done? I wonder now not only what is inside him that made him turn violent, but what is inside of me that I followed him, put myself in danger, and what is inside my husband that he can't reach me.

I feel Mitch's chest rise and fall as he holds back something that wants to come pouring out—anger at Wade, frustration at me, impotence within himself that he can't make it all better. And I think back to what I said in Landyn's office about never really knowing anyone.

I want it back. I want us back the way we were before I walked into Nichols to buy towels. Before I followed Wade Austin to that back road. I want to breeze about the kitchen, cleaning up after dinner, rattling off the facts of a new case, or hearing about his late supply deliveries or a funny anecdote about the whims of the wealthy—someone wanting marble imported from Italy or a light fixture exactly like the one they saw at some dinner party. I knew the things that made him laugh to himself because he told them to me and only me. And he knew how my cases churned inside, the rabbit holes I went down and obsessed about. He would take me in his arms and tell me all the ways he would pull me out of them, his hand running up my thigh, knowing just where to touch me. I want it back. I want it all back. I pull him tighter, my arms around his neck, but I can't get through.

Mitch leaves, takes the girls downstairs, and I move slowly through the bedroom, putting on sweats, brushing my hair. Finally, Rowan calls.

I grab the phone, my heart already racing. "Tell me . . ."

"Where are you?" he asks. He's out of breath, walking somewhere.

"I'm home. With Mitch and the girls."

"Is the detail outside?"

I go into the hallway and the window that faces the street. I see the black SUV parked two houses away. I tell Rowan, yes, they're here. Ask him what the hell is happening.

"I'm sending you something—open it."

My hands tremble as I pull the phone from my ear and open his message. There's an image attached—a picture of a man I've never seen before, with gray hair and a double chin, easily past sixty.

"Who is this?"

Rowan is back inside the station. I hear the familiar sounds of phones ringing and people talking.

"That's Wade Austin."

CHAPTER EIGHT

THE KILL ROOM

The forensics team finds nothing useful at the shelter except the rifle under the counter and the red jacket. Traces of OxyContin are found in the pockets. There is no hair or other biological material on either.

The bones found in the cremation oven are damaged. They provide insufficient DNA sequences to run through CODIS. They have assembled the teeth and can match them to an X-ray once they have a lead on the possible victim. They do this in a matter of three days, even with a backed-up lab.

They focus next on the behavior of the criminal because that's all they've got. The execution of the crime was meticulous but also unusual. The way many surfaces were not wiped for prints—only those the perpetrator touched: the doorknobs at the entry to the shelter, the basement, the cremation oven, the rifle and mount beneath the counter. The only area wiped clean in its entirety is the Kill Room. That—and the removal of the plastic sheeting on the floor—solidify their belief that the victim was killed there, rolled into the plastic, and dragged down to the oven.

One of the state investigators is interested in the tire tracks—or the lack of them. So she has the team measure the marks that are left behind—the parallel lines spaced evenly five feet wide that pulled up the dirt and leaves along the clearing that leads to the shelter. She finds

---

---

it "quirky"—and eventually discovers that the marks were left by a pull rake. These are used not by farmers, as the team initially presumed, but by homeowners with tractor mowers who want an easy way to remove debris from lawns. They are lightweight, and some are retractable—they can collapse into a small size and be stored in a shed. Or the back of a truck.

The team traces the manufacturers and retailers that sell them but finds the list prohibitively expansive. Anyone anywhere can order one online, brand new from Amazon or any major hardware store—Home Depot, Lowes, etc. Or used ones from an even longer list of sites—Craigslist, Facebook Marketplace, eBay. There were also forums like Quora and Pinterest where people sell things to one another directly.

No. That was a dead end.

What becomes more interesting is the type of person who would know about using a pull rake to destroy evidence of tire tracks. It wasn't an obvious choice. Most criminals altered their tread with chains or other devices. But, of course, those attract attention on a well-traveled, paved road.

The team searches for similar cases on every database they have. They call other departments and ask actual human beings if they'd come across something similar.

They find a hit in a newspaper article from the *Denver Post* several years back. It comes up with the key words "murder," "tire tracks," and "pull rake." In that case, a man killed his estranged girlfriend and left her body in a pile of dirt off a highway. It was miles between exits, towns, rest stops. There was no reason for anyone to go looking. He didn't even bother to shovel a little dirt over her, to show some effort at a burial for a woman he supposedly loved. When asked about this, he said he wanted the vultures to get to her. He said he thought about them pulling at her flesh, and this prolonged the revenge he had taken when she got the restraining order. *Fucking bitch.*

But after he drove home and was cleaning off his truck, spraying down the dirty tires with a garden hose, having to work into each groove to get them clean, it occurred to him that if there was that much dirt caked into the tread of his tires, there would be tracks off the side of the road leading right to the body. If—and it was still a big if because his plan was so clever—someone did find the body, maybe because of the vultures, they would surely see the tire tracks.

He first returned at night with a hand rake, parked the truck a mile up the road, walked back to the place he'd gone off road, and started to erase the tracks by hand. Anyone who's raked their own yard knows that raking is hard work, and he soon grew tired and frustrated.

Back home he went, to his computer, where he googled the problem and discovered the versatile pull rake. He picked one up at a nearby garden store, waited for nightfall again, then erased his tracks in under twenty minutes. One more cleaning with the garden hose, a trip to the local dump to get rid of the pull rake, and he figured he was good to go.

What he forgot to do was remove his search history from his computer.

Within two days of the girlfriend's disappearance, he became the prime suspect as he knew he might, given their relationship. His house was clean. His truck was clean. Spotless clean, in fact. But then there it was—the Google search. After that, it was simple deduction. Finding the garden store. Searching the dump. Tracing the soil. It took six days of driving roads lined with that kind of soil to spot the parallel lines, five feet wide and evenly spaced. But once they did, it was game over.

The question that came next was this: who would know about this case all the way out here in Connecticut?

CHAPTER NINE

Reality sets in before the sun rises. The pain from the bruises wakes me. I sneak out of bed to see them in the bathroom mirror. They are darker today, which I expected. Still, it feels unexpected, exposing the chasm between intellectual thought and emotional turmoil. In my brief sleep, I had erased the facts that I did not want to be real. They are back now, bringing a new struggle between exhaustion and adrenaline. I feel like a fugitive who's been on the run for weeks—first from myself, and now from this man who called himself Wade Austin.

I take two ibuprofen and get dressed for work, even though it's only 4:00 a.m. I think I might get away with a silk scarf since fall is here. I have to dig it out from the back of my closet. I haven't worn a decorative accessory since my teaching days, but it covers the discoloration around my neck. I head down to the kitchen.

I have not asked whether the attack has interrupted my plan to return to work. Whether it has raised new concerns about my fitness for the job. Whether I need to go back to see Dr. Landyn. Unlike the shooting, there is nothing in our guidelines that requires a delay or more head shrinking under these circumstances, and I suspect Rowan will advocate for my return. He knows I will fare much better if I'm allowed to help solve this new puzzle of Wade Austin.

Confusion has morphed into understanding about the situation. The real Wade Austin is an employee at Shield Insurance. The man in the blue truck, the man who assaulted me, the tall man from the shooting, is now a ghost.

The number he dialed from my phone was from a burner. Untraceable.

The man whose name he used has no digital footprint. No social media. And no photo on the firm directory. He was a bookkeeper, not a salesman, so there was no need to have him on the company website. As Rowan said yesterday, Wade Austin was "just a guy with a name that's impossible to search."

Rowan told me how they went through everything, the whole list of questions we ask people who have had their identity stolen. About IDs and credit cards. About new friends, theirs or their family members'. Wade Austin is married with two grown kids, and he called them while Rowan stood by. He checked his credit cards and bank statements while our office ran his social security number for any loan applications or title searches.

His identity wasn't stolen. Just his name. Just as a cover.

There was no way to know how long the tall man had been using it.

They went through other possible leads and came up empty-handed. There was nothing found on me or my car—no fibers or skin or hair. The flowers were cheap and came in no wrapping. Probably from a grocery store.

Rowan sent me photos of blue trucks, hoping I could narrow the search by make or model, or even the shade of blue. But I had not been focused on the truck. There might be something on the surveillance cameras from the parking lot at the station yesterday to compare with what they had from outside Nichols. Maybe we could get a glimpse of the license plate sticker taped inside the back window. Maybe we could get an expert to ID the make and model. Lots of maybes.

An hour later I'm still in my kitchen, the sky pitch black, wearing the scarf, two bags of frozen vegetables pressed to my hip bones. I stare at a cup of coffee, piecing together what happened on that deserted road, seeing it in flashes of fragmented moments. I try to distance myself, to see it as a case, one we've just pulled from an old file.

What would we notice? How he turned on a dime when he stopped believing that I trusted him. When he lost hope that he could forge some kind of connection between us. Was this what Dr. Landyn had warned me about? The worship of rescuers? The need to believe that something larger than chance had brought us together? Because then the horrors of that day would not be random, but purposeful. Preordained. Random acts implied they could happen again for no reason and with no warning. They could happen walking to the park or going to a movie or shopping for pants at a department store.

Or was it something deeper? A personality disorder? A dissociative psychosis? A more dangerous pathology?

He accused me of knowing things about him. He'd cast himself as a hero, willing to draw fire to save those who'd run or hidden. To save the pregnant woman. Did he believe this? Or was he using it to pull me in?

I search online and see that Rowan is right. Nothing comes up for Wade Austin except a bare-bones LinkedIn profile. The last name— Austin—makes it impossible to home in beyond this. He's an insurance employee. If I take away that one word, *insurance*, I start to see every man named Wade who lives in Austin, Texas.

I get pulled deeper into my mind by the growing fear of this stranger I let into my world.

The clock ticks on the wall above the sink. The sky turns from black to blue with the rising sun. The frozen peas and carrots have thawed. I put them back in the freezer. The swelling has gone down, so I wipe off my skin with a dish towel, zip up my jeans.

I'm good at thinking, I tell myself. I've learned to channel the disquiet in my brain. Now it's my job. It's what I've done as a teacher and, before that, as a student. Spinning thoughts. Tornadoes. Rabbit holes that have no end, burrowing deeper and deeper into darkness. But sometimes they lead to the truth.

I go back to the beginning. To why I followed Wade Austin out of town.

It was basic. Primal. The screaming toddler that had hijacked my brain.

Human need. Every crime I've ever studied. Every crime I've ever solved. Every story I've lived and heard about people hurting people. It all funnels down to this one concept.

The need for love. The need for money. The need for revenge. The need for justice. The need for safety, self-defense, the protection of others. The need for power. The need to protect pride and ego. The need to soothe some beast inside. A beast of anger. A beast of fear. A beast of disquiet. A beast of pain.

What I needed from Wade scares me. The chorus had been loud, telling me it was irrational. That I had done everything right, regardless of the unanswered questions about Clay Lucas and his reason for firing his gun in that store. That it was just my anxiety taking control. I didn't listen. Not to Mitch or Rowan or Dr. Landyn.

What I did to satisfy that need is terrifying.

But the question lingers in my mind—what had this man needed from me? His crime against me does not feel like the place to begin this investigation.

A stripe of orange appears at the edge of the sky that I see through my neighbor's backyard, just as I hear heavy feet come down the stairs in the front of our house. They stop in the foyer outside the study, then continue, growing closer.

Mitch joins me in the kitchen. He looks surprised. "I thought you'd gone to the sofa," he says.

I shake my head, and he pulls me into an embrace. He'd held me through the night, and for the first time since the shooting, I'd stayed in our bed. I run my hand down his back, press my face into his shirt. He sighs before releasing me.

"There's coffee," I tell him.

He pours a travel mug to the top, screws on the cap.

"Is that for the girls?" he asks, peeking behind the scarf to see the bruising.

"And the office. They don't need to know the extent of it."

He moves through the room, grabbing a PowerBar and a water bottle. Mitch is a proud man, but he knows he can't get involved. He knows Rowan and the rest of the department will be looking for Wade with resources he can't begin to match.

None of this placates him. He needs to do something more than hold me while I sleep.

"Hey . . ." I stop him as he begins to turn away. "I couldn't get through this without you."

His expression grows weary with frustration, both at his powerlessness to help me and my insistence that he is. He knows he's not. He knows he can't.

We share one last hug, and he kisses the top of my head as we let this sink in.

I wonder how much of this our broken teacup can hold.

I follow him to the front door. We kiss, and he walks down the path to the driveway where he gets in his truck. I see the unmarked detail parked down the street. Our houses sit on quarter-acre lots. We all know when someone's kid is home from college or someone else's in-laws are in town. And we all have garages and driveways. The street is usually clear. The cops stand out like a sore thumb.

I don't linger. I go back inside and think that maybe I'll make muffins for the girls to have after school, like I promised them. And that maybe I'll make a fresh pot of coffee. And that I can't do this now—worry about our marriage. It's been four years, and I still react at the slightest provocation, anxiety taking over the rational part of my brain.

I take the coffee from the bag in the freezer. Close the door, turn to the counter and the coffee maker. A flash comes then. A memory of the conversation I had with Wade before he turned angry. Violent. When I was lost in the moment. The euphoric relief when he told me I did, in fact, save his life. That I did have to shoot Clay Lucas to save him. And then the frenetic outpouring from both of us about what we saw and felt that day and what it's done to us since.

I told him things that went beyond the shooting and its aftermath—about sleeping on the sofa and how I hadn't done that for four years and then Wade asked me, "*Why were you sleeping on a sofa four years ago,*" and my answer.

Fuck.

I stand now, paralyzed as I drag the memory from the place it wants to hide.

"*Because my husband had an affair.*"

What else? I force myself to remember.

"Her name was Briana . . . he was remodeling her house . . . his father had just died, and I had a baby and a toddler . . . I've forgiven him . . ."

And then, *"Still, you must hate her."*

"Yes, sometimes . . ."

"Of course you do . . . that's human . . . just like I hate Clay Lucas even though he was sick."

"I don't hate Clay Lucas . . . I hate the person who put that gun in his hands."

The conversation plays as I stand in the silence. The things I told Wade, that I confessed because he mirrored those confessions, matched the vulnerability they created. I needed to relieve myself of them so desperately that I ignored the alarm bells. And he played on that need with an instinct that now seems predatory.

Suddenly, I hear another set of footsteps on the hallway upstairs. Fran racing to my room to see if I'm in my bed, if there's still time to crawl under the covers for a morning cuddle against a warm body. My heart sinks, knowing she'll be disappointed and now I realize I've also forgotten about the muffins.

I turn on the oven, pull out the mixing bowl and baking pan. I call out, my head turned to the opening that leads to the front hall and then the stairs to the second floor. "I'm in the kitchen!"

The feet move again, down the hall and then the stairs. I quickly pour flour, eggs, milk into the bowl. Sugar, butter, baking soda. I find a bag of chocolate chips. Despite the chaos in my mind, I follow the recipe I know by heart.

I see her in the doorway, a little bundle of crazy curls and sleepy eyes and pink pajamas. Her blanket is still clutched in her hand.

"Good morning!" I say, lifting her. She wraps her legs around my waist and her arms around my shoulders and presses her face into my neck. Intense pain shoots through the bruises on my hips.

"What's this?" she asks me, feeling the silk against her cheek instead of my skin.

I put her down, remembering the bruise, remembering the back road. Remembering Wade.

"I thought I would look nice on my first day back."

She is quickly distracted by the bag of chocolate chips. She claps and jumps up and down. "Are those for breakfast?" she says as she looks at the muffin tin.

"You wish!" I say. She sits at the table, and I bring her a bowl and a box of cereal. I get the milk from the fridge and some blueberries that will likely remain untouched. "They're for the snack I promised to have ready for after school. Kelly will be here today, remember?"

She says okay and pours her cereal and watches me mix the batter. I need to wake Amy. The bus comes in half an hour, and she likes to take a quick shower, then carefully consider her wardrobe choices. And just as I have this thought, I hear my phone chime.

I stare at it on the counter. Fran stares at me.

"Mommy, your phone," she says.

I look from Fran to the counter and slowly walk toward it. I don't recognize the number. There's a text message, which reads simply, *Nice scarf.*

And my heart stops.

He was out on my street when I opened the door, kissed my husband. He was outside my house. Watching me. Watching us. With a police detail parked right there.

I look at Fran. I think about Amy asleep upstairs, and Mitch on his way to work. My family. God . . . no . . .

"Mommy?"

I take her hand and pull her away from the table.

"Let's go wake Amy!" I say. I need to have my girls in my sight. In my arms.

Fran doesn't ask why I take her with me. She follows, instinctively aware that something has just alarmed me.

Suddenly, I feel a new need—one that is more powerful than the search for answers that brought all of this upon me and my family.

The need to make him stop.

CHAPTER TEN

The texts come rapid fire as I get Amy dressed and fed and drive both girls to school. The principal is informed and alerts the security guard, who now watches the entrance with more care. There are already cameras and door alarms. The school is a virtual prison. We're in the same state as Sandy Hook, and the precautions put in place after that horror are now routine. My boss, Sergeant Aaron Burg, agrees to add one unmarked car as well, and I fight the urge to have the place locked down by the National Guard. I don't want to alarm the children, and there doesn't seem to be a need to take additional measures until we know more about this man.

Still, it's not easy to drive away. I remind myself that I'm the one he wants and so my children are safer away from me.

His messages sway and swerve like a car with no one at the wheel.

I just want to see you.

We are connected. You can't change that.

Don't believe their lies.

Why won't you answer me?

Answer me!

Bitch.

Cunt.

I'm sorry. I didn't mean to say those things.

I need to see you again.

Mitch wants to take us all away, but *where?* I ask him. We're safer here with the detail and the department and the neighborhood that knows us.

Rowan is a live wire when I reach the station. He meets me at the elevator on our floor.

"Let me see . . ." He reaches for my phone and reads the messages. Then his eyes turn to me and the scarf around my neck.

"He was outside the house," I tell him. "He must have seen me then."

We walk quickly to our shared desk where I set down my bag, but we don't stop. We continue to the back corner, where Aaron waits for us in his office.

The squad room is a large open space except for one row of enclosed rooms against the back wall. One for conferences. One for interviews. And one for Aaron. We work at shared desks and behind cubicles with computers and files, and there is normally a buzz that never stops from phones and machines and people. I don't hear anything today. Maybe because my return and what is now happening to me has silenced my colleagues. Or maybe because I can't hear anything beyond the fear that rings in my ears.

Aaron stands as we come in. "Elise," he says. "How are you holding up?"

It's been less than twenty-four hours since I followed a blue truck to a back road where I laid myself bare to a stranger. Where I was assaulted and left choked out in my own car. I can still smell the flowers he left in my lap. And now this. The texts. He isn't going away. I think about the moment I walked out of Landyn's office. How the shooting was already being forgotten since no one was shot besides the shooter. How everyone was satisfied with the conclusions about the kill—my kill—and had moved on. Except for me and my inability to live with the unknown. My unrest. The emotional turmoil that caused me to follow that truck and engage with an unstable man. This was my doing. I brought this man into my life. Our lives.

"I'm okay," I tell him. "Where are we in finding Wade Austin?" I realize I called him Wade, but that's not his name and a gust of concern passes through the room. "What are we calling him, then?"

No one's decided this because it's only just begun, this new investigation. A moment passes before Rowan finally breaks the silence.

"He's a 404," he says. A 404 is a missing person. But it also has another meaning in our squad: someone who is worthless or pathetic. We throw it around here as a joke among colleagues or to derogate a suspect. Rowan is taking this personally, which means we're both emotionally charged. I don't know where that leaves us. One of us has always been on steady ground. We usually aren't triggered by the same types of cases. But this one has us both unhinged.

Aaron motions for us to sit, and we all take chairs. Rowan leans forward, elbows on knees, fists laced together and punching the air. His anger has nowhere to go. I sit perfectly still as my mind spins, searching for rabbit holes.

"First things first," Aaron says, "Vera Pratt is coming in this morning to help with the facial composite."

Vera Pratt is the pregnant woman who was in the dressing room with Wade.

"Between the three of us, we should have something close," Rowan adds. I remember now that Rowan saw him briefly, just before he left that last stall, the one with the closed door.

My phone chimes.

"Is it him?" Aaron asks as I pull up the screen.

"More of the same," I tell him. "They've been coming in pretty steady all morning."

Rowan catches him up. "It's a burner. Untraceable."

Aaron nods, tells me my number is now being fed to a technical unit that will monitor the messages. They can look for patterns in his words, check each phone he sends them from. "Just let them come," he tells me. "Let's keep him talking, try to get a profile. Maybe he'll give us something we can use."

I nod and silence the phone.

"For now, do not respond. Nothing. Let's see what he does. If we can't get an ID from the composite, we'll move to a protocol for engagement."

Yes, I think. This is all by the book. All of the things I know to do as a cop but now have to live as a victim. A target. First came the self-loathing because I'd made myself vulnerable. Then the humiliation of a forensic exam. Then the anger. Now the fear. The helplessness. It overwhelms me as I try to focus on the instructions and the case I am about to dive into. They push and pull inside my head. Raw, hot emotions and the knowledge of what needs to be done, calmly and with precision.

There, too, is the uncertainty about Clay Lucas and whether I needed to take that shot, but that is now pushed aside to make room for these new emotions. I know it will come back.

Aaron continues, "We've got nothing from the station lot, but the blue truck was parked in the Nichols strip mall. There's a nail salon and toy store that might have more security footage. We're going to see what we get from that. Maybe there'll be a better angle of the plate number through the back window."

I've gone through the images Rowan sent me last night of makes and models and shades of blue and haven't been able to narrow it down to a remotely useful range. I wasn't looking at the truck, even as I drove behind it. My mind was on the man inside and the answers he might have to ease my suffering.

There were four doors, I remember that. An open flatbed. It looked new or well maintained. Mostly what I see when I remember yesterday is the man who stepped out from the driver's side after we stopped on that back road near the park.

"When we have the composite, we'll send it to the press and also have a team go back through the witness list. Someone else might have seen him coming or going."

We cover all of the dead ends. The flowers and the gifts I'd dropped at Goodwill, which then either got tossed or sent to stores across the state. They were long gone and, in any case, had been unopened. They could have been candles or coasters or chocolates. None of my neighbors remembered the truck on our street. No one knew to look, and besides that, maybe he drove a different vehicle or dropped the gifts off after dark.

None of the images from the cameras at Nichols had a clean shot of his face.

Rowan jumps in now. "There's something else," he says. "It may not be related but worth checking out."

This is the first I'm hearing about anything related to the case. Rowan has kept me at bay, thinking I should focus on my family and the sessions with Dr. Landyn. He had no idea how hungry I was to know more about Clay Lucas, what he was doing in Nichols that day, and how he got his hands on that weapon.

"We've put together a list of everyone Clay Lucas may have had contact with after leaving his home three weeks before the shooting— old friends from school, doctors, caregivers, roommates at the facilities he spent time in."

Aaron leans forward. "I thought we'd been through all that," he says.

"Yeah, we have. But there was one woman, an employee at the adult day care center the family used until early last year—we haven't been able to make contact. Her name is Laurel Hayes, and she hasn't been to work since the day of the shooting. They didn't think much of it at first. A lot of people from the center were upset about it and scared to come back. Clay Lucas had been going there for months, and they have other patients with similar conditions."

"But she's been gone this whole time? Over two weeks?" Aaron asks.

Rowan tells us that her parents live in Oregon, and they were the ones who finally called the department. They spoke to her the day of the shooting to make sure she was all right. But she hadn't returned their calls seven days later, and now fourteen. That wasn't like her. They said it wasn't unusual to not hear from her for a while, but she always replied when they reached out.

I grab hold of this and don't let go. It feels like something, finally, and not the empty space we've been sweeping our arms through.

"So someone connected to Clay Lucas has been missing since the day of the shooting?" I ask.

Rowan nods. "Yeah. Could be nothing. Could be she decided to get out of this place after what happened. Maybe she felt guilty, having taken care of Clay, not seeing what he was capable of doing. Could be she's somewhere just trying to get her head around it. Everyone at that center—Clear Horizons is the name—was pretty shaken up."

"Or maybe she's scared," I say. "What if she knows how he got the gun? Or helped him get it?"

Aaron mulls this over. "Either way it's a solid lead. Okay. Good. Good," he says. "What's next with that?"

Rowan tells him there's a unit investigating the case as a missing person. They've already gone through her apartment and called friends and coworkers. The parents are flying in tomorrow, and there's an alert out on her car, which wasn't in the lot at her building.

I look at Rowan. "We should help with that."

Neither man speaks. And I get it. They're worried about me.

"I need to work," I tell them. "And it will send a message to Wade— the 404—that he's not impacting my life. That I'm not going to stop work and run away with him, or whatever the hell he thinks he's going accomplish."

Aaron bobs his head, mulls it over. None of us has any idea what his endgame is. But that's true with every stalker. It's a powerful compulsion. It feeds a sickness inside them. They fantasize about things that will never come to be. And contrary to my argument, they rarely give up until they're made to. Until someone stops them.

"Okay," Aaron says when he's done thinking. "But first the composite. That's the priority. Let's find out who our 404 really is."

Vera Pratt waits in a conference room. She's past her due date and expecting her baby with excited anticipation. I remember that feeling. I'd had it with Amy. It changes after the first one, when you know what's coming. You remember the joy, of course, but also the sleepless nights and long, hard days. And then there is acclimating the firstborn who's been ousted from her throne as the only child. The social worker who made rounds at the maternity wing told us to expect some emotional upheaval after Fran joined our family. Amy would feel like a wife whose husband had suddenly brought home a younger version. A second wife. *"That's what it will feel like to her. Like a betrayal."* I remembered that description fiercely when I discovered Mitch's affair.

We enter the room and make brief introductions. Me, Rowan, and the guy from tech who's going to create the image of the 404 from our descriptions.

Vera is a tiny woman with a big belly. She's young. Long dark hair, big round eyes.

"You must be excited," I tell her. "I have two of my own."

She smiles, though there's something sad about it. "I'm tired, mostly," she says, and I imagine the Nichols shooting has stolen much of the joy from her and her husband. "He wanted to be here," she explains. "He's already missed so many days at work. I told him to go. It's not like he can help with this."

Vera Pratt had been in the men's department to buy a sweater for him. His birthday was that weekend. I've read her statement, though it felt light to me—like something was missing. She told the investigator that she'd run into the dressing room and gone to the very last stall. She'd left the door open and stepped up on the bench where people place their belongings and the clothing they removed to try things on. She did this to make the shooter think no one was in there.

Wade, the 404, came in soon after. He joined her in the room and insisted they lock the door. She didn't argue with him. When he heard Rowan call out that it was all clear, he opened the door and left. She had started to have cramps and was hyperventilating so Rowan came to her aide, laying her on the ground and having her breathe into his cupped hands. The paramedics came soon after and took her to the hospital. That was it. That was all she remembered. She never set her eyes on the shooter.

I think about this and what Wade told me. How he saw Clay fall to the ground and then went into the dressing room to see about the pregnant woman. To help her. The stories don't match. But that's not why we're here, so I leave it alone. For now.

We work for an hour. I have the most to offer because of the time I spent with him on that back road. The composite is close, but there's something about it that doesn't capture him. I think about his expressions, how they changed so drastically. In an instant. And how an expression can make the difference between Wade's picture being noticed or passed by. I tell the technician that we have to include his height. Anyone over six foot four is distinct. That's something he can't hide with a smile.

When the tech leaves, Rowan and Vera push back from their chairs. I know I should do the same. Get up and say goodbye. This woman has been through enough. But I can't. I don't. There's something she's not telling us.

I reach out and touch the back of her hand.

"Can I ask you one more thing?"

CHAPTER ELEVEN

It's 4:22 in the morning. I stare at the clock on the cable box in the study. I came here thinking I might find more sleep on the sofa, as discouraging as that was, after waking in a cold sweat, heart racing, head on fire. I must have been dreaming the dream for a while.

Clay Lucas, his back to me. Wade, hands in the air, pleading for his life. Vera Pratt flashing by, disappearing into the dressing room. Then Clay turns. He sees me and I see him and Wade starts to move. Clay turns back when he catches a glimpse of this movement. I fire my weapon, but the bullet moves in slow motion. Clay turns one last time, he sees the bullet, his face is so young, and he's so scared. He opens his mouth and calls to me. Just one word: *Stop!*

I shake off the dream and watch the numbers turn, minute after minute. I go over Vera Pratt's statement, the new one, the appendix. The one that's changed everything. The one that's caused this nightmare. I hear her voice, apprehensive at first when I told her about my conversation with Wade. The 404.

"He said he came into the dressing room after I killed Clay Lucas. He said he wanted to help you, but then why would he insist on locking the door if he knew the danger had passed?"

She looked at Rowan as though he might save her from having to tell the last part of her story. The part she left out when she was interviewed the day after the shooting.

"My husband was at the hospital the whole time. I didn't want him to know."

And there it was. The start of her confession.

Rowan took the lead when he saw I was suddenly without words. "He doesn't have to know. The reports are not public."

Back and forth they discussed what would happen with the story until she was finally convinced she should tell it. Then she did.

"It was after he came into the stall. Like I said, he locked the door, and I whispered to him, 'No—leave it open so he doesn't know we're here.' I don't think he really saw me until then. I was sitting on my heels on the narrow bench, trying to be as small as I could make myself with the baby.

"He looked at me with surprise or fear, like he didn't know what to do. But then he locked the door anyway. He said something about the shooter knowing we were in here and that I should stay quiet."

She looked at her folded hands again and thought about this last part. Then she drew a breath as though bracing herself for the discomfort of her own words.

"What he actually said was 'Shut the fuck up or I'll kill your baby.'"

Sometimes I think Rowan is made of steel because he didn't flinch. I don't know what I did, but it was more than that. A gasp, maybe. A look of shock, wide eyes. It was immediately apparent that Vera Pratt had never spoken words like this before.

She continued, "He grabbed me by my wrist and pulled me down from the bench. I didn't know what to think. I didn't know if he was the shooter, maybe, trying to pretend he wasn't. I saw a movie once where a bank robber did that—took off his mask and hid among the hostages when he knew he couldn't get out. I thought maybe he was a killer. I started to feel the cramps then and the baby kicking. I couldn't catch my breath, which means he wasn't getting enough oxygen, and then I feared I was going to suffocate him, my son, and I told the man, 'Please—just let me go. The baby . . .'"

But Wade didn't let her go. He held her in front of him and stood with his back to the wall. He crossed his arms around her chest so she couldn't move away. He used her as a human shield.

I felt myself steel then. The alternative was to fall apart, right there in front of our witness.

Now I knew what he meant when he asked, "What have they said about me?" and then, "You think I'm a coward." This is why he turned on me so suddenly. He was afraid I was playing him, luring him in. That I knew what he'd done to this woman and was trying to get him to confess or maybe arrest him. I can only imagine what twisted web he'd been weaving in his depraved mind. That if I never found out what he'd done, I would feel an attachment to him that went beyond that moment on the back road.

Rowan wrote everything down, asked more questions. The rest was the same. They heard Rowan call out, and Wade let her go, opened the door, and left when Rowan started tending to Vera.

"I'm so sorry that happened to you," Rowan told her.

I said the same, though my mind was on the implications of this story.

"If my husband knew," she said, "he wouldn't rest until he found this man and killed him. Please—this is his son, his wife."

Rowan told her he understood. He assured her the statement would be kept in the file, confidential, even though we both knew he couldn't promise that. We would try, both of us, but lying to witnesses had become second nature. Rowan went through the usual list of follow-up inquiries. These had already been covered in the first interview, and we got nothing new from it.

I asked her one last question before we helped her up and walked her to the elevator. It was self-serving. Still, I couldn't stop myself. "Did you hear the last shot?"

"Yes . . . I think so."

"Do you remember if it came before or after the man came into the stall?"

Rowan's eyes shifted from Vera Pratt to me and back again. The only good thing that had come from following that blue truck was hearing that Wade had been in the line of fire when I killed Clay Lucas. That I had taken a life to save a life. That Clay Lucas had fired at Wade, right at him, not off to the side. Which meant that he was there to take lives and not have someone take his. Even if Wade's actions that followed called all of it into question, it had remained a possibility.

But now . . .

"I don't remember," Vera said. "But if he knew we were all safe, why was he still so afraid?"

Exactly. If he'd seen Clay fall the way he told me and then gone into that dressing room to help Vera Pratt, why would he lock the door and use her as a human shield? Vera and her unborn child? Why would he pin himself against the wall, shaking with fear?

The clock turns again. It's 4:37.

I grab my phone and check the news feed. There's nothing since last night when the composite went out. It only reached the local outlets, but that was enough. We assume he is still in the area. They included his height and the description of the truck. They said he was a material witness to the shooting at Nichols Depot. I stare at the composite. It looks inhuman, this computer-generated image. Still, I stare at it for a long while. His face. Wade. The 404.

I'm back to where I was before I followed him out of town. Back to not knowing if I needed to kill Clay Lucas. But there's no time to indulge in anguish or self-loathing. I have a bigger problem now, and all I can feel is rage.

It's 4:57 when I hear a buzzing sound. I'm holding my phone, so I know that's not the source. But it is some kind of phone or device. I think through the possibilities. The alarm system Mitch installed last night, which chimes anytime a door or window opens. Does it do more than that? I go to the box in the front hall. I hear the buzz again. It is louder, but not coming from the alarm system. I think next about the smoke detectors. Maybe one is low on batteries. Only those chirp, and they chirp loudly and a minute apart. This is a buzz, and it's coming every few seconds.

I follow the sound into the dining room, of all places. I scan the room and see nothing, but I'm drawn to the small chest in the corner where we keep the nice linen and silver that we only use on special occasions. I open the top drawer and stop, frozen.

On top of a stack of neatly folded napkins is a phone, and I think, pray, that maybe it's Amy's. Maybe she found a way to get one after we told her she was still too young. But where would she get a phone? How would she pay for it? She's only nine. And why would she leave it here? These thoughts lag behind what I already know but don't want to know. What I don't want to be real.

I pick it up and see a message. I know who it's from.

Open me, it says.

There's an attachment. An image, which I open. It loads slowly because this is a burner phone and it doesn't connect to the internet. I see the walls and the furniture, then the body, lying still on the sofa, covered with a quilt.

I can't believe what I'm seeing. It's a picture of me, asleep in the study. It's from the first night. The night of the shooting. I know because of what I'm wearing and the quilt I'd brought from the closet upstairs.

No, I think. This can't be right.

The photo is taken from inside the house.

I remember the next morning, the open window I couldn't explain but was too preoccupied to think about.

Wade was in my house that very first night. The 404. And he was here again, planting this phone.

When? How?

My head spins as I stare at this picture of me, sleeping, this person standing over me. A new kind of violation covers me head to toe, and I shiver from the disgust. The repulsion.

And then another buzz. A new message.

Sound asleep, it says. *Just like a baby.*

And then,

Like little Baby Doe.

Baby Doe—the name given to a case decades old but solved about a year ago. A newborn baby girl was found in a dumpster outside an apartment complex. We extracted DNA from a sample of blood that was still in the file, something they couldn't do back then. We tracked down suspects who had since scattered far and wide and found a match to the mother. Once we had her, we got a confession and arrested the father, an older married man who lived down the hall. He'd picked up his newborn baby daughter and literally threw her away.

How does Wade know about a case we solved a year ago? I was a stranger to him then. My name wasn't in the news about the story. I never give interviews or statements to the press. I don't like to come up in Google searches.

Think! How does he know?

I stare at the phone, waiting for a new message, but nothing comes.

Hands shaking, I unlock the box that holds my gun, then race through the house, checking locks on doors and windows, checking room by room, top to bottom like I would a crime scene. I'm careful not to wake my girls or Mitch as I look under beds and in closets. Searching for the boogeyman the way I sometimes did as a child when my parents went out and my brother left me alone.

It doesn't occur to me to wake my husband. This feels like something I need to contain inside myself before I tell anyone else. Mitch. Rowan. Aaron. I need to understand what it is and what it isn't. This is the curse of anxious people, prone to overreaction, overthinking. Everyone is safe, so I give myself the time to settle my nerves and let the thoughts fall into the right places.

It's 5:14 when they finally do, bringing the answer. I make my way back down to the study and sit on the sofa. I find my laptop in the kitchen and pull up the portal where I post cases for the college. And there it is—*Solving Baby Doe*. I'd shared the case with students, past and present. Anyone can sign up for a class and gain access. And Wade told me he'd found my class. He'd said it was clever.

Wade is not going anywhere. He's been on my street. In my home. And now in my head. He'll know everything I've ever done with forensic evidence. Something tells me he'll be a quick study.

Wade. The 404. No—*Wade*—the name sticks in my mind because I'm still on that road, letting him into my life.

I think about the plan we made today with Aaron. How they're watching my phone, searching for clues. Wade has found a way around that now, which means he knows the protocol.

And he'll know what comes next.

CHAPTER TWELVE

The "situation" with the raked path leading to the shelter and the similar story from Colorado cannot be mere coincidence. Using a pull rake to remove tire tracks from a crime scene is so unusual that they have still only found this one prior case. They decide that whoever planned and executed this crime that has left them with a burned body has been using the internet for information about forensics and evidence and, more specifically, how to evade detection. The case from Colorado made the local news, but they have yet to find it in other online sources. They consider the possibility that the killer moved to Connecticut from Colorado, where he first learned about the rake. They wonder if he has killed before, using knowledge he acquires as needed. They work quickly as the leaves fall, searching the other, smaller shelters, the woods in between. After the leaves will come the snow, and then any evidence on the ground will be buried.

They gather a small team to do nothing but search for online materials that match the forensics found at the shelter and inside the Kill Room, but just like the evidence, it's either too much or too little to be useful. For example, when they search for ways to dispose of a body, cremation is right at the top, along with acid and in large bodies of water.

One of the investigators recalls a story from thirty years ago when he worked homicide in New York. Yes, he should be retired, but after trying it out for six months, he decided to take some of his pension from New York and work part-time in Connecticut. It was that or his marriage, his wife told him. He wasn't built to play golf or fiddle with shit in the garage.

The case involved a mob soldier—the guy who kills people and disposes of their bodies, when needed, or leaves them for all to see as a message to a rival or snitch. They had been after him for years, hoping to turn him.

He tells the team how the guy was finally caught and convicted using evidence found in his apartment and one severed finger unearthed by a dog in Queens. His MO was to cut up his victims and bury their body parts in different boroughs. He knew each borough worked its own cases, so a hand found in the Bronx and a torso in Central Park and a finger in Queens were not likely to be connected. But, he said, there was a book in the suspect's apartment about hiding bodies. It was a self-published how-to guide only sold in the places one might suspect—S&M shops, the classifieds of fringe magazines. Step by step, the guy followed that book. Cutting up the bodies in his bathtub. Pulling the teeth. Burning the fingertips and face with acid. Then burying the pieces in different jurisdictions.

Once investigators found that book, they reached out to neighboring jurisdictions and coordinated their investigations—in the end they had partial remains of nine different bodies. From there, they looked into missing persons cases to identify the victims. The bodies, the book, and traces of blood in his bathtub drainpipe were all used at the trial.

The trouble here, his colleagues reminded him, was that they didn't have a suspect. If they did, they could, possibly, connect him to some browser history that matched the forensics. Even that would be a stretch, though. They would need the equivalent of blood in the drainpipe to seal the deal.

Still, it was all they had, so they looked, for hours on end, for anyone or anything they could connect to the pull rake story, and for a possible victim.

One of the areas of focus is the killing from three years back, the one that made the Kill Room a thing people talked about. The one that exposed the shelters and the cremation oven. The media attention was fleeting, not enough to get any kind of momentum to tear these things down or put an end to the hunting season. They compile a database of all the sites that carried the story, from major news outlets to chat rooms and social media. They plan to do this for the pull rake story from Colorado, specific information about cremation, and eventually, perhaps, find one source where all of these stories have been present. Where they'll go from there, they don't know. But at least they'll have an idea of what site this killer frequents to add to his toolbox.

They have yet to discover the local community college that allows a former professor to update her online materials with new cases. Access to that portal requires enrollment, which costs money, and does not appear in their Google searches.

What seems promising is a new lead from missing persons in West-chester County. Because of the traces of Oxy found in the red jacket, and the fact that the killing here three years ago was drug related, and also a new discovery made in the well that fed the water pump in the Kill Room—a rope connected to a mesh bag that had balloons of Oxy, indicating the well was used as a hiding place for the supply—they had focused on narcotics CIs and missing persons who had not been re-ported as missing.

The CIs knew who came and went and who didn't return. This was not uncommon. People in this line of work moved around, changed locations, went to jail in other jurisdictions. Their families didn't file reports when they failed to show up for Sunday dinner. No cops. No cops. No cops. Not ever.

But now a CI from a small city halfway between the shelters and the Bronx had been asked and given the answer that became the subject of this new lead. A young guy, a kid really, who'd been on the scene for over a year or so hadn't been around lately. The CI gave a description, and the cops working that area matched it to a surveillance photo. He went by the name Nix.

That photo was then circulated to narcotics units in other areas, including Connecticut.

There was nothing local, but "sure as shit," they got a match from surveillance down near the river in the town where the Nichols shooting happened just last month. The river under the bridge.

One of the investigators recalls that the shooter, Clay Lucas, had been seen under that same bridge days before walking into the department store and shooting up the place.

But unlike the "situation" with the rake, they write this one off as a coincidence.

CHAPTER THIRTEEN

I don't tell anyone about my discovery in the early morning hours inside my home or what the message on the burner contained and what all of this implies. I don't have a plan. I just know that it gives me options beyond Rowan and Aaron and the department that is tracking Wade's communications with me. I can see the risks if I tell them, so keeping it a secret, for now, feels safer.

Wade wants a direct line to me. A private way to communicate. He wants my attention while he plays his game. Is he proving himself to me so I'll see that we are somehow connected? Is he torturing me for not wanting it? Whatever this is, it has to do with me and only me, and if I let people get in the way of that, I could push him into a deeper psychosis. Force him to take more drastic measures.

This limits my resources. He's accessed the portal at the college where I posted my updates, which means he's registered for a class or hacked his way in. He might have stolen a student's ID and password. There are so many ways he could have gained access, and our techies might find it. But that feels remote. He'll know how to cover his tracks.

Maybe I'm the delusional one, thinking I can contain him on my own. That by having complete control of my chessboard, without others telling me what move to make next, instilling doubt and second-guessing,

I can beat him. But it feels like the only way out. To play this private game with him. If I tell the people who love me, who want to protect me, I know they'll stop me. And if I bring the department in, they'll make me follow rules. So I walk down this road—alone. I hope I'm taking small enough steps that I can find my way back if I'm making a mistake.

Rowan and I visit the missing social worker's parents when they arrive from Oregon. Their daughter, Laurel Hayes, has been out of touch for two weeks, and it is only now sinking in that she might be in danger. Or worse.

They move as though they are two parts of one person, finishing each other's sentences, anticipating the needs of the other without a word.

Richard Hayes gets his wife a glass of water from the bathroom of their hotel room. They are visibly shaken and aren't sure where to go or what to do. Laurel's apartment has been turned upside down by forensics, and they don't want to be at the police station. So they stay here, waiting for news.

Cora Hayes sits on the edge of the bed while Rowan and I lean on the bureau across from it.

"Did she ever mention a patient named Clay Lucas?" Rowan asks her.

"The man from the shooting?"

"Yes," he confirms.

Cora seems surprised. "Well, of course. He was at the day care center not two months ago."

Richard is back and chimes in. "We called her when we heard about the shooting, made sure she was safe and sound. But then she called back later that night to tell us about this young man after his name was released. She was pretty upset."

Rowan looks at me, wondering if I'm going to pick up on this and ask the next question. Partners develop a kind of dance with interviews, and this is ours. But I'm not paying attention to the music. Wade's burner phone is in my pocket, and I feel like a walking time bomb—like he could trigger it at any moment.

Rowan gives up on me. "Did she say why she was upset?" he asks.

Cora answers, "Well, obviously it was unsettling to her that someone she spent time with every day for several months had that kind of violence in him. I still get a shiver thinking about it."

Richard sits beside his wife and gently places a hand on her knee. "It was more complicated than that," he tells us. Cora hangs her head, and I know that look. She's worried about what we'll think when her husband finishes his thought. What conclusions we might jump to about her child.

"Laurel has always been a compassionate person," he explains. "Always taking in the stray animal. Making friends with the kid no one wanted to sit next to at lunch. It's why she went into social work."

"She has a big heart," Cora adds. "She only sees the good."

Richard nods. "She took a special interest in this young man. When she called back that night, she told me she was afraid she'd gotten too close to him. That she'd crossed a line. She said he was like a friend. There weren't a lot of patients around her age. She's just twenty-three. Most of the patients are older than her grandparents."

I jump in now. "Did she know about his condition?"

"Yes, of course," Richard says. "She told us that, when he was taking his medication, he was a gentle soul."

"'A sweet kid' is how she described him," Cora interjects.

"She felt that maybe she missed something. Apparently, he grew quite fond of her. He would always do whatever activity she was leading, sit by her when they were watching TV. Things like that. She was so upset when she called that night. She felt responsible, even though it wasn't her fault, and we told her that. Both of us, didn't we?"

Cora takes her husband's hand in her own and reassures him. "We did. And she knew, in her mind, that she did nothing wrong. But her heart was heavy. His family withdrew him from the center because they couldn't afford it anymore. They thought they could supervise him at home. Laurel had no contact with him after he left."

Richard looks at us now. "No contact. She made sure to tell us that. She hadn't seen him for several weeks."

Rowan nods his head to reassure them that no one is judging their daughter for her compassion. He then looks at me, and this is my cue to play the bad cop and ask the harder questions.

"Did she say anything else about Clay that was bothering her—things that in hindsight might have been warning signs? Did he talk about guns or killing, for example?"

They answer in unison—no—which under different circumstances would cause suspicion. But this felt genuine, like they had been thinking it themselves.

"There was nothing like that. She felt guilty because she *didn't* see any of those things," Richard explains.

We switch gears to her friends, possible love interests, coworkers she spoke about. Then to her history, college, graduate school, former employers. No red flags appear, and we leave after reassuring them that maybe she just needed to get away, sort out her ambivalence about her interactions with Clay Lucas.

Richard says that she does like to hike, and Cora agrees—yes, she likes to be alone sometimes. Unplug for a while. They make a plan to call some of the hiking hostels she used to stay at.

"She even walked part of the Appalachian Trail," Richard tells us. "There was a place in New Hampshire she stayed."

We leave them to this task, knowing it will keep them busy and hopeful. We do not share their optimism, but don't let on. There's no point.

Ten minutes later we're headed back to the station, running through theories and initial impressions of Laurel Hayes and her family.

"I think she was more involved than she let on," Rowan says.

"A hundred percent," I agree. "She overstepped somehow. Maybe kept seeing him after he left. Checking in on the family. The guilt doesn't make sense. She was well-trained. She knew anything could happen if he went off his meds."

"Didn't tell her parents the whole story because she didn't want them to be disappointed."

"Right."

"Do we think she might have been suicidal? Over the guilt?"

I shake my head. "I don't know. The parents seem like pretty forgiving people. But let's not rule out anything."

We take a beat to consider where to turn next. The team working the case already spoke to the Lucas family, and they said they didn't know Laurel Hayes. We consider circling back to Clear Horizons and looking for a coworker willing to come clean about just how close Laurel and Clay Lucas had become and whether she spoke about seeing him after he left.

We're almost at the station when my phone chimes. It's not the burner phone, so I take it out and check the message.

Rowan glances at me the moment I see the number. It's Wade, using this phone again.

I let out one word, a whisper of disbelief. "No."

"What is it?"

I don't answer. It's a link to some kind of live feed, which I open and watch.

"No . . ." I say this one word again, louder, as the image registers.

A school playground. Recess. Kids on swings and monkey bars and climbing towers, throwing balls and kicking balls and standing in small groups, talking. Running, chasing each other in games of tag. I've been in this scene. Recess at my girls' school. The video plays in real time because it's after lunch and that's when they go out. I've been there on enough visiting days to know what I'm seeing.

I search the bodies for Fran's yellow sweater and Amy's black skirt. For flying curls and a long ponytail. For Mitch's eyes and my nose.

And then my search is assisted by a zoomed focus—first on Fran running across a stretch of grass, then Amy with two girls just beyond the basketball hoop. In and out the camera takes me. To my children.

My children being watched by Wade.

"The school," I say. I don't even look at Rowan. I just tell him. "Go to the school!"

Rowan puts on the lights and the siren and steps on the gas.

I hold the phone in my hand and stare at the feed, which zooms out again. My eyes dart between different pieces of Wade's show, following Fran, checking back on Amy.

Rowan calls the school. It goes to the automated system, then a prompt, and I say the extension with a trembling voice. We're transferred to the principal's office, where a woman named Marjorie answers. Every parent knows Marjorie. She's the one to call if your child is sick or didn't finish her homework or needs an extra day for vacation. She's the one who now asks what's wrong when she hears the sirens. She asks with great alarm, and I take a moment to think this through.

I grab Rowan's phone from the dashboard mount and take it off the speaker, and he calls in for backup on the radio for any cars that might be closer to the school. He tells them to proceed cautiously. No lights or sirens.

"Sorry about that," I tell Marjorie. "It's Elise Sutton."

She asks me if something is happening, and I know she's thinking back to that shocking day when everyone within ten miles of Nichols heard sirens as responders raced to the scene.

I tell her there's nothing to worry about, a fender bender on the highway, some units dispatched to deal with traffic, and that's not why I'm calling.

I ask her to give my girls a message, tell them that I will pick them up today so they shouldn't get on the bus.

"I think they have recess now," I say, and she says, "Oh, yes, of course. I'll get the message to them."

I need her to go outside and call my children to one place. I need her eyes on my babies.

Even as my voice trembles, we say polite goodbyes, and I keep watching until we pull up on the street across from the playground. When we do, the video cuts off.

"Look for the truck!" I tell Rowan. He drives around the perimeter of the school. We don't veer off because the children are still outside. Luring cops from an active scene to chase after a suspect is one of the things I used to teach in my classes.

Wade knows. He knows because he's accessed my online materials, which means he's inside my head.

There's always a way to get around the police. I can see the words as I typed them into a case study about a kidnapping.

I make Rowan park across from the playground where I can watch. I see my girls now, in the flesh. Marjorie is there speaking with their teachers, giving them the message, and then the teachers find them and pass it along, and then recess is called to an end and the kids meander slowly back to the side entrance of the school.

When they close the door, I lose it. Everything I'm holding in pours out.

"I'm going to find him, and I'm going to kill him." The words come between heaves of breath and streams of tears. I pound my fist into the dashboard. "I will kill him!"

Rowan doesn't react except to reach for my phone.

"Is it still there?"

He pulls up the message, but the link has expired.

"Maybe they captured something at the station," he thinks out loud. But I know they didn't. Wade wouldn't take that chance.

Rowan scrolls for a bit, then looks up at the playground. "What was the angle?" he asks me. "Where was he filming from?"

I take a deep breath and wipe my face. I look across the street and try to remember what I saw on the screen. The back of the school is directly across from where we're parked. The playground is a large rectangle that flanks the building. A wire mesh fence surrounds the perimeter. To the right, there's a patch of woods, the backyard of an abutting property. To the left is the street corner and across from it, a row of hedges and then the front lawn of another parcel.

"I saw Amy with her friends. She was there—behind the basketball hoop." I point to the area and try to remember. "Fran was running away from the camera, on the grass—there," I say, pointing to a different spot. "The building was to her right." I look at the vantage points, the woods, the hedges, the streets, and it falls into place. "He was on foot."

Rowan gets out of the car.

Thinking through the scene changes my focus, and I settle enough to do my job. I join Rowan, then walk to the spot where the scene matches what I saw on the feed. We're in front of the woods.

It's impossible to gauge exactly how far away from the playground he was. He was zooming in and out.

"He was close," I say. "The view wasn't obstructed." I walk four or five yards beyond the tree line and stop, turn around, and walk forward a couple of feet. "Here," I say.

Rowan checks the brush for anything he might have left, but of course, there is nothing.

He turns slowly in a circle, looking for ways in and out. We walk through the woods to the house, around to the front, and ring the bell. No one's home. Beyond their front yard is another street, and we think that maybe he parked there, walked the path we just did in reverse, and used the cover of the trees to observe and film the playground—and my girls.

We go to the street and do all of the things we know to do, not because we're remotely hopeful we'll find a damned thing, but because I have to do something and Rowan knows it. When we're done, when we've exhausted everything we know to do, I walk back toward the school.

One thought echoes in my head: *Get your children!*

Rowan follows. "Wait . . ."

But I keep moving, faster now. Around the corner until I see the entrance. The instinct overwhelms me. I need to get inside that building.

Rowan grabs my arms and stops me. "Elise—wait!"

I try to break free. Rowan does a visual sweep.

"Think," he whispers and holds me to him, tighter and tighter until I can't move and my body stops fighting.

He doesn't have to say more. I know what it will do to them if I enter the building, calling out their names, hysterical, terrified. The moment will stay with them. It will never leave. It will change the way they see the world. The way they see me and our life. The wires inside their heads.

"Okay," I tell him. Promising. "I'm okay."

He lets me go and takes my face in the palms of his hands. "They're safe, Elise. They're safe."

And I repeat the words until I know it's true.

"They're safe."

The moment passes, and we find ourselves back at the car. I'm wired but also exhausted. We get inside, but Rowan doesn't drive. He takes my phone and looks at a message that preceded the live feed, searching for something that might help us find Wade.

"He's said this before," Rowan reminds me. "'I just want to see you.'"

I nod and catch my breath. Wipe my face. I'm a mess, inside and out. "And now he's threatening my family." I stare at the phone, even though the live feed is gone.

"What do you want to do?"

For the first time in my life, I don't see a path forward. Wade is a ghost, and we have nothing to go on. No prints or hair or soda cans or coffee cups. No vacuum dust from a dumpster or tire marks or even a license plate. We have a facial composite. Witnesses to a crime that happened over two weeks ago, their memories now compromised by time. A community weary of the story, changing the channel. It's next to nothing.

The resignation begins to settle in. I know how to do this work. Take my time, be patient and methodical. But Wade is a lit fuse. We don't have that luxury.

I think about the burner phone. I think about telling Rowan, pulling it from my pocket and handing it over. I picture his face when I do—the anger that I waited, then the determination to find this man and make him pay. And then what? I go down one of two roads—the first, traveled with my partner and the department, following the rules, keeping me safe first and foremost. It feels narrow and confined, and I know it will come to an end. Wade will stop using the phone and find another way to get to me. The second road feels wide and endless. And under my control.

Looking at the crossroads, having taken my small steps, I can still see the way back. This feels like the point when I have to choose.

I keep the phone in my pocket as a plan takes shape.

"He wants to see me," I tell Rowan. "That's what all of this is about. It has to be the reason."

Rowan shakes his head. "No. No way."

He's said this before when I've had an idea he doesn't like. I know how to get around him.

"A meeting in a public place. I'll go alone but wear a wire. You'll know everything that's happening. You can be close by. He can't hurt me in a Starbucks."

Rowan looks at me like I'm crazy. Maybe I am. But these are my children.

"I don't think he's going through all of this just to have coffee with you."

"So I'll ask him what he does want. Maybe if he sees me, if he can see that this is over and whatever he thought he could get from me is gone, he'll move on."

I think it through as I talk.

"Hear me out," I plead with Rowan, my eyes back on the school where my children are safe—for now. "What if he was just a man who was shopping for pants, and the things he did in that store came as a shock to him—so much so that they shattered his ego and made him seek a way to go back to his life? To his real job and his real name and the man he saw himself to be? He told me that was why he left Nichols—that he wanted to be the man he was before the shooting."

Rowan wears a new expression now. Something I haven't seen before.

"What?" I ask him.

"He was filming your girls at their school. And now you want to have a friendly chat and send him on his way? Back to his life before all of this?" He reminds me of the assault on Vera Pratt. "*That's* why he left the scene."

While he's talking me out of it, I begin to type a message.

"Elise," Rowan says. "What the hell are you doing?"

I type until I'm done and hit Send.

"What will he do next? What will he do to my family if I don't see him? If he shows, we'll get him. If he doesn't, then we've called his bluff. Given in to his demands. And we'll move on to the next demand, and that will give us more information and buy us more time. Right now we're the ones resisting, and it's making him angry. Look what he did today—to my girls . . ." My voice shakes, and my face flushes with a surge of blood. These words are somehow bigger after they leave my mouth.

Rowan takes the phone from my hands and reads the message.

Tomorrow. 2:00 p.m. Ridgeway Diner.

"You're not doing this," he says.

The phone chimes. I lean over, and we read the reply together. Wade doesn't say anything I'm expecting—something like *Come alone* or *This better not be a setup*. He doesn't insist we meet somewhere more secluded. He doesn't make any demands at all, and the burner phone remains dead silent in my pocket.

He simply says, *See you then.*

CHAPTER FOURTEEN

I lie in bed with Mitch curled behind me, his chest tight up against my back. His arm tucked under mine, hands clutched together by my heart.

So much has left us. Moments like this one had bound us together. The simplest gesture of how he held me saying more than a million *I love you*'s. I hadn't thought about it before. I'd taken it for granted. His hand in mine, pulled to my heart. Every morning before we climbed out of bed to begin our days in our separate lives, we'd had this. Hands to heart. Proof of our connection. Our love. Binding us together.

We are bound together by something else now—fear. Both of our hands tremble.

We went through the options, not as a police family, but as terrified parents. Take them away somewhere. Send them to his mother in Florida.

We've been over this already. If Wade wanted to get to them, he could follow, and to a place we couldn't control.

Here, we knew the neighbors and the teachers and the kids who played in the street. We had an entire department looking out for us, that now saw this as personal. One of their own being threatened. New measures were being put into place at the school, and our house was on virtual lockdown with an upgraded security system.

Again, we decide to stay so I can find Wade and put an end to this.

I leave our bed around midnight, as soon as Mitch has drifted off. I tiptoe into the girls' room, stare at them both a good long moment. Then down the stairs to check on the detail. I can't make out their faces, the two colleagues who have given up their night to protect my family. Rowan says they like the extra pay and the time off during the day to see more of their kids, or sleep if they don't have kids, or do their laundry and binge-watch their shows. He tries to alleviate the guilt.

The alarm system has been activated, and now any break of any seal—door or window—goes out to the detail and the dispatcher. No middleman. No well-check phone call before the troops come storming in.

None of this settles my nerves.

I go to the kitchen and pour a glass of Mitch's scotch, the good stuff, which feels like magic when it hits my blood.

Sitting at the kitchen table, I stare at the burner phone and think through the day that's passed and the day that's about to come. If Wade believed I had any intention of meeting him alone, he would have used this phone, which isn't being monitored. He would have asked to meet in a place he could control. He knows that I'm awake, here or on the sofa, thinking about him and his motives and why he's letting me go through with this bullshit.

It's hard to think through rage. It causes a physical reaction that produces chemicals. Rage begs and pleads for a reaction, and the body responds. It's primitive.

I drink the scotch to fuck with the reaction. That's how I think of this battle being waged inside my head—with irreverence and determination. I will not succumb to any of it. Not the rage or the fear. Wherever the guilt over Clay Lucas is hiding, I let it stay there. The shooting and whatever else it's done to me locked away with it.

In one of my classes, I presented a case study on stalking. I told the students that, at the end, I wanted an answer to the question *why?* It's the one crime that is certain to fail.

Our case involved a woman who broke up with a man. There were no children, and they had only been together a few months. The man could not accept her decision. It began with text messages. Dozens of them each day. Protestations of love. Analyses of her emotional flaws, why she couldn't accept his love. *I'm not like the men before, the ones who've hurt you.* Warnings about her future if she didn't take him back. How she would never find love again. How she was a piece of trash and lucky to have him. He used the same words Wade has used in his messages to me. *Bitch. Cunt.* The transition from "love bombing" to violent threats happened over a matter of days, the communications and actions starting with all love and ending with all hate, the ones in between mapping the shift within his mind. He didn't want to hate her. He didn't want to hurt her.

Next came the sightings. He was outside her apartment. Outside her office building. Outside the grocery store, then inside, an aisle away, making sure she saw him and knew how close he was.

She told the police. Got a restraining order. There was nothing they could do. There were no stalking laws back then, and there is nothing uniform today. Even the states that have them do little in terms of enforcement.

What did this man think would happen when he broke into her apartment, left a rose on her pillow? Then a dead mouse? Then a pile of dog shit? He found ways in, no matter what she did. He dedicated his life to her every movement. Just like Wade getting into my house, spying on my children.

Breathe in. Breathe out. Don't give in. My heart still races as I see the pattern.

I asked my students, does he believe this woman will take him back? That threats and coercion will lead to genuine affection? If this is the motivation, it is delusional.

Or is he simply unable to control his behavior? Is his obsession with her so big that he cannot turn away from it? That he has to satisfy it any way he can?

Or is this about power and control? Does he know that every time he stalks her, he is causing a reaction—fear that disrupts her life? Does this replace the satisfaction he felt when they were together? Has he accepted the rejection and moved on to revenge?

And, in any of these scenarios, how will it end?

I made them answer before we got to the conclusion of this one story. When he was outside her door demanding to be let in. When she called the police and begged them to come. When they arrived, walked him to his car, waited until he drove off, and then left. And finally, when he returned half an hour later, broke down the door, and stabbed her to death in her bed.

Most of the students concluded that he was mentally ill. No sane person would believe that stalking behavior would lead to love, and his final act was certain to (and did) land him in jail for the rest of his life.

In that case, they were right. The stalker was eventually diagnosed with a delusional disorder. But the research on stalkers and outcomes varies wildly. There are few predictors of the outcome, and the psychology of the stalker is usually not fully understood until the behavior stops—one way or another.

I down the rest of the scotch and stare at the phone. What is happening here? There has to be a cause for this. Who was this man before the shooting? What did the shooting do to him? I cannot make assumptions. I have to gather evidence and apply possibilities and likelihoods, without assuming one is right and the other is wrong.

This unsettles me. The not knowing. The unsolved puzzle, the missing pieces I have to work now to find. I have to be clever enough to find them, even as the rage begs and pleads.

That's what this is now. A game of wits. Maybe this is one of the pieces. Wade is enjoying this game with me. Maybe it's giving him back the power he lost when he stood on the other side of a loaded gun. Maybe he is having the response Dr. Landyn warned me about—that he soothed himself with delusions about fate, that we were meant to be together. Whether it's true or not, he believes I saved his life, and now he craves a connection with me, even if the only form that takes is through this game he's playing.

Maybe, maybe, maybe . . . The word reignites more rage inside me as I hear it with every thought that searches for an answer.

I pour a second glass of scotch.

It's after one when I return to bed and crawl beneath the covers. Mitch finds my body with his and wraps us up together again, like people do when they love one another. I take from it what I can, the warmth. The safety in this moment.

Five hours later my eyes dart open, and a deep, shocking breath rushes in. I wake from sleep like I'm waking from the dead.

I listen to my house—to the radiator popping and Mitch snoring and something ticking, his watch on the dresser or the clock in the bathroom. Antiquated sounds from an old house, old fixtures and accessories, an older man than the one I married. I listen and feel at peace. For a moment.

Fran finds us, beside herself that we are both still in bed. She jumps in between us and snuggles all the way under the covers until she disappears. I hear her giggle when Mitch tickles her feet. He's good at this. At keeping things normal. At pretending. Just the sight of them triggers the same fear in him that it does in me after what happened at their school.

My baby giggles and squirms and seeks refuge by climbing up and over me to the other side where her father can't reach her. She pleads for me to help, and I run my hand softly on the inside of his ear, which makes him yell "*Stop!*" because that's the most sensitive place on his body.

And I don't know why, or maybe I do, but I wonder if Briana knows this about him. If they made love that way, exploring every inch of skin with their hands, mouths. Or if they just fucked half-dressed over a desk or against his truck or her car. It's a horrible thought. Four years have passed. But it has been unearthed because of Wade. Because he asked me things and I told him things that day on the outskirts of town, and now he's inside my head, making me think about what's inside of his. And from there, what's inside of anyone's.

The not knowing is familiar and has brought me back in time.

I had not seen the change in Mitch four years ago. I had not smelled her perfume on his clothes or felt her touch lingering on his skin. I found out through an acquaintance, someone who'd seen them in her car at a time when Mitch said he was still at the jobsite. And then I waited. And I watched. I investigated my own husband for six days—the way I would a suspect in one of my cases. The moment I finally caught them never leaves me.

I hadn't seen it coming. Even with all of my training, I ignored the signs that were right in front of me. Just like I ignored the alarm bells sounding off as I followed Wade to that back road. I wanted to believe my husband would never stray. I needed to believe Wade would save me from myself by giving me the answers I needed about the shooting. Human want. Human need. They can be unstoppable.

Rowan doesn't want me to meet Wade today, but Aaron has approved the operation, and he's the boss. We have to call Wade's bluff. Force him to come out of hiding or move on to his next demand and see if that can tease out more information. More clues. There is nothing to be gained by staying in this stalemate, forcing him to escalate his behavior because I refuse to meet him. Aaron has assigned two units to stand by—one in the kitchen of the diner, one in an unmarked car parked outside.

None of this will matter, though I keep this to myself.

Wade knows how we work. The things to look for. He knows how to spot us and get around us because I posted it online and now he has it. All of it. Beyond this, we still have no idea who he is, where he's from, and what he might have learned before he ever met me.

I hadn't seen my own husband having an affair. I would be foolish to think I can see Wade for what he is.

Not yet.

I pick up my daughter and set her down on the floor. "Go tell Amy to get in the shower. I'll get breakfast."

I give her a big kiss, and she runs off screaming her sister's name, knowing it will annoy her to be woken so abruptly. Years from now Amy will remind her of what a pest she was. Maybe at a graduation or a wedding, and with the laughter of shared memories and endearment.

They will have that. Whatever I have to do now, I will make sure they see that day.

I take my horrible thoughts about my husband with me to the bathroom and try to scrub them off as I wash my face and brush my teeth. I barely notice that the bruises have changed color. I've become used to them, accepting that they'll remain a part of me until this is all over. I'm still in my sweats from the night before, so I put on some deodorant and return to the bedroom. I'll shower later, after I get the girls on the bus. I'll need to choose my clothes carefully so I can cover the wire, and I can't think it through until they're gone. Until the house is quiet.

Mitch is still in bed when I open the door.

"What?" I ask him because his eyes follow me as I walk across the room.

He smiles. It's sincere but sad. "Nothing," he says. But then, "I'm just happy you came back up last night. I miss you."

I crawl beside him and kiss him and say all the right things back. And he pulls me to him, thwarting my escape from the bed and the room and the thoughts that did not wash clean.

He brings me into a giant bear hug, and I want to disappear, melt into his body. I am no longer steeled to what I have to do, and my breath grows short and erratic as I hold back a swell of emotion. Mitch can feel it. We've been here before.

"Hey," he says, lifting his head to look at me. "You don't have to do this."

He doesn't want me to meet Wade. He doesn't want me used as bait.

I exhale long and hard. Then I answer him with as much truth as I can spare. "I can't take much more of this. I have to find him and stop him."

He squeezes me tighter, and I think he's about to say something comforting and consoling. But he doesn't. Because there's nothing he can say that isn't just wishful thinking.

The Ridgeway Diner is clearing out by two. It's in between lunch and dinner. I sit at a booth across from the counter with the red leather stools. A waitress has poured two cups of coffee.

Tape pulls at my skin where the wire is adhered, and I think that Wade will know it's there. He'll know everything about today because he is thinking backward, just like I taught him. He's pictured himself in an interview room, in custody. Me and Rowan across from him. A folder on the table between us. He's thought through how he got there. The unmarked car in the parking lot. The unit in the kitchen, Rowan probably among them. He's thought about the thing he said that went through the wire and into Rowan's ear and the recorder stuffed into my bag—the thing that was enough for them to make their move. A confession. A threat. And then back before that, he's seen me at the table by the window, across from the counter that leads to the kitchen. Halfway to the front entrance and halfway to the back. No easy way in or out.

And so I wait, letting the coffee get cold. Knowing he won't show. That he never planned to.

And yet he needs to see me. Whatever his motivation, he isn't done with me. We won't catch him today, but it will provoke him. Something will come of this.

I could have waited to contact him. Told no one. I could have made promises that I would meet him alone. And he would have no choice but to assume I was lying. The time in between the making of the plan and the execution of the plan would make it impossible for him to know for certain. Whenever there is time, there is doubt.

The element of surprise is a criminal's best weapon.

I remember the examples I wrote about in that case study. The woman walking alone in a parking garage with her keys laced between her fingers, glancing over her shoulder, ready for anything. *That's not your victim.* It's the one who's forgotten about the danger, the one who hasn't pictured herself trapped in the trunk of a car on the way to that notorious second crime scene where she is sure to die—*that's the one you want.*

I had written all of this down. *Trust and distraction are common mistakes.*

Wade isn't coming. But planning this without Rowan, without Aaron, would have eroded their trust in me. I need that trust so I can continue to deceive them. The thought sounds crazy and rational all at once.

Wade isn't coming—because he can never be certain I'm being honest when I say I'm alone. He will always assume there is a car in the lot and cops in the kitchen and a wire on my back.

The next time we meet face-to-face, I won't see it coming.

CHAPTER FIFTEEN

The number one reason criminals get caught is lack of discipline. The ones who get away, the so-called masterminds, have impeccable self-control, motivated by calculation rather than emotion. Theft, for example, driven by desire for greater wealth can be calculated. Theft driven by desperation, homelessness, starvation, especially involving a child or other loved one, will always involve emotion, and therefore be vulnerable to mistakes.

Murder, kidnapping, assault—the same rules apply. A crime of violence committed to send a message or eliminate a competitor for example, can be calculated. A violent crime driven by anger, fear, jealousy, revenge—these will come littered with evidence that can be found and analyzed. Whether there is justice can't be predicted, of course. So much depends on the resources and intelligence of the good guys and the bad guys. But mistakes are most likely to be made when the brain is compromised by feelings.

I am about to officially give up on Wade showing when I see Rowan rushing out from the kitchen, the swinging doors slamming against the sides of the cake displays.

"Go!" he yells. "Go!"

So I go. I race out after him and the second officer from our squad.

I don't ask what's happened. I assume that they've spotted him or the truck and that he spotted them back and took off.

This doesn't make sense to me. There's no way he would come this close.

We get outside and survey the parking area. It's a small strip mall with parallel parking at the curb and angled spaces on either side of a grass median. Our people were in the last space at the end of the curb so they could get out quickly, which they have now done. They've popped the flashing red light on the roof of their SUV and are in full pursuit of a blue truck, both vehicles now out on the main road.

We can't catch up to them, so we stand on the sidewalk and watch.

Rowan holds his phone, pacing. Excited. "Do we have him? Tell me we have him!"

We watch as both vehicles pull to the side, two lights down the road. Specks off in the distance. And for a second, just one second, I let myself believe it's over.

"What's happening?" I ask Rowan.

Our colleague steps away, also on his phone, also getting an update. They hang up at the exact same time.

Now the burner phone buzzes, and my hope leaves as quickly as it came. I knew better than to let it in.

Rowan stares at the scene unfolding down the street, hands on his hips, shaking his head. "It's not him," he says. "Just some kid with a blue truck."

Some kid who got paid two hundred bucks to drive through this parking lot, slow down in front of the diner, then drive at least two lights away—no matter who followed him. Some kid who got paid in Bitcoin. Who communicated on Reddit with an account that is now gone. Vanished.

"Fuck!" Rowan says. "Fuck!"

I don't tell him about the messages that wait for me on the burner phone. Guilt tugs at my heart, but the plan is in my head and I cannot let it go. It has become my lifeline. The only way I see out of this. I have convinced myself, and there is no turning back. This is a game Wade and I must play alone.

My nerves settle as we get back in our cars. Me in my Subaru. Rowan and the other guy in the SUV parked around back.

"They're bringing the kid to the station," Rowan tells me, and I agree we should talk to him and find out everything we can. I know already there will be no trace.

Rowan doesn't take any chances. He watches me get in my car and lock the doors. I drive around back as they walk, then follow them. If Wade was hoping to create a diversion, pull the first unit away with the truck, then send me back to my car alone, it doesn't work. Of course, he knew it wouldn't because it's the first thing I consider when we get the news about the truck. Wade is in my head the way I am in his.

I check the messages only when we're back inside the station, waiting for this kid with the blue truck who will be useless.

The first is a video clip. There's no time stamp, but it's recent. Mitch grew a beard after the shooting. I think he felt exposed the way I did, and this made it better for him. It wasn't rational. Still, he'd never grown a beard before the shooting. Now here he is. With Briana, with the beard. With Briana, sometime after the shooting. Within the past three weeks.

I know the scene. The house. The truck. The people.

It's Mitch, standing in Briana's driveway. They are at the end of something, a conversation perhaps. I see them hug. Mitch rubs her back and then lets her go. They don't kiss, but they do linger. I can't hear their parting words or even see their mouths as they move, but I can tell they're speaking even as Mitch gets into his truck.

Wade was on the road in front of the house when he filmed this. It has a fully exposed, sprawling front lawn so he would have no trouble parking and recording through the window. There's an unobstructed view from the curb up the entire driveway to the house. Mitch would have noticed the blue truck there, which means Wade has access to a different vehicle.

This is confirmed by the second message, which contains a photo of our officers in their SUV at the Ridgeway Shopping Center. I can tell from the angle that it was taken through a car window parked across the median.

Wade was there today, in a different car.

A third message comes in now—short and to the point.

They don't deserve you.

I am disturbed by the video of my husband and his mistress. I can still feel his body wrapped against mine just a few hours ago. But this photo from the parking lot causes a different reaction.

I study the angle just like we did at the school. Where he must have been in the parking lot with the median. Then I think about where I'd left a bicycle, chained to a rack, with a camera attached beneath the seat. I told no one. Not even Rowan. I've already kept so much from him, gone down this road too far.

I can tell from Wade's picture catching our team outside the diner that I have also caught him on my camera. He's in a car. I can see a piece of the rearview mirror in his photo. I am not arrogant enough to think that having this information will lead me to his door. But it is something. A loose end he never should have risked.

The only calculation devoid of emotion would have been for Wade not to come near that place. But he did. He needed to see me, and he needed me to know how smart he is.

Emotions. Feelings. Fucking up his perfect plan and feeding right into mine.

CHAPTER SIXTEEN

THE KILL ROOM

The state team puts eyes and ears under the bridge by the river in the neighboring town. They continue to work the theory that the remains found in the cremation oven belong to a drug dealer. It's a good theory, which they have little trouble selling to their commanding officer, a young lieutenant with a lot on her plate. They tell her about the murder three years ago and the traces of Oxy found in the red jacket and the balloons in the well. Now they want to investigate a dealer who might have gone missing. If they can get an ID, maybe they can track down dental records. They need to identify the victim.

The lieutenant is impatient with them, so they do not linger on the details—how there is too much evidence or not enough. How the killer knew what he was doing. Knew about the unpaved road leading up to the shelter that would need to be raked and the cremation oven and, of course, the Kill Room. They don't tell her about the team they have scouring the internet for a source that might contain all of this information. A website or forum. Maybe on the so-called dark web, which isn't all that dark anymore when it comes to stuff like this. There is a newfound sense of freedom in the world, a *what the fuck are you gonna do about it* sentiment. The only things that stay buried, or at least try to, involve money and sex—child pornography, human trafficking, tax evasion. It feels like a long shot. Likely to fail. No point drawing attention to how quickly this case is getting cold.

The missing dealer goes by the name Nix. The CI who gives them the lead describes him as young, definitely under thirty, maybe even in his late teens. Pinpointing age within a pool of criminals is harder than people imagine. The distinctions that can serve as starting points are often absent—clothing, grooming, gait, speech. There is a tendency to conform, to fit in. No one wants to stand out and later be identified by a witness, surveillance camera, or undercover cop. Some things really are the way they're depicted on TV. Nix wears loose jeans, sneakers, T-shirts, and hoodies. Sometimes a denim jacket, but then with a baseball cap. No team logo. He is like background music, the CI tells them.

It only takes a day to find someone who knows where he lives.

The girl won't give her name. She is somewhere between a runaway and homeless—not that there is a clear line. It has to do with time, really. And hope. The runaways still think they can get out from under the condition of not having a place to stay, their addictions, their poverty. Like somehow this is only a temporary situation. The brain isn't fully developed until well into the twenties, and the last part to finish forming is the part needed to make decisions. Executive function.

The girl calls herself Honey, which of course is not her real name. But they call her Honey and give her some cash, and she leads them to an apartment over the border in New York. She doesn't know how old Nix is or his real name. Just that he shares this apartment with some other guys and let her stay there a few nights when she first left her shitty home. She has turned eighteen and has big plans now that she is an adult. They don't ask Honey what she does in exchange for the shelter or what drug has sucked her in and has yet to spit her out. They buy her lunch and give her a blanket and deliver her back to her new home under the bridge.

With the help of the local NYPD, they sit on the apartment for eight hours—enough time to get a warrant. The application cites behavior that indicates drug trafficking, including a visit from a "known offender." They are not asked how they made this identification and will have to come up with something more than they have, which is a visual ID in the middle of the night from across the street. The apartment surveillance shows that this man also wears a hoodie covering most of his face, so if a lawyer ever got into it, the whole case could go up in flames. A bad warrant would negate whatever evidence they find in that apartment. But they don't want evidence to use against the tenants. They just want to identify a possible victim of a homicide. They are trying to help this young man who goes by this strange name, Nix, so they are not concerned with the legality of their search.

It is late afternoon and the place is empty when the super lets them in, opening the metal door with two different keys on two different locks. The smell nearly knocks them off their feet when the door cracks open.

Some of it they can place—the stale meth residue, the kitchen filth, the lingering stench of unhygienic humans. One of them asks, "What the hell is that?" And the other shrugs as they step inside.

The super is the one to answer. "There," he says, pointing to a cage in the back corner. Inside are several puppies. "Pit bulls," he tells them. "The kid found them on the street and brought them home. The owner of the mother dog probably didn't know what to do with them. Easier to dump them on the street than find a shelter, I suppose."

Whatever the situation, there they are—seven pit bull puppies shitting and pissing all over each other in a crate meant to hold maybe one medium-sized dog. That is the smell that makes them pull their shirts over their noses.

They move quickly, one of them searching for mail and papers labeled with names and the other grilling the super about who is on the lease and does he know the other tenants and what about someone who goes by the name Nix?

They leave with more than they bargained for. First, the kid's real name: Billy Brannicks. He isn't on the lease, but one of the bedrooms has a letter with that name, and it clicks instantly. Brannicks. Nix. He is twenty-four years old. Later, they trace him to an address in the Bronx and, from there, to his mother's house in Queens. He had been to a dentist, she thinks, when he was a kid, but the practice closed and she never asked for the records. Still, they had to be somewhere, and this feels like a significant lead.

As exciting as this is, matters are complicated by the stash of guns, drugs, and cash found in a hole behind a bathroom mirror. Later that day, New York cops arrest two men connected to the apartment. They are not told Nix might be dead. They are interviewed separately and wonder if, perhaps, their third roommate has also been taken in and is pointing fingers at them. Naturally, they both claim ignorance. It must be one of the other guys, they each say.

Lastly, the team at the apartment leaves with seven pit bull puppies, which are brought to a shelter.

The mess with the drugs and guns and the possible issue with the warrant are left to New York. The investigators working the shelter in Connecticut have their possible victim and get busy tracking down the dentist who closed his practice and might still have his patients' dental records that are now a decade old.

It is not long after that the other team working the case finds something else. It starts with a chat on Quora. A question about "disposing of a body" asked by a podcast narrator who is following a "true crime" disappearance in Montana. He needs to fill some airtime and thinks he could bring on a few experts to talk about possibilities if this missing person has been murdered. Answers come in from several members, but one entry catches the attention of the team working the shelter killing.

I took a class in college, it begins. The member says she never forgot this one thing. When a student asked the teacher how to commit the perfect murder, she said:

First, you burn the body.

CHAPTER SEVENTEEN

It's difficult to be at the station. The adrenaline has subsided now that the driver of the blue truck is a dead end. We cut him loose, then explain to Aaron how the operation got so fucked up.

"And you're sure he wasn't there, maybe in a different car?" he asks.

Rowan shrugs. "If he was, he didn't make a move."

I say nothing about the camera still hidden beneath a bike seat at the Ridgeway Shopping Center. I can't retrieve it until we finish here and I know the area is clear. Wade could be waiting for me to return and sort out where he must have been parked when he snapped that photo of our guys.

I feel the burner phone weighing down my jacket, and I come so damned close to telling them everything. About finding it in my dining room and about the photo from the Ridgeway and the video of Mitch, and before that, the photo of me asleep on the sofa and the reference to our case from last year. Baby Doe. The case he could only know about by accessing my online materials. Now he is studying them. Learning from them.

Aaron says something like *put it behind you* and asks us to go over everything we have and don't have in the search for the 404. He wants us to come up with a new way forward, look for stones we haven't overturned. "I don't like that we're still waiting around for him to make his next move. We have to get out in front. Stop playing defense."

We both agree and retreat to a conference room.

"Coffee?" Rowan asks me before sitting at the table where we've laid out the file.

"Sure."

I don't need coffee, but I'll take the chance to be alone.

Running side by side with the urge to drive back to the Ridgeway and collect that camera are new emotions that have my heart exploding. I don't even know what to call them.

I take out the burner phone and watch the video of my husband and his mistress again. I study it, looking for anything that might tell me when it was taken. I have nothing to go on except Mitch's beard, and the leaves that are starting to turn. But they've been turning for at least two weeks. Soon, they'll begin to fall.

I put that phone away and take out the other one. The real one that's being monitored. I call Mitch at his worksite. I've already texted him that the meetup was a bust and confirmed I would pick up the girls from school. I read his messages back about how he's relieved I'm safe and he loves me. I texted back the same. *I love you too.*

But now I need to hear his voice.

"Hey, what's going on?" he asks, sounding worried.

"Nothing. Just had a break," I tell him. But the truth is that I need to hear the sound of his voice—or, more precisely, how his voice sounds when he has a secret.

He sighs and whispers, "Maybe I should get the girls. You must be spent."

"I'm okay. How's the job? Did the marble get there?"

He pauses now because I don't always remember the things he tells me about his work. Invariably, it involves people and materials not being where they should be when they should be. Subcontractors. Wood. In this case, marble tiles for the foyer.

"Yeah. Finally. Set us back four days."

My face flushes and tears start to pool, but I fight it, hard. This was how things played out four years ago. I didn't tell him I knew. I waited.

I drew from him moments just like this one where we spoke of ordinary things in ordinary voices. I tried to memorize how he sounded, his tone, and his words. Was he being too kind, too interested? Was he overcompensating to hide? I wanted a benchmark like we take with a polygraph, asking benign questions we know the answers to. We measure heart rate and pulse and sweat when the witness is telling the truth. Four years ago, in those few days when I kept the truth to myself, I collected benchmarks for how my husband sounded when he was cheating.

It's not the kind of thing you can write down, and I find that I can't remember. As he speaks to me now, after he's seen this woman again—Briana—I don't know if it's how he sounded four years ago because he sounds like my husband, and then I think maybe he's just that good a liar. Some people are. Especially when they feel justified.

Rowan comes back soon after I've ended the call.

"What?" he asks me. I'm not as good at hiding, and he sees the distress on my face.

"It's just . . ."

"I know," he says. "This was a tough break. But we're gonna get him, Elise. I promise you that."

I nod, take the coffee he's brought me from the kitchen. It's stale and bitter, but I drink it anyway.

The loneliness has returned. I don't think it's ever been this deep. When I learned about Briana the first time, I turned to Rowan. When work had been hard, frustrating, I turned to Mitch. When I need more than they can give, there are friends and my brother, and my girls, of course. That love has guided me through the darkest nights.

Now I keep secrets from all of them, hiding behind another invisible wall.

Rowan sits across from me. He takes a long sip of coffee then makes a face. "Fuck, that's bad."

I manage a smile. "Yeah. Seems to be the theme of the day."

He lays his palms flat on the table. "Okay. I'm just saying it. That was a shit idea from the start."

It's not what it seems, I want to tell him. I need to get to that camera.

I need to get to my husband. Thoughts spin. Emotions churn. I feel like a tinderbox.

Rowan studies me longer. He knows something's off, but it would be strange if it wasn't after the morning we just had and the day we had yesterday. A man is stalking me. Stalking my children. And we aren't any closer to finding him.

"Okay," he says. He takes a clean sheet of paper and puts it down between us. Then he stands and finds a red Sharpie and starts to write. He makes a list of the dead ends.

First, the name Wade Austin. Not only was he not Wade Austin from Shield Insurance, he wasn't any Wade Austin we could find.

Second, missing persons. No one matching his description has been reported missing in any jurisdiction that feeds into the FBI database.

Third, there were no matches with criminal complaints—stalking, domestic violence, and the like. We've had prosecutors and PDs throughout the state looking through their case files for male suspects matching Wade's description.

Fourth, none of the tips called in about the facial composite have led to a positive identification of the 404 or the blue truck.

The list goes on—no cell phone to trace, no license plates, no tips that panned out, and nothing of use from any of the security cameras at Nichols or the parking lot. Just that one image as it drove away.

Rowan sits back down, and we stare at the red ink and the list that looks very long.

"He really is a ghost," Rowan says. Then he leans forward and stares at something on the page. "Why an insurance company?" he asks me. "Wade Austin from Shield Insurance. He could have used any alias that was hard to search, but he chose this guy."

I know where this is heading.

"I think this asshole works in insurance," Rowan continues. "Or used to. That way he could talk about his job if you ever asked and not raise suspicion. He must have thought this through. He had two weeks from the time of the shooting until he approached you. Two weeks to come up with a false identity."

Rowan gets up once more and begins to pace. "So let's assume he's local, since he was shopping for pants here. That's not something you do on vacation. And now let's assume he works in insurance or used to."

I listen to my partner and I'm right there with him, sharing his thoughts, remembering what I used to love about my life and how desperately I want it back.

"So we check with every insurance agency and broker within, say, thirty miles. If we don't get a hit, we expand the radius."

It's genius, and I tell Rowan this.

"Okay," he says. "Let's get on it!"

I help him gather the papers from the file, lingering longer than I should on the facial composite of Wade. I think about that face and the hundreds of expressions that moved across it on that back road. I think about that face standing in my house, watching me sleep. I think about that face in the woods watching my children play. And I think about that face standing just beyond the young man I was about to kill.

I tell Rowan to go back to the desk without me. I'll be right behind him. "Just need to make a call."

I take out the burner phone and read the message he sent with the video of Mitch and the photo of our team at the Ridgeway.

Now there's a new photo. It's Rowan, sitting at his favorite bar, a beer and a shot on the counter in front of him. The same shirt he had on yesterday. This case is getting to him, triggering things from his past.

And then the same message as before.

They don't deserve you.

I assume implications from this. Mitch is a cheater. Rowan and my colleagues are unable to protect me. But I think now, as the weight of my crimes grows heavy, that maybe he means something else entirely.

Maybe they don't deserve me because of the secrets I keep and the ways I now deceive them.

CHAPTER EIGHTEEN

I make excuses to Rowan about errands and picking up the girls early from school, and instead I drive to the new site where Mitch has been working. I don't warn him I'm coming. I fantasize about the conversation, which is crazy. Just as crazy as my thoughts about Briana and whether she'd found that spot on his ear and caressed it with her finger. Brushed her lips across it as she whispered something sweet, or dirty.

I thought I would be stronger than this, but I'm not. I can't find it in me after everything that's happened. Wade has unearthed this scar from our past—but then she wasn't really in the past, was she? The video is from a scene that was missing a before and after. There is no time stamp. No context. No audio. It's impossible to tell what preceded it or what followed. She looked upset. He was comforting her. Their embrace was brief, but it was in the open. In her driveway.

This is the problem with discrete pieces of evidence. They can be misleading, create misperceptions and then reactions that can cause damage. Dominoes falling.

Mitch had been home every night since the shooting, and before that he'd never given me any reason to think he was still seeing her or anyone else. It had not been like that before. The signs I missed. The distraction from having a newborn and a toddler, and then the sudden death of his father.

There have been moments of weakness these past four years. Moments that caused me to check our credit card bills and bank statements for anything that might be a second phone or a token gift. I have fought them off like enemies, insurgents. I've been winning this battle over the voices that rise from the darker places inside me because there was always light to shine on them.

Thousands of moments of light over fifteen years. Small moments—a soft kiss as we stood side by side doing dishes, one that lingered and grew longer until we stopped with the dishes and found our way upstairs. Not a word spoken. And large moments—taking over the reading of the eulogy when I broke down at my mother's funeral. Reading my words when I couldn't get them out. Knowing I needed them to be said to honor her memory. Holding our babies the moment they were born. Holding me when a case got too hard. There was so much light.

But then there is Wade and the piece of the conversation by his truck that lingers in my mind, about Mitch and Briana. He'd been fascinated by my efforts to uncover the truth after a woman I hardly knew told me what she'd seen and what she suspected after seeing it.

I'd rented a car. I'd parked it along the road half a mile from her driveway. Mitch and his crew were renovating her house, so the driveway was littered with vehicles and building materials. But then five o'clock would roll around, and they would thin out until all that was left was Mitch's truck.

Briana's husband was a corporate litigator. He worked long hours and had a commute on top of it. They had one child who was away at boarding school and now college. Briana was alone in the house, day and night, lonely and bored and approaching fifty. A midlife crisis waiting to happen. And then, there he was. A strong, handsome, younger man in need of comfort. The kind of comfort women know how to give. With their words and their compassion and their bodies.

I'd thought of it like a case. Rowan and I had gotten into some situations by then. Things we would laugh about because at the time they'd felt absurd. Dumpster diving in Vermont. Sneaking into a block party in the city on the Fourth of July. We got a soda can from one, a wine glass from the other. Neither of the DNA had matched our samples from the case, but we were able to rule out two suspects. One by one. We ruled out suspects like shooting fish in a barrel.

I had a camera with a professional zoom. I knew where they'd be, my husband and his client. All I had to do was wait.

The photos caught a kiss through the kitchen window. They moved out of sight after that, but that had been enough. I left them in her mailbox for her to find. No note. It was just a warning. And it scared them both enough to make it stop and for Mitch to tell me before someone else could. I pretended to be shocked. I couldn't manage tears because I'm not good at lying, although I'm beginning to wonder. We all see ourselves a certain way. Then we catch a glimpse in a new mirror or a photo we haven't posed for. We hear our voice on a recording and are stunned at how we look and sound. And then a situation happens. A cheating spouse. A shooter in a department store. A man who threatens our family.

And we're shocked at the things we do.

I pull into the jobsite and find Mitch standing outside with some of his guys. He rushes over to meet me as I get out of my car, his face flushed with fear about our girls because I never visit him on a job.

"What's happened?" he demands the moment he reaches me, and I blurt out that the girls are fine and I'm fine.

"Then what is it?"

I open my mouth to find the words. To ask the question. "I couldn't do this at home," I tell him.

"Do what?" He pulls me aside where no one can hear us. He spins me away from the crew, who begin to disperse, so no one can see my face.

"I know you saw her again."

"How?" he asks. He doesn't deny it.

"It doesn't matter." I don't tell him about the burner phone or the video. I don't have to.

"So you know."

My heart breaks. This can't be happening again. I thought I was prepared, but now I realize that I've been clinging to every other scenario but the most likely one. "Mitch . . . no, please tell me something else."

"I didn't want you to find out. He's caused enough trouble in our lives."

"Who?"

"That fucking psycho."

"Wait . . ."

We go around in circles until I tell him to start from the beginning. To put this discrete piece of evidence into the puzzle where it belongs.

He doesn't use her name. He's careful about that. "Someone slashed her tires—in her own driveway. She was upstairs in the shower when it happened. She'd just come back from the gym."

He lets me process this for a moment. The details. It's not just the vandalism, but the fact that it happened while she was alone, naked, trapped inside.

I stare at him in silence as my heart catches up to my mind. Mitch is not cheating again. Our life together is not coming to an end.

"She asked me—" he begins to say, but then stops himself.

So I finish his thought because more pieces are finding their places, the picture coming together. "She asked you if I did it."

Mitch hangs his head. Sighs hard. "There were marks, scratches, a word engraved in the paint just above the driver's side handle."

"What was it?"

He pulls out his phone and opens the photos to show me. The word is small. Discreet, even. But unmistakable.

Whore.

"Mitch," I say now. "Do you really think I would do this? After four years? And that word—I would never use that word. Not even about her."

He looks to the sky, hands on hips, frustration written across his face. "No, Elise. I know you didn't do this. Not intentionally."

"You think it's him?"

"Who else?"

"You think he did this to her so she would call you and you would go to her and I would find out?"

Now he throws his hands in the air. "Yes. That's what I think."

"Why didn't you tell me?"

His face reflects the questions back, as if I should know the answer. As if it's obvious. "I told Rowan," he says. "He spoke to her, looked at the car. Checked for prints and asked her some questions. He agreed with me, Elise, that you didn't need this right now. On top of everything else."

I can't speak. I don't have the words. What should they be, I wonder? Where should I begin? He told Rowan and not me. Rowan then hid the truth, this new piece of evidence. But it really wasn't evidence of anything we didn't already know. Wade wanted to infiltrate my life. Use the forensics road map I'd created to destroy it. And I'd kept things from Rowan and Mitch. A circle of lies now exposing the fault lines in each relationship.

"When did this happen?" I ask.

Mitch tells me it was before the video of the girls. Right when all of this started. "I haven't seen her again, if you're thinking what I suspect you are."

"I wasn't thinking anything," I tell him. But this is a lie.

He knows what I thought when I learned he'd seen her, what he might be capable of. I know what he thought when Briana showed him her car, what I might be capable of. He knows what he felt when he went to her rescue. And I know what I felt when I thought he had been with her again and I could finally have an answer to the question I've been asking myself for four years.

Knowledge may be power, but it's not always working on the side of good.

Mitch looks up, and we stand there, both silent.

Wade set off a bomb, and now the pieces were falling around us. He's coming at me from all sides and every angle. Physically and emotionally. This whole exercise, vandalizing Briana's car so he could create doubt, remind me not only of what Mitch did, but what I did. It wasn't enough to use words. He made us relive it. Trigger the wounds of the past. It was all one carefully planned mindfuck.

I have to be smarter than this. Stronger than this.

"I have to go," I tell my husband. "I have to get the girls."

But first, I have a camera to retrieve.

CHAPTER NINETEEN

It isn't easy to get away, and nearly two days pass after I retrieve the camera from the Ridgeway Shopping Center. Everyone is watching me. Everyone is worried. Mitch is with me in the mornings and evenings. Rowan is with me on the job.

When I'm done at the office, I go straight to the school to pick up the girls. Unless there's ballet or soccer or a play date, I don't leave the house once we get home because where would I be going? It would confuse the detail, who wouldn't know whether to follow me or stay with them. And besides that, Mitch and I agreed to tag team, to be with them at all times when they aren't at school.

When Mitch gets home, it's game over. He watches all of us like an eagle tracking field mice. We never leave his sight. Even me. Even after all that's happened.

I can't stand not knowing. But I'm patient and I wait until the weekend when I can lie to Mitch about going to the office and lie to Rowan about being at home and when the detail is off duty until after dark.

The texts have been short and carefully planned. He's gotten control of himself. He sends them only to the burner phone because he knows, somehow, that I haven't told anyone.

You're such a naughty girl, keeping secrets . . .

The camera I hid under the seat of the bike caught him. The car was a Ford Focus—a small two-door. He barely fit inside. It was white with Connecticut plates, blending in with all the other cars that day that circled the lot, making that one-way turn around the median to cross in front of the stores, including the Ridgeway Diner.

I ran the plates at the office and contacted the owner. Female. Twenty-nine years old. Recently took a work-from-home job in data entry, so she loans out the car to make extra money. The app she uses is a direct rental service—owner to renter. It operates similar to Craigslist. No middleman. Waivers of all liability required. Everyone on their own to work out insurance and payment, pick up and drop off. But unlike the transaction with the kid who drove the blue truck through the lot that day, this one required the exchange of the keys to the car—which meant the owner met him, face-to-face.

We spoke briefly on the phone. She said he paid cash. She said he wore a baseball cap, jeans, T-shirt, and a red jacket. Casual but neat. Nothing to raise suspicion. He arrived on foot, which meant he must have parked his truck somewhere in the neighborhood and walked to meet her. I asked her if she thought it was strange that she hadn't noticed how he'd gotten to the house she shared with her mother. She said the renters always came alone and without a vehicle. They usually got a ride or took an Uber. She rented the car out for days at a time.

Wade had her car for the afternoon. That was all. But he paid her for the twenty-four-hour minimum without any attempt to talk her down.

She lives twenty miles away. I imagine he chose her because of this. She lives outside the reach of our local paper and her age is well below the demographic that would pay attention to news about a tall man wanted for questioning.

I leave the burner phone under the stairs of the porch in case it has a tracker. Then I make my next move. I arrive by midmorning, and we sit in her living room. She doesn't offer me coffee or water or anything because she's twenty-nine and still lives with her mother. She is still the receiver of caretaking, not the giver. I don't give this a second thought.

I am irrelevant to her, and she is irrelevant to me beyond what information she has to offer about Wade, so I get right to the point.

I hand her the sketch. "Is this the guy?"

She squirms a little because I'm a cop and now I've just asked her something official. "Is this about the insurance?" she wants to know.

I imagine now that someone has warned her about using that app to lease her car. The little research I've done revealed issues with theft and damage to the vehicle, parking tickets, speeding violations, and in the end, no recourse against the renters who leave no credit card or license number. The average age of the car owners is twenty-six—kids, really, who overextended themselves and were now using every resource they had to make ends meet.

"No," I assure her. "It's nothing like that. It's not about the car, but about the man who rented it. We're looking to question him about another matter."

Her eyes widen. She still hasn't looked properly at the sketch, and my patience is running out. I don't have much time.

"What did he do?"

"Nothing for you to worry about."

"But he knows where I live. He's been in my car . . ."

"Really," I tell her again. "You aren't in any trouble, and I doubt very much you will ever see him again."

She stares at me blankly, and I think for a moment she might recognize me from the coverage of the Nichols shooting. But, of course, it's not that at all. She can't get off the concerns about herself. She can't comprehend the world beyond her own, and it makes me wonder how I'm going to survive parenting my girls in this day and age.

A flash runs through my head, about how I have Mitch so I won't be alone, and then to the video clip Wade sent me—Mitch and Briana together within the past few weeks—and the flash ignites, goes up in flames. Will I have Mitch? Do I still have him?

"Look—I really just need you to tell me if this is the man who rented your car."

Something in my voice must have changed because she quickly

looks down at the paper in her hands and studies it intently. "Yeah," she says. "I'm pretty sure."

"Just pretty sure?" I ask.

She looks up, nervous. "Was he really tall?"

"Yes. Over six four. Maybe six five or taller."

"Then yeah. I think that's him."

"And did he ever rent your car before?"

"No."

I ask her about the cash he handed her—four twenty-dollar bills. She tells me it's gone, that she gave it to her mother, who used it for groceries.

"Most people Venmo," she explains. "I don't really use cash. But I didn't mind."

We go over the entire exchange a second time. How she was in her room upstairs when the doorbell rang. Her mother works during the day at a dry cleaner, so she was home alone. She came to the door and walked outside with him to the car parked on the street.

"I never let them come inside," she said.

She gave him the keys, and he got in, turned the ignition to make sure it started.

"He checked the gas gauge and the mileage. I charge extra if they use more than half a tank or a hundred miles."

The car is out with another renter so I can't see it. She tells me she's rented it twice more since that afternoon. "I'm booked pretty solid."

I think about fingerprints and shoe prints and fibers from clothing. *Too much evidence.* The cash is gone now as well. *None at all.*

"And when he came back with the car?" I ask her. "Same thing? He rang the bell and you came to the door from upstairs? No look at which direction he'd come from?"

"Yeah," she says.

"And when he left—did you see which direction he walked?"

She squints and looks out at the street through the window, trying to remember. "No. Not really. I just kind of went inside while he was walking back to the sidewalk."

I try to slow myself down, stop worrying about the time that's ticking away.

Options come and go. A door-to-door canvass asking about the blue truck parked on the street would take hours and likely lead to nothing I could use. I've already confirmed he was here. I need a plate number for the truck.

I picture him in that car, scrunched down low so his head doesn't hit the roof. This was intentional on his part. He's tall and drives a truck, so any association made would gravitate toward large vehicles. It's basic psychology, how our minds crave order. The first time I looked through the recording from the parking lot, my eyes were drawn to SUVs. I had to force myself to overcome the assumptions and search every vehicle. Then I saw him, barely fitting in this small car. The baseball cap, just as she described. Sunglasses as well—classic Ray-Bans or knockoffs. The red jacket.

He turned the corner, drove right past our people parked at the end of the row. He didn't slow down or turn to look at them. He was smarter than that. But when he got to the diner, he couldn't resist. A car was pulling out so he stopped to yield, even though he had the right of way. He stopped so he could look in the window and see me sitting at the booth. Desperate to meet with him. To make him stop. Knowing he wouldn't do either. When the car in front had pulled out, he didn't delay. That would have caused a scene, someone honking behind him. He drove off, a big smile across his face.

I think about what I've started, and it scares me. Yes, he was careful. But all of this—renting this car, exposing himself unnecessarily—something was driving him. Something emotional just as I'd thought. He had nothing tangible to gain from making contact.

If what he craved was power over me, he could have gotten that by watching me from afar. Across the road from the diner, there must be dozens of places he could have observed me driving into the lot. Parking. Getting out of my car and walking inside.

It had to be more than that. More than being able to make me do things. He was showing off his newly acquired skills. Finding the perfect car to rent. Leaving no trace of himself beyond this one witness. Driving right past us to see me in the booth waiting. Using a decoy—the kid in the blue truck. Committing small crimes and evading detection by me and by Rowan.

Still, he took the risks because he wanted me to know. He wanted me to see just how good he was becoming.

I think about what he's been texting me.

Your life will never be the same now.

You've killed a man and you can't take it back.

I'll show you. Just wait. It's coming.

Yes, I think to myself. He wants to show me what he can do, and that there's more. I move from thoughts of what he might know and what he can do, even what he's learned from me through my posts on the college portal, to who he is. What is it he wants to show me? And what will that get him? Does he crave my approval? My admiration? Or does he want to regain control? And from there, what's next? I think about the class on stalkers. About how it's a crime that can never succeed. Yet Wade must believe he can get around this rule. Whatever he wants to show me holds the key to that belief.

I barely hear the girl when she speaks again.

"What?" I ask her.

"He had something with him. A plastic bag."

"Can you describe it?"

"It was folded up when he got the car. Neatly, like in a little square. And then when he dropped off the keys, it was crumpled up in his hand, like he'd used it for something." The bag, she tells me, was white. And it was empty both times. Only he had obviously unfolded it while he had the car.

"What kind of mats are on the floor?"

She shrugs like she can't remember.

"You must clean it," I say. "Vacuum it sometimes so it's presentable?"

Her eyes light up. "Oh yeah! They're just like the rug kind. You know, like the same stuff that's on the roof."

He used the plastic bag on the floor, to keep it clean. He could wipe down everything he touched inside. But if we got to the car before it was used again, his shoe prints might be left on the floor mats.

Now I have another thought. "Did he leave the keys in the car when he returned it?"

She nods. "Yeah. In the ignition."

So he wiped those down as well, I think.

His thoroughness is both satisfying and disturbing. It makes me feel less of a failure to see that he's having to work this hard to evade detection. But then it terrifies me that he's succeeding.

I'm about to leave when she stops me.

"Hey," she says.

I turn, distracted, thinking about how I need to get home and lie to Mitch about what I've been doing at the office and lie to Rowan about what I did over the weekend with my family. But she quickly brings me back to Wade.

"I know where I've seen that bag. It's from a Getaway Inn." She pulls out her phone and does a quick search. Then she shows me the photo. "See—the bright green square with the giant *G*?"

I look at the logo. "It's a laundry bag. The ones they leave in the closet for wet clothes or shoes."

"We used to stay there in high school when we'd travel for hockey tournaments. We always used the pool if they had one. They're so gross. I don't know what we were thinking. It just seemed cool, you know? Staying in a hotel with a pool."

"You put your wet suit in the bag."

"Right! Then we'd shove them in our duffels."

I try not to get too excited as I thank her and say goodbye and walk to my car. But this is something I didn't have before. A lead he may not know I have. I get to my car and search for Getaway Inn locations within fifty miles.

This is another mistake he didn't need to make. A loose end that wasn't necessary. And I've found it. He's not as good as he thinks. He may be a fast learner, but he's still the student and I'm still the teacher.

No tattoos. No logos. Nothing the eye will catch and remember.

That was an essential step—knowing what catches the eye and causes the memory to stick. We erase on average fifty percent of what we see every day. Cars we pass on the road. People inside them or standing at the gas pump or a pickup line. We are still primitive creatures built to assume there is danger around every corner, and therefore we focus on what is new or different. The images from the past have left us alive and safe so they fade into the background.

Wade must have missed this when he was studying my materials. If this was a test, he would have failed.

Knowing this feels so damned good it scares me.

CHAPTER TWENTY

THE KILL ROOM

A new lead comes in while they investigate the materials they find online—the supplements to a class on forensic evidence that looked through the lens of the criminal. They have a call into the head of the school. They have another call into the tech department that manages the school website and the portal used for class materials. They build a spreadsheet matching the topics of the posts and original curriculum with the facts relevant to the shelter killing. Some things are distinct, like the rake and the shelter itself. But others are not. Cremation. Leaving too much evidence. Plastic used to catch blood spray.

Once they have all of the relevant posts, they hope to trace the IP addresses of people who have read them. It's a ridiculous long shot, but it keeps them busy enough to remain in a state of denial.

The new lead has nothing to with any of that. It comes in the form of a missing persons case. The woman's name is Laurel Hayes. Oddly, she is also from the neighboring town where Billy Brannicks was seen dealing shit under the bridge by a girl named Honey and where they had that department store shooting. They find her name in the FBI database.

The first call they make is to Sergeant Aaron Burg, who runs the department where the case originated. He lets out a heavy sigh when they tell him they have a body. That it's been cremated and so all they have are teeth and evidence of drugs in the hunting shelter where the remains were found. Burg says he remembers that place and the execution from three years ago. They talk about the scourge of OxyContin and commiserate about their difficult work trying to wrestle it to the mat. The state investigators tell him which cities have been hit the hardest, and Burg tells them it's everywhere, and they all agree that if they could stem the traffic in the larger cities, that would probably trickle down to the smaller towns, but there would always be communities like "the one under the bridge," and if it isn't one thing like Oxy, it's another. They all recall the crack epidemic in the 1990s, except one guy on the state team who wasn't born until '95.

It does not occur to them to discuss Billy Brannicks because he lived in New York and just because he was seen under the bridge in Burg's town doesn't mean he's connected to Laurel Hayes. They do not think to compare the guns found in Brannicks's apartment to the gun used by Clay Lucas.

They finish exchanging war stories about the drug trade and circle back to the missing woman. Burg tells them he doesn't have any leads. Her parents have been staying in her apartment for almost two weeks after leaving a hotel, hoping she'll return. Forensics found no prints that match in any database, and there were no signs of a struggle. Friends say she was doing some online dating, but nothing that sounded risky. Just the usual shit—guys lying about their looks and money, texting and disappearing.

Their working theory is that she left on her own after the shooting at Nichols. Burg tells them that she had gotten close to the gunman, Clay Lucas, while he was a patient at the day care facility where she was a social worker. Yes, of course, they'd been over the security footage at her apartment building and the day care, Clear Horizons. And yes, they had entered all of the interviews in a digital file.

Burg has the team heading up Laurel's case send that file to the state investigators. He also agrees to ask the girl's parents for dental records. There'd been no point in asking them before. They had no body. No abandoned car. It still seemed likely she had run away. Burg confesses he worried about suicide, but she was close to her parents. Surely if that had been her mental state, she would have at least done it in a way that allowed them to find her body so they could grieve properly. But young people these days—hard to say whether they give a damn about things like that. Probably doesn't even cross their minds. *Gen Z, you know.*

When the file comes, the investigators are not looking for Clay Lucas, though his photo is in the digital file. Burg's team had already done that, hoping to find some contact between Hayes and Lucas outside of Clear Horizons. Something to shore up their theory that she felt responsible for what he did that day and what it cost him. Instead, they look for other men. She was a single woman. Young. Attractive. Most women are hurt by a man.

They also find the notes from the interview with her closest friend from college—a young woman who lived up in Bridgeport. She had little to offer, and yet Laurel Hayes's phone records show numerous calls between the two women up until the day she disappeared—the same day as the shooting. That was also the last day Laurel Hayes used that phone.

A woman on the team picks up on this. *No way they talked that much and she doesn't know more.* This friend in Bridgeport had been Laurel's confidante. And the calls increased in length around the same time the text messages started to fade. They went from texting to calling, which is significant. When people stop putting things in writing, even private texts, there's a reason.

They make a plan to reach out to the Bridgeport friend. They wait for the dental records from Laurel Hayes's parents. But first, they go over the security footage.

It's the young man from the team, the one who didn't remember the crack epidemic, who spots the red jacket. Had the jacket not been such a significant piece of evidence found at the shelter, it would have passed him by. A man with a red jacket sitting on a bus stop bench across the street from Clear Horizons—not just once, but four separate times.

The last time was on the day Laurel Hayes disappeared.

They go over the possibilities—two completely separate theories. First, the remains belong to Billy Brannicks, killed over drugs or illegal guns. Similar story as three years ago. Or they belong to Laurel Hayes, a young woman who's gone missing in the neighboring town—close enough for the killer to know about the shelter, that it was a good place to kill, or to dispose of an already dead body. The dental records will decide which theory to follow. If it does turn out to be Laurel Hayes, they may have to find this guy with the red jacket.

But for now, they wait.

CHAPTER TWENTY-ONE

My secret investigation into Wade Austin is full-on after I get the lead from the car he rented. No one would approve of my methods or the chances I'm taking to execute my plans. I weave a complex narrative to justify it to myself. Rowan, Mitch, Aaron—they'd make me stop. They'd question my moves. They'd get inside my head and make me question them myself. I am now a criminal thinking backward, not a cop trying to catch one. I am plotting a crime against Wade, stalking him now. Infiltrating his life.

Wade. The 404.

There are four Getaway Inn hotels within a fifty-mile radius. The plastic bag he used to cover the floor of the rented car likely came from one of them. This is the best assumption I have to work with. I have to believe this and move forward. If I stop moving, all hell will break loose inside me. I know it. I can feel the emotions wanting to be set free. If there is guilt, I have locked it away along with the impact from the shooting, the stages of trauma I should be going through. I am high as a fucking kite on surviving, on hunting my predator. I can't stop until this is over.

This is my own painstaking work. I do not ask the managers or the clerks or the cleaning staff if they've seen a blue truck or the man in our facial composite. I do not even set foot inside the hotels. I use remote cameras now because I had time to purchase them and set up an online account. I attach them to bike seats like I did at the Ridgeway. Each one feeds into a website, sending images of people and cars, coming and going from the hotels. I find locations where the bikes won't be out of place and where the cameras lodged beneath the seats can capture the entrance. Three are on main roads with one way in and one way out. The fourth has a back exit as well, and this will require two cameras and more time going over the surveillance. I watch the recordings in the kitchen while my family sleeps. I limit the recording hours from 8:00 a.m. until 10:00 p.m. I assume he won't come or go when he could be easily spotted. Still, I am always behind, watching scenes over the course of three days.

I find time to replace the batteries, but it's not easy. There are only so many times I can tell Rowan I'm home with Mitch and tell Mitch I'm on the job with Rowan. I wait in fear of getting caught and remain in a constant state of anxiety. But then, I suppose I'm used to that.

I park half a mile away or more. I make sure the car is hidden from the road. If Wade has seen me, then he's seen me. What will he do about it? Move locations? It's a risk I'm willing to take. He may have studied my classes, but I remind myself that he's already made mistakes. I have to believe I can stay ahead of him.

His messages continue. He knows I'm reading them. He tells me so.

Elise? When will you answer?

Are you waiting for my surprise?

Maybe he's studying. Learning new tricks. But he can't catch up. I've been doing this my whole life. And yet I am waiting and wondering. I still don't know what he wants to show me and what he thinks it will get him. I do not delude myself into thinking it's insignificant or foolish. I assume the worst, but I don't know what that could be.

At least that's what I tell myself when I stare at my girls in their beds, breathing in and breathing out, lost in their dreams. When I feel my eyes closing in spite of my attempts to keep them open. I have to believe this will come to the kind of ending I can live with.

It's now the third night I've had footage, and I'm watching it on my laptop at the kitchen table. It's just past midnight, and I've made a fresh pot of coffee. I replay the footage as fast as I can without missing a car or a body, coming or going, throughout the day and night. I look for the truck, but I also assume he's on foot, having parked somewhere else. Somewhere hidden from view. The BOLO they issue is across the state, and even with no plate number, it stands out. We've had hundreds of sightings of blue pickups, run the plates, then pulled the owner's photos from the licenses on file. The effort has been futile, which means the officers assigned the task grow weary with each useless lead. Still, he won't take that chance by parking in plain sight.

So I look for bodies, tall bodies leaving their cars and walking to the entrances, the front or the sides. I watch for a head towering over others as they move from all directions, in and out. It's the one thing he can't hide.

The search feels essential. It feels ludicrous. It tests my sanity and my perception of that sanity, as I recall the wild-goose chases of the past that have turned up nothing, but then the ones that solved a case. And then the broken, damaged faces of those who have lost their loved ones and finally have some peace. Justice.

I am now one of those faces. I am working my own case. Saving myself.

This is what I tell myself in the middle of the night when I should be sleeping. These are the whispers of the unsolved mystery. Of Wade Austin, the man who has hijacked my life.

One message haunts me as the chemicals in my brain fuck with my thoughts.

They don't deserve you.

He told me I'm a killer. A liar. And I am those things. I don't know what they've done to me, but he's right. I am forever changed.

Maybe I'm fortified. Stronger. Better than before. Superwoman.

Or maybe I'm damaged. The Titanic after it hit the iceberg. A sinking ship. Maybe the people I love don't deserve this person I've become.

I think about my girls and see the pieces of me, not just on their faces and in their bodies, but the way they are. Fran's irreverence. Amy's cautious calculating. I wonder if I've had enough time to give them what's good in me. If I am the Titanic, I will send them off on lifeboats, far away from me, and watch those good pieces drift to safety. If that's where this is heading, I will make sure they don't get pulled under.

I hear Mitch coming down the stairs and close the computer screen. I hear him stop first in the study where I usually am at this time of the night when I'm not in our bed.

He pauses, and I feel his heavy sigh through the walls and across the floorboards.

Then he is in the doorway of the kitchen.

"Hey," he says. He's been asleep. I can tell from the way his hair stands up on one side and from his deep breaths and heavy eyes.

"I was just coming up," I lie.

He looks at the coffee maker, which is gurgling to a finish, the fresh pot taking in the last drops. "Is this what you did before?"

He walks to the counter and pours the coffee into a mug. Next, he goes to the fridge where he grabs the half-and-half, adds some to the coffee, and returns it. He carries the mug to me and places it carefully on the table. And while he does this, while he delivers me coffee the exact way I like it because that's the sort of thing he knows after fifteen years, I contemplate my answer.

"Yes."

There's no use pretending I don't know what he's talking about. Or that I didn't do what he knows I must have done four years ago when I got a tip that he was having an affair. When I was also solving my own case. He's had time to think since we stood together at his worksite and I confronted him about the recording Wade sent.

He sits at the other end of the table—as far from me as he can get—and he places his elbows down and looks at me in a way I've never seen before. Then he waits for my defense, but instead I deliver the brutal truth.

"I would feed Franny, rock her back to sleep. Then I'd go through the house and cars, yours and mine because sometimes you took my car when you had the girls. I didn't expect to find hotel receipts because you had her empty house all day. I didn't look for messages on your phone or emails on your computer. I knew you'd be more careful than that. It was easier knowing who it was. I guess I got lucky. Small town. Everybody knows everybody else."

His face changes now as he pictures me having these thoughts about him. Analyzing him like one of my suspects. A fish in my barrel.

"I used a lint roller on your coat and the clothes you tossed in the hamper and the seats of the car. Hair sticks to things. People don't realize it, but it can even be in the air, if there's enough physical activity, and it lands on a shirt that's on a chair, or maybe the hair was on the chair already, before the shirt. Mine is dark. She's blonde. It just took one. One long blonde hair. I also used a blue light in the truck because sometimes her house was full of workers—so, you know, there was that possibility. That you were with her in the truck."

Another shift on his face. Another expression I don't recognize as my words roll right off my tongue like a robot. I should feel things now—remorse or anguish at what his affair led me to do—but instead I feel detached from him, separated by the anger I'd felt years before, which has now become a scar. No longer painful but dull to the touch where the nerves have been severed.

"From there, I gathered evidence. Two afternoons I had the sitter come, so I could run errands."

"The pictures," Mitch says, almost as a question even though he knows the answer.

"I just said—I ran errands."

He drops his head so his eyes can escape mine. So he can not look at me—this woman who is suddenly a stranger to him the way he had become a stranger to me four years ago and again just this week. I have spoken to him not as his wife, but as a cop relaying facts—distant and cold—and he knows I couldn't help it. That the scar is still there. And that all this time he thought it was gone.

How easy it is to make this shift, from thinking we know someone completely, to thinking we don't know them at all. When, really, it's always somewhere in between. Until the day comes when we can read another person's thoughts, this will be true. Of friends and enemies. Of family and foe. Of lovers and haters, spouses and exes. We never truly reveal ourselves, and we never get to see the true reveal of others. *Never.*

I wonder if we are all destined, then, to the kind of loneliness Dr. Landyn described during our sessions.

"Why didn't you just ask me?" Mitch says as I sip the coffee.

The question has an air of absurdity to it, but I give it an honest reply. "Because I wouldn't have believed you if you told me it wasn't happening. And then you would have either ended it or been more careful and I never would have known."

"So you did surveillance? After you used the lint roller and the blue light—you watched her house and got close enough to take those pictures? My God." His mind reels now with the implications. "You were at the window."

"Yes," I say. "I couldn't get a shot from the street."

"And how long did you stay there? Watching us?"

"Well," I tell him, "I stayed until I couldn't see you anymore. You started in the kitchen and then moved from sight. Where did you go?" I can hardly believe I ask this, but I do and then I don't stop. "I've always wondered. Did you go upstairs to a bedroom? Her bedroom— the one she slept in with her husband? Or the living room sofa? Or a guest room?"

He is stunned, and when I come to my senses, I am as well. Stunned at how easily I have slipped into this role of the curious investigator. Out of the role of the betrayed wife. The heartbroken woman. I am all of those things, all at once, but they don't know how to coexist. They have never had to before.

"I'm sorry," I say now and reach out for his hand, which he pulls away. "I had to know the truth. I would have gone crazy. You know that about me. The uncertainty, every time we were together as a family, and again as husband and wife. How could I have been that woman without knowing if it was a lie?"

This shift from the facts of my investigation to my desperate hope to save our marriage brings a swell of emotion I can't hold back. I love this man, in spite of everything. The scar is there, and yes, it is dead to the touch, but it is not all of me. It is not everything.

For the first time since Fran was born, I see tears well in the corners of his eyes. "You put those photos in her mailbox."

"Yes."

"All this time, I never knew. How is that possible? It's your fucking job, and I never even suspected. We thought her husband hired a PI. That's why I told you and why she told him. And it ruined her life, Elise. You ruined that woman's life."

He looks at me with incredulity through red, swollen eyes. And I can see that he believes this. That I ruined his lover's life by capturing evidence of their affair.

"She didn't have to tell him. I just wanted it to stop. And I wanted to see . . ." I can't finish. I choke on the words and the emotions, new and old. All of them devastating. He had the affair. And now he's upset that I was the one who unearthed it.

Mitch finishes my thought. "You wanted to see if I would tell you. If the fear of being found out would make me come clean. And all this time you let me pretend I did the honorable thing. That I came forward on my own, out of guilt and shame . . ."

"And respect for our marriage!" Where is this consideration? How can he not understand that I did what I had to do to be sure of him? Of us? "What would have happened if I had been the good wife who came out and asked you? Or maybe said nothing? Would it have just died out after I got back on my feet? After Fran started sleeping through the night and I could see straight enough to meet your needs? Or would you have lied about it and kept it going? Lied about it and stopped? Do you even know?"

Mitch shakes his head. He still hasn't lifted his gaze. "Maybe I don't know. But the way you frame it, that you were exhausted from the baby and up all night, that you couldn't even see straight. And yet you saw straight enough to investigate us. To stalk us and take photos . . ."

"Us? Now you and Briana are 'us'?"

A raw, bitter silence comes between the "us" that exists in this room. This kitchen where we had gone on living our lives until that day at Nichols.

I can't undo the things I did. I was trained to do them. I had the skills and knowledge, and I found the strength because my life depended on it. And Mitch—he can't undo what he did, desperate for something I wasn't giving him. Finding it with someone else.

I think of saying more, about how I resented him for needing things from me, new things he hadn't needed before. Things that scared me, especially when I felt so vulnerable. But when the words form, the sentences come together, I realize how horrible they are. There is no reframing them to make them better. I hated that he needed things from me when I needed things from him. So I withdrew into myself. And he turned to Briana. Then I stalked them and planted evidence that ruined her marriage.

We should never have allowed these revelations to rise to the surface. They should have stayed buried with everything else we hold inside—big things and small things, a million things every day and over fifteen years.

But it's too late. I wipe my eyes and take a breath. "I'm asking you now what you wanted me to ask you that day I confronted you after work. Was that the first time you saw her again—when she thought I'd slashed her tires and keyed that word into her car door?"

Mitch looks up finally. His face is empty. Spent. Like he's felt everything he can tolerate.

"Mitch . . ." I prod as he gets up from the table.

I reach for his arms as he passes by, and he stops long enough to peel my fingers off of him.

With every step he takes away from me, down the hall, and up the stairs, I examine the regret he wants me to feel. The shame at what I've done. And I see it for what it is and have no regret and feel no shame. The thoughts return—I am an investigator. I have these skills and this knowledge, and asking me not to use them to find an answer to a question that involves my marriage, my family, my heart—well, that's simply too much to ask.

For four years I've stayed and worked and worked and stayed. I've swallowed down the thought of her touching him, knowing about that place on the inside of his ear, the sound of his moan, the feel of his hands, his body. I have done it because I accepted my role in making him vulnerable. My neglect of him. I've done it because I knew that I loved him and our family and because the moments of happiness have far outweighed the pain I've had to swallow. I've done it because he's human and worthy of forgiveness.

Now, I imagine, he will have the same journey to forgive me. He will have his own pain to swallow, the images of me invading his privacy in every possible way. Of ruining his lover's life. Of forcing him to stop being with her. I can't take that journey for him. I can't make him want to take it.

And if that journey isn't hard enough, I add to it with my new list of crimes.

And yet I am not deterred.

I wipe away tears and drink some coffee. Then I open the laptop and resume my secret hunt for Wade Austin.

CHAPTER TWENTY-TWO

The morning is still. Not so much as a hint of a breeze as I walk back from the bus stop. A neighbor is beside me and remarks about this weather phenomenon I would not have noticed otherwise.

"The calm before the storm," she says.

I look at her then because this expression hits a nerve. I haven't heard from Wade in twenty-eight hours. Over a full day with nothing. It doesn't feel right. Just like she said. It feels like a premonition.

My neighbor turns her gaze to the sky. "They said late morning, but I don't see any clouds."

I do the same. "Nope. Not a one."

"Storm season's here, and the leaves are still turning. Suppose it's climate change."

We pass the detail, the gray SUV. Both of us hold up a hand and give a quick wave. Two officers, rookies as usual, nod back at us. It's almost comical. A parody.

"Sorry about the trouble," I say because I like this woman, whose name is Sunny and who used to invite me over for a glass of wine now and again. I suppose I could count her as a friend. She moved in next door three years ago with her husband. They have twin boys in fourth grade.

I feel a hand on my shoulder and then a quick squeeze before it leaves.

"It's no trouble," she says.

We're at my house and the flagstone steps that lead to the door. She doesn't say her usual quick goodbye. She doesn't keep walking to her own flagstone steps and walkway and door. Instead, she stops and faces me.

"People always say they can't understand why celebrities aren't happier. They're so lucky to have all that attention and money and never have to worry about anything."

I think I know what she's trying to say, and it makes me deeply uncomfortable. "I'm not exactly a movie star," I tell her. I try to be lighthearted. I sweep my hands in front of my body. "Not that Hollywood isn't banging down my door to get a piece of this."

She laughs and nods but then returns to what she wants to convey. "You saved those people in that store. You saved their *lives*. And now you deserve to be protected. We owe that to you. And whatever pain it's caused you—well, I'm sorry. It shouldn't be that way."

Sunny has me on the brink of tears, and I don't have the energy. I've been up most of the night again, scouring footage from a hotel parking lot, and now I have to get to the job and function until it's time to pick up the girls from school, and Mitch will work late because he can't stand to be around me, so I'll retreat to our room and let him spend time with his daughters. I won't think about what is happening to our marriage. Instead, I'll wait until the house is dark and my family is in bed and I'll make a fresh pot of coffee and it will all begin again. This endless cycle of watching and waiting and wondering when the storm will hit and whether I can stop it.

Sunny sees the tears well, and she cuts me a break. "When this is all over, whenever that is, let me take you out. I think you could use a few cocktails."

She looks away, smiles. Glances toward her house. I follow her line of sight, and we both spot an Amazon delivery truck. It's one of the smaller ones. A white van.

"Oh my God—*Silence of the Lambs*, right? Vans still freak me out," she says.

"Yeah, definitely. Never park next to a van in a parking garage."

"See—now we have to go out! You could give me useful advice, and I could cheer you up. Think of it as public service outreach."

In spite of myself, I lean in and hug this woman whom I barely know but who seems to know more about me than I do at the moment. I am lost inside my own mind, the trees in the forest whose edges have disappeared. When I let her go, we use banal pleasantries to detach from this moment of connection because it is intense and we both have things to get to. There's no graceful exit.

She walks away, and I give it just a quick beat before heading up to my house.

Inside, the quiet mirrors the stillness of the weather. I close the door and turn the lock. I purge myself of the tears and the sunshine and the hug. I move quickly now because the two young officers out on the street are waiting for me to leave so they can leave too. It's been a long night for them, and I imagine they have normal, ordinary lives waiting. Hot showers and sound sleep.

I go first to the kitchen where I bring two cereal bowls and two juice cups and one coffee mug to the sink, rinse them, and put them inside the dishwasher.

Upstairs, I turn on my shower and let the water run. And while it runs, hopefully from cold to hot, I check the girls' room, drawing comforters loosely into a shape that covers each bed, turning off the lights. Their bathroom is across the hall, and I see the light on there as well, so I make a final stop before checking the water.

Fran left her pajamas on the floor. I pick them up in one hand while I reach for the light with the other, and it's then that I see a pink towel on the floor, just beneath the hook behind the door where it must have fallen. I don't reach for it. I don't move a muscle.

The water runs next door. Fran's sweet baby smell rises from the pajamas. And my heart pounds, just from the sight of the towel, and I realize that all this time Mitch has been cleaning up after the girls so I wouldn't have to see them. The pink towels. He hangs them up behind the door, washes them every week. Tucks them into the drawer beneath the sink. In spite of what's going on between us now, my husband has been doing this for me. I don't know what to feel. Has he done this to appease his guilt? Was I supposed to notice before today and return the kindness somehow? What used to be so easy between us now feels like a maze I can't get out of. There is nothing but confusion around every corner.

I bring that thought with me as I drop the pajamas in the hamper and then take off my sweats from the afternoon before, which have carried me into this new day, and enter a room now filled with steam. I leave the door open to let it out, then get into the stall. The water shocks my senses away from everyplace they want to take me. But the thought stays, lingering through pathways of memories—small acts of love like picking up towels and holding me through the night, strong arms, warm body—until it can't find any more and slowly recedes.

I'm wired as I wash my hair and soap my body, moving quickly because I'm running late. Through closed eyes, I picture the cops in their SUV checking their phones for the time and sighing with irritation. And then I see Sunny walking to her house, not even at her flagstone before I turned away.

These thoughts, too, find small memories and bring them out for me to examine—my subconscious asking a question I can't quite articulate.

Sunny walks. My eyes are watering. The sun shines, and the air is still. But the sound—what is the image that wants to be seen again? A van. A delivery truck. White with that orange arrow. The one we're so used to seeing we don't even notice anymore. The truck from Amazon. Squeaky wheels parking across the street a few houses up. It arrived while we were waiting for a different set of squeaky wheels—those from the school bus.

After the shooting, Mitch ordered the pink towels from Amazon. The truck delivered them in a brown box. The driver left them right at the doorstep. Only that vehicle was bigger. They come in all sizes now, I think. I've seen some as big as moving trucks, which are brown, and the small black ones with electric motors that remind me of Europe because of their odd shape, and others that are just white vans.

White vans with an orange logo.

And how hard would that be—to rent a van and have a logo made and stick it to both sides? Not hard at all, especially if that's all you had to do all day. Not hard at all, especially with the websites and apps that connect renters with car owners. And owners of white vans.

Fear crawls from these thoughts to my body, down my spine, and through my blood where they find a pulse. I gasp for a breath but otherwise stand frozen, my back to the open door that leads to the bedroom, the stream of water hitting my chest.

Slowly, I reach out and turn off the faucet. The air stirs with steam, but all sound fades as the pipes settle. I wipe my eyes with my hands and move to face the glass door, which has fogged.

It's only a shadow, I tell myself as I look through to my bedroom. It doesn't move as I lift my hand and press it to the glass, clearing my field of vision from left to right.

And when I can finally see clearly, when the steam is wiped away, the shadow becomes a figure and the figure becomes a man who lets me see his face before disappearing.

Wade. It's Wade, in my bedroom! Inside my house!

I try to scream, but my throat closes. I'm back at Nichols. I'm pinned against my car on a back road. I'm watching a live feed of my girls on a playground. Images of my husband and his lover.

It's becoming familiar, so the reaction passes quickly through me. In mere seconds the shock is gone, and I am moving with clarity and intention.

I grab a towel and wrap it around my body. I take a nail file—the metal one with the sharp end—from the shelf against the wall with the window. I see my sweats on the bed just through the door and think that my phone is in the pocket and the burner phone is in the kitchen where I left it and that Wade is making his escape. If he'd wanted to get to me, he could have.

He could have come into the bathroom and locked the door behind him. The water was pounding, and my back was turned.

I stop at the entrance and exhale quickly to even out the adrenaline.

I picture the sharp end of the nail file plunging into his neck, his left carotid artery because I am right handed. I will have to reach for it.

And then I make a move.

I scan the bedroom in an instant. It's clear, so I go to the bed and shake the clothes, then feel them with my left hand because my right hand holds the weapon and my eyes do not leave the open door to the hallway. Nothing falls from the pockets. The phone is gone.

No phone. No gun because it's still locked in the box downstairs. The windows face the backyard. I can't see the street. My voice will be muted if I call out to the detail, and even then, there would be too many words.

I hear footsteps on the stairs. I know every sound this house makes. He's taking them slowly, wanting me to hear the way he wanted me to see. But he doesn't want to catch me. He doesn't want me to catch him. This is a game he plays in his mind, and now in mine.

I put on the sweats. Drop the towel to the ground. Next, I go to the hallway, and the sound of the feet on the stairs quicken and then become steps across the floor that leads back to the kitchen. It's the same sound I hear at night when Mitch comes to find me.

I run after him because if this is a game, I want it to be over. I want to win or lose or draw—any way it has to happen.

I'm at the bottom of the steps when I see the front door but hear the back door and know I have a choice. It will take Wade fewer than ten seconds to reach the van, where he'll get inside and turn the ignition, his feet on a plastic bag or a rubber mat. He wears a uniform, polyester head to toe. A matching baseball cap with the Amazon logo. He's been back in my classroom, reading about diversions and hiding in plain sight. Reading about cases where a killer gained entry to an apartment building by posing as a cable repairman. Or a security guard. Or a mail carrier.

I think about the rookie cops out in that SUV. I think about them checking the time. Used to nothing ever happening on this detail. Not once. Everyone assumes that he is done with me because I've kept things to myself. Complacency has set in. This is why he's waited. Another lesson I taught him.

I can go for the front door. Race outside. But he will beat me to the van, drive right past me. I have nothing but my body to stop him. The detail is facing the other way, in the wrong direction. Five seconds to reach them. Fifteen to explain. Then they'll have to call it in while they start the car and turn it around and chase after the van.

And then what?

The sound of the back door is still hanging in the air as these calculations are made in mere seconds. They come not as thoughts now but instincts.

We won't catch him. The van will disappear before more units can get to the neighborhood. Once he leaves my street, he can choose left or right, then left or right or straight, easily five or six times before we could catch up, and that's assuming we guessed right at each juncture. The odds are against us. Against me. Because, I remind myself, I am alone with this man. With his obsession. With the knowledge about the plastic bag from the Getaway Inn and the surveillance from the Ridgeway Shopping Center and the secret phone.

I am alone, the way I was in Nichols that day.

I am alone now, in this house, as I look out the window from the front hall and see the van disappear down the road. The rookies don't even notice because they have grown weary of checking their rearview mirrors.

My body feels limp as I walk the same hall as the intruder, to my kitchen and the back door that is closed as it was before. He must have walked right in my front door because that was the only one I left open when I took the girls to the bus stop. He drove the van from the other end of the street. He parked. He carried a package, which I see when I open the back door, now unlocked.

He walked up my flagstone steps and into my open house and waited for me to return. I wonder where he hid as I cleaned the dishes and turned on the shower and then went to the girls' room and their bathroom and picked up the pajamas from the floor. I wonder if he pulled that towel from the hook and let it fall to the floor where I was sure to see it. And remember.

I wonder where he hid while I took off my clothes and got in the shower and how long he stood there, watching me through the doorway and the steamy glass, reveling in my vulnerability.

I take the package, place it on the table and open it with the nail file that remains clutched in my hand. Inside the box is a crisp new folder. I pick it up with clumsy, trembling fingers. The adrenaline has subsided, and I am left frail and limp. It's a struggle to stand. To remain upright.

I open the folder to find a stack of photos. They've been printed at an office store. The paper is glossy and the images sharp. These did not come from the hotel.

They are images of people, gathered in pairs and small groups. I recognize the scene. It's from the underpass, from under the bridge. These are the dealers and the sex workers and the homeless. These are the people who provided shelter to Clay Lucas, who gave him access to a gun. The photos then zoom in on the small clusters so each face can be seen in at least one frame. Faces of people from under the bridge. Faces of the dealers. Faces of people I told Wade I wanted to die. I think about the words I used. *Hatred. Vengeance. Justice.* I told him that it tortured me, having killed a man. But that I knew I could kill again if given the chance to rid the world of this evil. The person who put a weapon in the hands of someone like Clay. Someone sick and vulnerable.

I didn't mean it. Not any of it. Yes, I wanted to find the dealer. And yes, a part of me had been reeling with these raw emotions. When I followed that blue truck to the edge of town, I'd been holding them in for two weeks because I knew they were dangerous. It's what our brains do for us hundreds of times every day. Push against emotion with reason. With civility. And morality and judgment. The world would be a very different place if our impulses were left unchecked. If it suddenly became acceptable to behave however we wanted, moment to moment. Instead, we don't even speak of the things we want to do and say, let alone do and say them.

But for that one moment on that back road, Wade managed to tear down the barricades, to give me permission, and I did speak of the things I wanted to do and say after the shooting. It felt safe because he echoed each and every one. He, too, wanted to find the dealer and rid him from the world. He, too, felt rage and hatred. His eyes lit up when he said this. And again, when I said it back.

Christ, I know better.

The last photo zooms in on a young man. I don't recognize him, but his face is circled with a red pen. And I know exactly what this means.

I hear the burner phone, which he moved to the counter near the coffee machine along with the one he took from my clothing, buzz with a new message. It says simply, *You're welcome.*

CHAPTER TWENTY-THREE

I gather my thoughts and make a plan. I won't tell anyone that Wade was in my house. That he left me this gift. The fact that he came here means my plan is working. I have chosen the right road to walk down, and it's a road I have to walk alone.

I think about what this means, this picture of a young man. It has to do with Clay Lucas. More specifically, it has to do with the gun he nearly used to kill Wade, the gun that got him killed in the end.

The search for the original owner had led to dead ends. Guns are everywhere, and saying that is not a political position or opinion. It's an objective fact. They're purchased at stores and gun shows, resold on the internet and on the street, places like the one we have here under the bridge. They're stolen off delivery trucks and from manufacturing sites and from people's homes. They're smuggled in from other countries. They're even printed now.

This was just one gun. All identifying markings had been removed. The ammunition was indistinguishable. So it came down to assumptions about where Clay Lucas might have gone, might have been, people he might have seen, and who might have given him a gun or sold him a gun or been so careless with a gun that he was able to take it in the middle of a dark night while he wrestled with his demons and the chemical disorder that afflicted his brain.

I've seen the reports. The interviews with our detectives in vice and with the feds who came to dip their toe in our little pond until the media trucks drove away. They had done their own investigation and come up empty-handed. Yes, Clay Lucas had been spotted under the bridge, taking refuge with others who had nowhere else to go. The ones who were helpful had nothing to hide, and so they admitted to seeing him sometime before the robbery. They could not be more specific, except to say it wasn't that day or the day before. Time slipped away easily, marked by the weather. Hot or cold. Rain or snow.

They were less forthcoming about anyone who might have given him access to a gun. This was a community that functioned on symbiotic relationships. The homeless provided cover for the dealers. The dealers brought relief to the homeless—food, blankets, cigarettes, alcohol, drugs. Some were clean but down on their luck. Others had lost their battle with addiction. Others still, like Clay Lucas, were mentally ill.

Attempts to study them end in frustration. Diagnosis isn't a ten-minute process. It requires cooperation and submission and trust. The dealers don't want social workers and shrinks hanging around, and the homeless gain nothing by attracting them. They gain nothing and lose everything by biting the hands that feed and protect them. And would bite them back without a second thought.

There is a balance that cannot be disrupted by outside do-gooders. A social order, a culture built on rules and loyalty and punishment for disobedience.

Then there is the missing woman—Laurel Hayes. We don't know what to think. What to make of her disappearance. We consider the possibility she lied to her parents and her coworkers at Clear Horizons. Maybe she did see Clay Lucas after he stopped attending the day care. Maybe she gave him shelter or money after he ran away from home. Maybe she was somehow involved in helping him get his hands on that gun. Someone did.

There it is again—the word *maybe* clinging to every theory, every thought. I force myself to swallow the anger it provokes.

This picture I hold in my hand is the result of a different kind of investigation. It's the handiwork of the man I inadvertently trained and who knew about the people under the bridge from our conversation. He didn't think forward the way others had, starting with the fact that Clay had a gun and that he had been spotted under the bridge. He thought backward and asked the question I should have known to ask had I not been preoccupied with the pain of my numbness and my guilt and shame from killing a young man.

The day Clay beat his mother and escaped her care, he ran away. There was a short effort to find him, and it produced those few witnesses who'd spotted him under the bridge. He became another runaway in the wind. Another victim of a mental disease who had left treatment and disappeared. Finding the missing is how I've spent the majority of eight years. There's a reason for the dusty files that remain unsolved.

I can hear the question in my head as I move through my house, get dressed, lock up as if nothing has happened. As if Wade did not walk through my front door and hide and watch me in the shower and then leave this present at my feet.

Why did Clay Lucas go to the bridge to begin with?

He was too young to know about that place. He'd been sheltered in hospitals and at home for most of his life. He'd never run away or been out of the watchful eye of a caregiver since his diagnosis when he was just sixteen years old.

How did he know to go there? Miles from his home on the other side of town. No transportation. No phone. No money. And yet that was where he ended up.

I stop moving after I've gotten dressed. I stand in my bedroom and try to navigate through spinning thoughts and frayed nerves and a churning gut. There is a physical disruption inside me. A sickness that pervades every cell. Every function. Whatever decision I make now must be held to a higher scrutiny. Impulses cannot be trusted. They tell me to scream and cry and drive in circles until I find Wade and take him down. I fantasize about throwing him to the ground and cuffing him and reading him his rights and putting him in my car and delivering him to my partner, who then drags him to an interview room where he is interrogated and then, finally, thrown in a cell. Impulses tell me to fight, but they don't know how, and so I weave these absurdities.

I don't know if what I am about to do is right or wrong. But I think about it from every angle and run down every possible outcome and finally make the decision.

The Lucases live seven miles from my house. I tell everyone I need to—the rookies in the gray SUV, who missed Wade walking through my front door, and Rowan, who is already buried in paperwork—that I'm going to a doctor's appointment. No one wants to pry, and I think that maybe I can use this a few more times before it becomes suspicious.

I take the back roads and pull into their driveway twenty minutes after leaving my own.

They know I'm coming because I've looked up their number in our system and called ahead. I told them who I am. I told them I am coming alone. I gave them this time to prepare.

Aaron had been in touch with them several times and said they didn't blame me. He said they wanted me to know that. But time has now passed and whatever caused them to feel that way has likely shifted. Just after the shooting, their son was a villain and I was a hero. Scrutiny had fallen upon their family. Judgment for not supervising such a sick man.

In the end, though, we have the attention span of small children. The scrutiny has since faded, along with the spotlight. Just like a political scandal or a celebrity divorce or a storm system moving toward the coast of Florida, a category five, no wait, now a four, and then never mind, it turned out to sea. The media attention surrounding the shooting was long gone. Not even the plea to the public to help find Wade had renewed the interest. Once a story was gone and people had digested it, folded it into their knowledge of the world, they had little interest in going back.

So I brace myself for the likelihood that this has happened to them. The scrutiny has faded, and their feelings about me have shifted to what my feelings would be if they had killed one of my girls. Hatred.

The house is a one-story ranch. A weathered For Sale sign is posted on the front lawn. Two cars are parked in the driveway. One is a small SUV. The other a utility van with the logo for Lucas Electric on the side. Flowers hang from a pot on the front porch, along with two wooden chairs and a round table in between. The setting is out of place, likely staged by the realtor. I can't picture Clay's parents casually enjoying nights spent on the porch, waving at neighbors as they walk dogs and supervise kids on bikes. I can't imagine what they live with. What they now hold inside.

I pull into the driveway and don't hesitate. I brace myself for whatever I'm about to find.

Bruce Lucas is fifty-seven. His hair is silver, and he appears gaunt and thin but somehow not broken. Sandra Lucas is fifty-three, and she has the look I know too well. The grief has been ravenous.

They greet me at the door. As I walk inside, I glance behind me from force of habit, to where Rowan usually is when I'm in the company of the survivors. This time, he's not there, of course, and the reflex reminds me that I'm not operating at full capacity. I'm compromised by exhaustion, and the shock of having Wade inside my house. In my bedroom.

The Lucases are polite and cautious. They lead me to a cozy living room with gray sofas and a chrome coffee table. The floor is covered in carpet that shows signs of wear from a busy family. Photos hang from the walls and sit on the TV stand. My eyes catch a glimpse of Clay as a little boy. I would know those eyes anywhere. They haunt me.

This has been the Lucas family home for twenty-two years. Three children were born here, and the house beats with the memories of those lives. The babies learning to crawl. The toddlers learning to walk. Adolescents and teenagers coming and going, day in and day out. And then the sickness that crept inside and cloaked those memories with something heavy.

As we sit around the coffee table, I notice that the room is dark. No lights are on anywhere in the house, and the shades are all drawn—maybe this reflects their mood or maybe they are still hiding from the outside world. Whatever the reason, I fear that my calculations were accurate and my visit needs to be brief.

"I apologize for the intrusion," I say, looking at the folder in my hands as they study my face—searching for something that might tell them how horrible I feel, or perhaps not. Perhaps I am disdainful, among those who would judge them and cast blame. They knew I had struggled, taken a leave of absence. I had not smiled or shown gratitude at the award ceremony at town hall. I have not given a single interview. So they wonder.

I want to meet their eyes and let them see what this has done to me. That killing their child has killed a piece of me and now put my own family in danger. But instead I open the folder and take out the photo of the young man with the red circle drawn around his face. I reach out with the photo in my hand and don't look up until their eyes have shifted from my face to this image I have asked them to see.

They take the photo and huddle together to study the young man. Now I am the one who watches their faces, searching for any sign of recognition. This is what I am trained to do. This is what I would do if Rowan were here and this was just a case from a dusty box. But what I really do is look for a reason to blame them. I feel it suddenly, like a reflex. The pain of being here in their home, sitting where Clay might have sat, my feet on the carpet over which he might have crawled and walked and ran. I don't want this pain. I can't stand it. And so I search for reasons to blame these people for making a child I was forced to kill.

This meeting has to end. And quickly. We are, all three of us, too human to tolerate the intolerable situation I have created by coming here.

A moment passes, and I see it. Sandra Lucas leans back, away from the photo and the man whose image it has captured. Her face contorts into something unpleasant and then shifts to sadness.

"The rehab," she says quietly. Her husband nods, also remembering. "The last one." Her eyes begin to tear, and her husband strokes her arm as she closes her eyes, and then he looks back at me.

"At the hospital?" I ask, though I know the answer. I know every facility that treated Clay Lucas. Every doctor. Every therapist.

His father nods. "This boy was there with him. It was three years ago, and he was older than Clay, so he must be in his early twenties now.

He was there under a court order. Part of a plea deal for a drug charge. They put all of them together. Clay had been using. Self-medicating, they call it, but it doesn't matter why any of them do what they do. They pile them up in one warehouse and treat them all the same because they know none of it will stick."

I try to swallow, but my mouth, my throat, are too dry. Wide-eyed, I watch Clay's mother, who fights to hold back the tears, and Clay's father, who protects her by telling the story and whose anger radiates through the darkness in the room. I can't look away no matter what it does to me. I know the wounds are happening, but I can't feel them. Not yet. The pain will come later when I relive this moment. Over and over and over.

"His name was Nix. That's what Clay called him. He was on his meds while he was there. Have you ever seen someone on heavy anti-psychotics?" he asks me.

I nod.

"Then you know. It's not like he was just a different version of himself. To sedate what happened inside his mind—well, it acts like a medical lobotomy. He spoke like a child and needed help the way a child does. A small child. Help getting dressed and eating and using the bathroom. It was all day every day, the care he still needed when he wasn't—" He stops talking suddenly like he's remembered a promise he made to himself before I knocked on their front door. He does not want to start down this path, and I am grateful when he gets ahold of himself.

"Do you remember anything else about this young man?" I ask. I stare now at the parents of Clay Lucas, and I see his nose and his eyes and his jawline and his shoulders and then my gun pointed at his head and the bullet entering from behind, the explosion of flesh and the fall to the ground and the twisted leg.

I don't how much more of this I can take.

They both shake their heads. All they can tell me is when and where and why he was there with Clay. And the name Clay called him, which sounds like it wasn't his real name, but still a solid lead. All of it is solid. Not just for me, but for Wade, who has already found him.

I reach out, and they hand back the photo. I put it in the file and stand.

They follow me, each sighing with relief as we walk to the door. When we get there and I step outside, I turn quickly and open my mouth because the words are screaming to escape.

I feel the blood pulse as my cheeks flush and my eyes cloud with tears and I start to say them, "I'm sorry. I'm so sorry for your loss. I have children. I know . . ." I told myself not to do this. It is self-indulgent and cruel trying to take from these people more than I already have. Trying to extract forgiveness from those who need to place blame the same way others do. The way I wanted to do just moments before.

Bruce Lucas speaks as his wife walks away and lets out a cry that slices through my heart. "Thank you," he manages. Then he closes the door before I can finish.

He does not mean those words. He isn't thankful for anything. But he's a good man, struggling with what he wants to say to me as he hears his wife cry and what he feels he should say so that he has no regrets after I drive out of sight.

Which I do. I run to my car and peel away from the curb and don't look back.

I have a new mission now. A mandate. Wade is steps ahead of me—five, ten, a hundred. I can't possibly know. The student has graduated. I can't make assumptions. Just because this kid knew Clay Lucas in rehab doesn't mean he helped him get a gun. Just because he was under the bridge, his face captured and circled in red marker, doesn't mean Wade has done more than find him, watch him, and take pictures.

It could be a trap. Bait. A misdirection to cause me to react in a way I'll come to regret.

It could be a gift, a way to find peace if this kid was dealing guns and put one in Clay's hands and we can now find him and take him off the street.

When I'm far enough away from the Lucases' home that my heart settles and the adrenaline drains, I decide that what I need resides in the twisted mind of this man I helped create.

It's there I now have to go.

CHAPTER TWENTY-FOUR

Possible victims:

Billy Brannicks—suspected drug and gun dealer from New York; possibly the same motive and players as the shelter killing three years ago.

Laurel Hayes—missing woman from neighboring town; no apparent connection to shelter; killer assumed to be local.

The trouble with the Brannicks theory is that the killing three years ago wasn't all that similar. The only similarity, in fact, is that Brannicks presumably dealt drugs and traces of drugs were found at the shelter—in the well and the pockets of the red jacket hanging on the back of the door. The killing three years ago was an execution. The body left to be seen. To be identified. Drug killings usually serve more than the obvious purpose of taking a life. They send a message about power. It's business. There are things to sort out, like territories and loyalty. Why kill this kid called Nix and then go to the trouble of hiding it by burning his body?

As for Laurel Hayes, the dental records take longer than expected. Her parents, it turns out, have returned to Oregon. They've cleared out her apartment, settled up the lease, and gone home. They have trouble finding her new dentist in Connecticut where her records have all been transferred. Her childhood dentist made copies before sending them to her new one, but the copies are in storage with a company that handles thousands of practices. A request like this can take weeks. Richard Hayes promises to do what he can, but he lacks the urgency they are expecting under the circumstances.

The woman on the team wonders if he doesn't want to know. If maybe he's delaying the identification of the body so he can hold on to hope that his daughter is still alive.

Others think it might be shock or the manifestation of a passive personality—the kind that succumbs to any and all authority, including the receptionist at his daughter's old dental practice.

Regardless, they are stuck with two possible victims, each seemingly unrelated to the other. Of course, there are other possible victims who have yet to be reported missing. So they stop waiting around and work with what they have.

And then lightning strikes.

The class is called Leave No Trace: How to Commit the Perfect Murder. They find it by tracing the IP address from the Quora chat discussing the disposal of bodies—the member who said she'd taken a course in college and wrote about what she learned. *First, you burn the body.* Her name is Bethany, and she works as a clerk in the county court. She took the class when she was in college over nine years ago. At the time she thought she might go into forensics, but it never panned out. Working in a criminal courthouse was as close as she was going to get. Now she feeds her interest in crime through chat sites like Quora and listening to podcasts.

The portal is open to faculty, students, and alumni. It has materials from classes going years back. They can be anything—from old tests to curriculum outlines to lecture videos. The portal has a search engine so students can look by class name, topic, teacher—anything, really. As an alumna, Bethany has access to the portal. She says she uses it just to read the posts linked to this one class but isn't sure who's posting them. She assumes it's the teacher. But really, it could be anyone with access. Including former students.

Bethany has a long list of gruesome crimes she is following on her podcasts. She says she never forgot that class and thinks about what she learned when she listens to the evidence used to track down criminals. She distracts the investigators longer than necessary. People get sucked in by stories of crime and criminals. Career criminals. Sociopathic criminals. Everyday people criminals. Crime is inherently fascinating.

Once they have the name of the class, they are able to search the portal for every entry posted under the class name. The last time it was held was five years ago. Since then, there have been twelve new entries. They are case studies, some pages long, with facts and news articles, but also an analysis of each crime and criminal. And, of course, a detailed breakdown of the evidence.

Just like they suspected, the materials tagged to this one class contain information that could be connected back to the shelter killing.

First, the case from Colorado involving the pull rake. Takeaway: *Don't use your own computer to research your crime.*

Second, a case involving a dead baby found in a dumpster twenty-seven years before the mother was finally found. There was no DNA at the time. Takeaway: *Never leave the body.*

Third, a case about a husband who killed his wife wearing a different size shoe. Takeaway: *Don't buy your supplies in person near your home.*

Fourth, the drug killing from three years ago at the hunting shelter with a room designed for dressing a kill, the floors covered with plastic sheeting, a cremation oven in the basement. Takeaway: *Kill where there's been other killing.*

The materials from the course itself include extensive notes about every piece of evidence a forensics team could find. It's both fascinating and disturbing to read—all told through the eyes of a criminal. A killer planning to kill.

Bethany say it was "awesome," that it was her favorite class in her four years at the school.

This lightning strike does two things. First, it narrows the search for the killer. The tech department gathers IP addresses for anyone who has read all of the posts submitted for this class. Bethany is one of them, but she is easily eliminated.

Second, it gives them a name. The professor who taught the class. She doesn't appear on the portal, not for the original class or the twelve sub-sequent entries. Bethany doesn't remember it, but the school has records.

Detective Elise Sutton.

The young man on the team puts the next piece together. Elise Sutton is the officer who took out the gunman at Nichols Depot—the cop who killed Clay Lucas. And wasn't Clay Lucas the patient at Clear Horizons, the place Laurel Hayes worked? Wasn't he the reason the cops down there thought she'd left town on her own?

They make a call to their new friend, Sergeant Aaron Burg. They ask about his officer, Detective Elise Sutton. They tell him about her class and the posts she'd made to the portal since she stopped teaching and how they link back to some pretty specific pieces of evidence they've found at the shelter.

Burg is both alarmed and concerned. He tries to reach her, Detective Sutton, who's gone back on leave. He calls her cell. The tracker is off. He leaves a message with her husband. Has a unit stop by her house. This isn't like her.

He doesn't know what else to think. Except that Elise Sutton has disappeared.

CHAPTER TWENTY-FIVE

The plan to find Wade by calling insurance companies and agencies takes longer than we expect. We assumed he worked as an agent because his alias, Wade Austin, worked at Shield Insurance—an agency. What we failed to consider was that he might work in a different sector of the industry.

We get a lead from an agent outside of Hartford, who says an employee at a small shop called Astor Life Insurance was fired a few months ago for sexual harassment. It's the fifty-seventh call we've made for this query, and Rowan reminds me of this as we drive north.

"Fifty-seven calls to insurance agencies looking for a tall male employee. 241calls to courts, lawyers, and stations looking for a tall male stalker or abuser or con artist . . ." He finishes the thought with an exasperated sigh.

"I know," I tell him.

I gaze out the window and try to mask my anticipation. It feels explosive. We've already made a positive ID from a photo in his employment file. The 404 is an actuary named Brett Emory.

Brett. No longer the 404 or Wade Austin. I try to replace him in my mind. Not just the name, but the entire image of him. The terrifying, terrified stalker. The ruthless tall man. The liar. The predator. And now, the insurance actuary.

Nearly two days have passed since he was in my house. Since he was in my bedroom while I took a shower. Since he left me a photo of a young man from under the bridge, a man I've now learned is named Billy Brannicks after calling the rehab where Clay Lucas had met a guy named Nix.

I've said nothing to Rowan about this. I'm too far down this road to turn back. I only told him about Mitch seeing Briana. I knew Mitch might talk to him, so I covered myself. I didn't say how I knew, and he didn't ask. That was a land mine, and he knew to tread carefully around it.

After I left the Lucases' home, I raced down this secret road faster than before. Brett's messages on the burner phone have a calm about them now—like he feels in control. He refers to the things he's done and to whatever he has planned next.

Did you like the gift?
I have another surprise for you.
Are you back on the sofa?
Is Mitch worried about the whore?
Are you?

The team monitoring my phone thinks he's gone silent. Dormant. There is a lightness at the station, like maybe he's moved on. Of course, we still need to find him after what he's done to me and to Vera Pratt in that dressing room stall. He could be a danger to others now, so we don't stop. But there is already talk about removing the detail from my house.

Their road leads in the opposite direction from mine.

Last night I sent the first reply.

Message received.

This pleased him. Excited him. He wrote back seconds later.

I'm glad you liked it!

He couldn't help himself. The speed of the reply. The exclamation point. The interpretation of my ambiguous message. All of it gave away a clue about his state of mind and convinced me the road I was on had begun to yield results.

My words could have meant anything—that I knew he could get to me anywhere, that he could get past the cops on the street and hide in my house, that he left the pink towel on the floor, or that he stood there watching me, naked in the shower, but then left me unharmed. Or the one he chose to believe—that I accepted his gift. The picture of the man who likely put the gun in Clay Lucas's hands.

He could have given me the name. But instead, he forced me to engage in my own investigation, one step behind him.

He revealed himself further.

It isn't rocket science, Elise.

Yes, he'd found Billy Brannicks before me. Thinking backward, about why Clay went to the underpass in the first place. And he was right. We should have been smarter. I should have been smarter.

You win, I wrote back. He answered with a smile emoji.

The drive is almost two hours. Astor Life sells life insurance as the name implies. Brett Emory worked as an actuary, making models that predict life expectancies and try to value policies. A woman named Georgina explains it to us as we sit in a small back office with four desks. She's our second stop, after HR.

"There are a lot of factors," Georgina tells us. She seems genuinely excited by her work. "Age. Gender. Medical condition. Medical history. Family history. Married. Divorced. Widowed. Did you know that men live longer when they're married, but for women it's the opposite?"

Georgina is attractive, well dressed. Warmth radiates from her. She seems approachable. Honest. Kind. An empath. Rowan and I know the type and the psychology behind it. They are rarely suspects and often victims.

She continues, "I used to joke with Brett. When he asked me why I was still single, that was my response. You know, not wanting a husband to steal years from my life. It was a way of deflecting."

Rowan leads our dance, getting the details from Georgina about the two years they worked together. Brett had been here longer—eleven years in total. He was hired right out of college, making him thirty-two. He went to the University of Hartford. Grew up nearby in Glastonbury. His parents are alive but in a nursing home, as far as she knows, although she reminds us that he could have been lying—men lie to her all the time about the oddest things on her dating apps, she says—and then she thinks a bit more and tells us she doubts it. He didn't seem like the lying type.

He has an older sister who lives in Alaska now. A photographer. A free spirit. Georgina said she wondered how someone like that and someone like Brett came from the same parents. He is tightly wound, she says.

Rowan gets every detail. How they spend their days compiling data and hunting down facts about customers, things they fail to disclose, like prescriptions for ED medication they got online, which could mean they have other problems like sleep apnea or alcohol abuse. Or maybe not. They have statistics for everything.

"Brett was very good at his job. Meticulous. Patient. He ran the department."

"And the department is just the four of you?" I ask.

"Down to three now. They decided to cut costs, so they promoted someone from our team to replace Brett and then didn't fill his position. His name is Pete. Anyway, we may be small, but it's a small company. Which makes every decision that much more important."

She becomes defensive, so I shut up and let Rowan lead again.

"So how did all of this start?" he asks. "The events that led to his termination?"

Georgina looks at the floor, swivels back and forth in her chair.

"I know this is difficult," Rowan says. "Why don't you start by telling us how you came to work here?"

We haven't told her why we're investigating her former boss. What interest we have in the man who sat four feet away from her in this back office, making models and predictions about people's lives.

So she starts at the beginning. How she was hired after spending three years at an accounting firm downtown. Better pay and benefits, she tells us. Less stress because there really are no clients. Just the company. No tax season to wreak havoc, no filings that could be missed throughout the year. "It was a lot to worry about. And too much pressure. This seemed much more nine-to-five, you know?"

I look around the small, windowless room with the beige carpet and white walls and sterile desks, and picture Brett Emory barely fitting through the doorframe. I picture him towering from the seat of his standard-size office chair and having to slump to see his computer screen where he sat for eight hours every day, crunching his numbers and searching for human defects that might make a policy more risky to underwrite. I picture him seeing Georgina with her bright white smile and alluring glow. I picture him smelling her perfume and hearing her bubbly voice and the desire creeping into his mind.

As if I knew him well enough to picture him doing anything.

"One day it just started. Little innuendos that I laughed off. Like he was testing the waters, you know? 'Nice dress,' he would say. Or 'How was your weekend? Any hot dates?' Then he would chuckle, or wink even. When I got coffee, he would join me and then keep us there, lingering in the break room, always asking me questions about my personal life. My friends. Where I liked to go out. What I liked to do. How I kept so fit and did I belong to a gym or do yoga or run. And each time I let something go, another thing would follow, slightly more personal. It felt like he was creating a file in his mind about me. Like a mental database. He remembered everything I told him . . ."

"And then he reflected it back," I say.

"Yes," she says. "How did you know?"

I shrug and lie. "It's a type, that's all."

I think about the way he pulled me in so easily. Effortlessly.

Rowan keeps it moving. "So what pushed it over the edge from flirtations around the coffee machine to the complaint filed with HR?"

The report was sparse, which is common. It spoke of conduct that made Georgina "uncomfortable" and that was "inappropriate *under the circumstances.*" Always a caveat. The young man at HR there had been charmingly evasive.

Georgina offers little more. She's been coached, and Rowan and I both see it.

"I just started to feel strange when I was here. Afraid to get coffee. Afraid to get lunch. Afraid to go to the ladies' room. I wanted to stay at my desk, with Josh and Pete at their desks—they're the other guys who work in the department."

"Josh and Pete—are they at lunch?" Rowan asks.

"They should be back by two. We only get an hour."

Rowan shoots me a look. We need to follow up with them. See what they saw. Check all the boxes.

"Were you afraid because he followed you when you did those things—going for coffee, lunch, even to the bathroom?"

She hesitates. We both catch it. Her eyes look away, and she draws a quick breath. Then she shakes it off, whatever it is she's not supposed to say. I feel an urgency to reach inside her and pull out the truth, but I don't. I sit back and let Rowan work his magic.

First, he gets up and closes the door. Next, he turns off his phone and motions for me to do the same. "It's just us now. What you say stays in this room, between the three of us."

But it's not that easy.

"There's nothing to say, really. Just what's in the report. What I told them in HR. They spoke to him twice and the behavior didn't change, so they fired him."

Rowan nods and smiles a little. "That must have been awkward—working in this small room, Brett right beside you, knowing you'd spoken to HR about his flirtations."

Georgina nods. "Yeah."

"How did he behave after that kind of public rejection?"

The second hesitation gives her away. I decide to take the lead again.

"It's difficult when you see an otherwise good person doing something he shouldn't. I sense that you felt sorry for him."

Now a long sigh. She closes her eyes and gets a curious look, like she's seeing something behind them. "In all the time I knew him, he never dated anyone. He was awkward. Insecure. It came from the inside, you know? He was a good-looking guy. Great at his job. But it didn't matter. So, yeah, I did feel bad for him, but I just wanted him to stop. And then when he didn't, when I had to tell them a second time and he lost his job, I think it was just too much."

Now Rowan. "Georgina—what did he do—after that?"

"I wasn't obligated to tell HR anything after he was terminated," she begins with a soft voice. "It was done. He was gone. He moved away a few days later."

Rowan and I hold back our questions. We sit and wait and let her come to us with the answers we can tell she wants to reveal.

"He did leave quietly that day. And I thought it was over. The guys took me for drinks after work to blow off some steam. I don't know what I thought—because he was always walking this line between good and bad. Malignant and benign. There was a desperation about him, like he needed a win in his personal life. Like he had a score to settle. I knew it was there. I should have been more careful."

She tells us then how she left the bar, drove to her apartment, and parked her car in the garage. And how Brett Emory was waiting for her in the shadows.

"He came out of nowhere. Right when the elevator opened. I felt his hands on my shoulders, and he pushed me inside with him. I thought . . . well, I thought that was it, you know? I thought he was going to kill me. That's when I knew that my instincts had been right. Even when all he had done until then was follow me around, try to get close to me. That was my thought—not that he wanted to yell at me or even try to, you know, be with me somehow. My thought was that he was going to kill me."

She describes her fear, how it must have been sitting inside her, waiting for a spark to set it on fire. We always want to see the good in people. To believe in a world where there are no monsters. So much that we pretend they're not standing right in front of us.

The assault lasted mere seconds. It was not sexual. He pinned her, then leaned down to see into her eyes.

"He was inches away from my face. I could feel his breath on my lips when he said the word."

"What word did he say?" Rowan asks now.

Georgina slumps back in her chair and crosses her legs and arms, folding into herself. "'Whore,'" she says, playing back the memory. "He called me a whore and then he started to laugh—like a little kid who's finally gotten the courage to do something naughty and then feels excited but also scared because he might get punished for it."

"Or," I say, looking at Rowan, "scared because he wants to do it again."

She tells us the rest. How he let her leave when the elevator reached her floor, and she ran to her apartment, scrambled for the keys in her purse, opened her door, and got inside. How she locked it behind her and then walked around, turning on lights and checking in closets and under the bed. Checking for monsters. How she stood still and cried.

We take turns asking more questions, like did she call the police or tell a friend or someone at the office?

She says she told her sister but then kept it to herself. She didn't want to provoke him. "I stayed with a friend for a few days—made up a story about them having to redo my floors. But then I heard he'd moved. HR told me they got a request to send his last paycheck to a post office box. I drove by his house, and sure enough, a rental sign was outside. And he changed his phone number."

There has been no contact since.

"I just want to forget about it."

We finish with Georgina, offering our sympathy and encouraging her to file a report. Rowan gently reminds her that what happened was an act of violence, and she says she knows. Then she reminds us that these things happen to women all the time. We can't argue with her. She just wants to move on.

The similarities between our stories are striking, and as terrible as it may be, this makes me feel better. I didn't create this monster. I didn't unearth what was hiding inside this man. His behavior that day at Nichols—how he first froze with fear but then followed Vera Pratt into that stall and threatened the life of her baby. The sudden violence is consistent with Georgina's assault, which happened before he even came to town.

But then I think that it happened to me as well, on that back road. I had been the doe in the herd with the broken leg. Easy prey. The kind a predator doesn't even have to work for. The shooting had made me vulnerable.

Rowan and I discuss our findings on the drive back after speaking with the two guys in the office, Josh and Pete, who painted the same portrait. Brett Emory was a geek. Socially incompetent. Neither of them wanted to hang out with him after work. His jokes were off color, and he couldn't execute them. He was trying to be something he wasn't. Someone people liked and wanted to be around. The more he tried, the further away he moved from these objectives.

"I don't know," Rowan says. "So he gets fired. And then what? Moves two hours away, creates a false identity? Maybe this was a last straw for him, this termination. Something cracked."

We get reports as we drive. About his last known address near Hartford, now rented to someone else, his bank accounts, tax returns. He was a good boy. No late payments. Meticulous in his money management. He'd saved quite a little war chest, which he'd withdrawn within days after his termination from Astor Life and which had yet to show up in another account under his name.

There were no hits on his social security number. No criminal arrests. No divorces. No marriages. No children. His credit score was 810, and he graduated college with a 3.8 GPA. The manager at the nursing home said he visited his parents twice a month and was always pleasant and polite. He visited them right before he left town, told them he was being transferred to a field office but would come see them as soon as he got back.

He played by the rules. And yet there was something lurking.

I read things off my phone as Rowan drives. "Hartford PD is doing a canvass in his neighborhood. Looking for contacts through his cell records. And they've got the plates for the truck. It's new. Registered two weeks after the move. He traded in a Prius."

"That's a 180," Rowan comments.

"There's no trace of Brett Emory after that. No transactions. No credit checks, which means no apartment leases."

"He came here to disappear. And we know he wasn't using Wade Austin to do it. We already checked that. Probably used a different name before the shooting."

"And listen to this," I tell him, getting a new report. "He withdrew his entire savings account and his 401(k). Two hundred grand in total. Withdrawn just after he left Hartford. About a month before the shooting."

"Shit."

We both know what this means. Every case we've ever worked with a drained 401(k), which incurs hefty penalties and taxes before retirement age, was done for one of two reasons. First, because of financial distress. And second, because the suspect did not plan to return to his former life.

Brett Emory was not in financial distress.

"There's no profile here," I say. "Nothing to understand why he didn't just run away after the shooting. He had all of that money. He could have moved to Mexico, lounged on a beach until we'd forgotten about him. Bought fake documents. Created a new identity. It makes no sense." I had been overly optimistic. "I don't understand any of this."

Rowan gets a curious look on his face—the one he makes when he can't believe what he's about to say. I watch and wait until, finally, he says it.

"Landyn."

CHAPTER TWENTY-SIX

Dr. Landyn meets us after his last patient. We've told him it's urgent. That it has to do with the Nichols shooting.

I feel many things returning to his office. The last time I was here, I was counting down the minutes to get cleared for work and escape the numbness that had me in a state of despair. I hadn't yet followed the blue truck to a back road where I was assaulted, where I'd opened the door for this man, Brett Emory, to infiltrate my life. Now I sit quietly, fighting to keep my new secrets from showing.

Rowan is quiet as well. He doesn't like shrinks. He says he spent enough time with them after his reentry to civilian life and not every pot should be stirred. Sometimes it just mucks everything up. Rowan keeps his demons at the bottom, like grains of sand that settle in the water. They sit there, perfectly still, letting the water glisten, crystal clear. But one shake, one stir, and they'll begin to rise.

I know this about Rowan the way he knows things about me, like maybe I need some alone time with Dr. Landyn after we finish our official business.

And he's probably right. But just like his grains of sand, I have my own pot I don't want stirred. I know the first thing Landyn will ask if we're alone is whether I'd found peace with the shooting. I've already done too much lying.

We sit in the waiting room while Landyn finishes his last session. He has two doors so the patients leaving don't see the patients who are coming. Cops don't need other cops knowing they're having their heads examined. It erodes confidence, which is absurd, really, if you believe in head shrinking. Theoretically then, every patient, coming or going, would feel safer knowing someone was sorting out their pots. But it doesn't work that way. Maybe we all just wonder if the person coming or going is crazier than we are.

"You look tired," Rowan says.

"Didn't sleep great." This is the truth, or part of it anyway. I don't say why I didn't sleep—that I was watching surveillance feed from four hotels.

"Is Mitch at the house?"

I nod. We're still tag teaming in the afternoons. I'm usually the one to pick the girls up from school since we stopped letting them take the bus and stay with Kelly, but seeing Landyn is important, so I asked Mitch to do it and he didn't argue. I don't know what it means, that we talk only of logistics and the investigation. I don't know what's left of our marriage, but I can't stop to find out. I tell myself I'm giving him space. I tell Mitch the same thing. I'm here if he wants to talk. But I'm not really anywhere but in the mind of Wade Austin—that name still won't leave me. Everyone else, including Mitch, thinks Wade has moved on.

The door opens, and I take a deep breath when I see Dr. Landyn's face. I return his smile with the exhale. We small-talk as we settle into his office. I take a different chair than before and remind myself that I am not the patient today.

Rowan manspreads, elbows on splayed knees, fists knotted together beneath his chin. His discomfort is comforting because misery loves company, and that's what we both are—miserable with anticipation of our pots being stirred.

"So," Dr. Landyn begins. "Interesting case."

The file we've given him contains a psychiatric evaluation of Brett

Emory that the Hartford PD got from his parents. They were as helpful as they could be, as was his sister over the phone from Alaska, but
none of them could believe that this gentle, kind son and brother could
do any of the things that had been described to them. They agreed to
let us monitor their phones, so we'll know if he tries to make contact.
But he won't.

"What's your take?" Rowan asks. "What's wrong with this guy?"

Landyn doesn't flinch, even though I can tell he wants to. *Wrong* is
not a word he likes to use. There is no right or wrong with mental health.

We haven't told him anything more. We want his impressions of
Brett Emory before he walked into Nichols that day. The lack of context makes him reluctant to weigh in.

"Without meeting this man or knowing more about him as an adult,
my hands are somewhat tied. But—he was physically different from the
other kids throughout his childhood. He was in the one hundredth per-
centile for height and the fortieth for weight."

"So tall and thin," Rowan says. "To the point of standing out."

Landyn nods. "Yes. He would have stood out. Add to that twelve
relocations around the world starting in first grade, and an extremely
introverted personality, and you have a recipe for social alienation."

"Why so many moves?" Rowan asks.

"It says his mother was a consultant. They followed her jobs."

"And this social isolation—what did that do to him?"

Landyn tilts his head left, then right, indicating his ambivalence.
"In middle school they had him evaluated for behavior that his parents described as reclusive. He had no friends that year after their latest
move. It was bad timing. The whole grade was moving up from lower
school—a hard transition to begin with. The kids who were at the top
are suddenly at the bottom and they search for ways to fit in, to find
their social rank in this new environment. Brett Emory went into that
situation not knowing a single kid."

"So he was without friends and didn't know how to make them.
He stood out physically," Rowan says, growing impatient. "That must
have made him angry."

Landyn nods but again with the tilted head. "There is some indication that he had repressed anger. He expressed it only with his mother, which is very normal. Kids often feel safest showing feelings that scare them to a primary caregiver."

"How did he express this anger?" I ask now, as flashes of that day on the back road come and go. Wade's arms around my neck. His body slamming mine into the side of my car. I stop myself before any more come.

"Look," Landyn says, closing the file and leaning forward. "The kid in this file had struggled with social interactions for most of his school life. It's likely that this was discussed at home, out of concern, but in a way that made him aware of the problem. He said in the evaluation that his parents were always pushing him to eat more, lift weights, be more outgoing. And his sister teased him. She had adapted to the lifestyle, moving into each new school with a successful strategy to make friends. Part of that was distancing herself from her awkward younger brother. It was survival for her. His home life and school life became part of a feedback loop—each one fueling the other."

Rowan leans back and lets out a sigh. This is not enough for him. Or for me. Lots of kids were awkward in middle school. They were tall or short, pudgy or skinny. There were budding breasts and acne, body odor and periods and hair in new places. Everyone was changing at different rates and in different ways. Some bodies were graceful about it while others seemed tortured. And everyone knew kids who were introverted, geeky. They survived it.

Landyn senses his frustration. "You know, society underestimates the impact of chronic childhood trauma like your guy suffered. It doesn't have to be one big event. Sometimes it's the accumulation of smaller cuts that causes the deepest wound. It would help me to know what this boy grew up to become," he says. "What he's done that now requires an understanding of his past."

Landyn is right. I was hoping for a diagnosis, maybe like the one we had for Clay Lucas. Something to connect the dots more easily.

I look at Rowan and nod, giving him my approval to tell the story of the tall man. Wade Austin. The 404. And now a geeky actuary named Brett Emory.

He starts with the shooting, and the second the words leave his mouth, Dr. Landyn looks at me.

"The tall man?" he asks, and I nod. And then he nods.

Rowan tells him everything. What he did to Vera Pratt and the woman at his office and how he was fired for sexual harassment, draining his bank accounts and disappearing, moving here, we think, shopping for pants at Nichols, and finally, his contact with me. The gifts and flowers and then the meeting. The assault, going off the rails. Stalking me, my children, my husband's former lover. And now, seemingly, dormant.

Rowan finishes with the last contact he knows about—the filming of my girls at their school and then our failed attempt to lure him to the diner. How he mocked the entire department by paying a guy with a blue truck to drive through the parking lot.

Landyn looks straight at me. "Is that the last thing? There's been no more contact?"

Rowan nods, and I do the same, trying not let the blood rush into my face. It hits me now, hard. I'm no longer just hiding, omitting facts. I'm actively lying.

The sessions we had in this office just weeks ago come rushing back. The investigation into my emotional state following the shooting, which feels almost irrelevant now. The assessing of my stability, my sanity. Talk of trauma recovery and what it can do to a person who interrupts the process, skips the stages. And I wonder if I've gone completely mad. Because the thing about that—about losing your mind—is you're the one person incapable of seeing it.

"Okay," Landyn says. "This is the best I can do without observing Mr. Emory or speaking with him directly. So take it for what it's worth."

He begins with shrink speak—the fragility of Brett Emory's ego from his childhood experiences, his ability to overcome them in college, at least academically. We have no information from anyone there.

No professors who really noticed him. No friends who'd come forward. Still, had he been emotionally unstable, it is unlikely he could have concentrated on his classes and attained such a high GPA.

And then his success at work, eleven years with multiple promotions. There were hits on his phone records, numbers of people who saw him socially. Rowan relays this to Landyn when he asks, and then he says this confirms his thoughts, which are that Brett Emory had found his place in the world. A job, enough friends to have human contact. His visits with his parents and demeanor with the staff at their nursing home—all of that indicated that the scars had either healed or he'd found a way to ignore them.

"The termination was a trigger," Landyn says. "No question. It tore down the life he'd managed to build. And all of the parts of him that he had come to see as positive were suddenly taken away. The assault on his coworker in the elevator at her apartment building, and then leaving town the extreme way that he did, indicate a mental break."

Landyn says he likely came here as an attempt to rebuild. He suspects he had a new fixation on a woman, whether she knew it or not. "The problem was that he could never go back. Any attempt to rectify the past, clear his name, would risk being exposed for what he did to his coworker. I also suspect there were similar acts of aggression that were not reported—in college, with people he met outside of work. The behavior toward this last woman shows underlying predatory tendencies."

"And now?" Rowan asks. "Are they worse—these predatory tendencies?"

Yes, I think. He has become a predator, and I've been using myself as bait. I want to run from this room and Landyn's eyes, which keep shifting to mine, searching. He knows something's not right.

"There are likely two things at work here," Landyn explains. "First is the compromised person he was before. Essentially, he already had one piece of a common stalking profile—delusion. Your guy deluded himself about his coworker, ignoring her social cues, inventing a scenario where she was secretly in love with him. The delusion was necessary to his emotional stability, the image he had of himself that he needed to protect at all costs—even his job."

"And the second?" Rowan asks.

"The second," he says, "is the trauma from the shooting. There are stages of recovery that must occur before mental health can be restored. Not everyone can tolerate them. People move at different speeds. Some take years, finding ways to muddle through life without going through them. They aren't easy."

Landyn looks at me again. This time I turn away. The water churns in my pot, and I need it to stop. We spoke about trauma in our sessions, I taught trauma in my classes, but now I've lived through it myself. I am suddenly agitated. Impatient. I want to get back to my kitchen and the surveillance of the hotels.

Landyn rattles them off, and I can sense Rowan mirroring my feelings. He's been through all of this as well. Once you get to the other side, you don't want to think about it ever again. There are no victory laps. No finish line photos.

Shock, denial, pain, guilt, anger, bargaining, depression, then, finally, an upward swing to acceptance and hope.

"Do you see the common factor?" Landyn asks. "Denial," he answers his own question. "It's closely related to delusion." He pauses to let us catch up. "Your guy, Brett Emory, has used denial or delusion to prevent what will come if he faces the truth—pain, guilt, anger, etc. The lingering childhood trauma, the acute trauma from the shooting. The causes are different, but the wounds are the same. And the power he feels from the stalking behavior is a kind of avoidance—a Band-Aid. Not unlike the way others use alcohol and drugs. Anything to avoid the painful process of recovery."

I tell myself to stay quiet, but I can't. I try to hide my concern behind a hypothetical. "And if he comes back, continues his contact with me? Where does it end? How does it end?"

I look at Landyn. Rowan looks at me.

Landyn, for the first time since I've known him, stares at his folded hands. "Given what he's been through, the extent of his denial—and the acquisition of these new skills and this new persona . . ."

He pauses.

So I finish his thought. "He won't stop unless I make him."

We take the elevator to our floor. We ride in silence, both of us thinking about this guy and, as Rowan finally says, how fucked up he might really be. If Landyn is right, it's not just his past behavior leading up to the assault of his coworker and the attempt to reinvent himself. It was as if he was a faulty machine whose parts had been slowly wearing down, fraying and fracturing as he hobbled his way through life. A piece finally cracked up in Hartford. And then the whole damned thing broke apart that day in Nichols.

So what is he now? He doesn't seem like a broken machine. He's managed to rebuild somehow. Stronger. Impenetrable.

Landyn would say that is all a facade. The armor of a sociopath is strong because underneath is a fragile, wounded child.

"Fuck that," Rowan says finally. "I don't care what he went through as a child or in high school. He needs to be locked up. Maybe some prison shrink can try to fix him."

But when we get back to our desk and sit down, Rowan leans forward and hangs his head.

"I'm sorry. That was just so hard to hear. But it shouldn't be. It's just information about a suspect. A possible psychological profile. We use them all time. I hate that I can't distance myself from this. I hate that it's become personal."

I nod. "Yeah. Very personal."

The secrets between us grow larger as we make our confessions. Here is my opening. My chance to tell him that I've lost my way more than he ever could. That I've gone beyond a momentary outburst to so many lies. About all of the messages. The rented car. The plastic bag. The cameras at the hotels. And Nix. Billy Brannicks.

I come so damned close to telling him everything, but something nags at me. What this secret is now doing to me is nothing compared to what it would do to him. And that's what Wade wants. He wants Rowan to lose his shit, put his job at risk.

I think about the message he sent with a picture of my partner at a bar. Sitting alone. A beer and shot glass in front of him. I won't put him in that position.

I change the subject to Laurel Hayes, the missing woman who knew Clay Lucas, and we lose ourselves in a case that doesn't stir our pots.

CHAPTER TWENTY-SEVEN

It's past eleven, and the girls are lost in their dreams. I hear the floor-boards above me in the master bedroom, Mitch moving about. A shower. Changing his clothes. Trying to sleep, getting up. Maybe starting to come downstairs to the kitchen where I spend another night, scanning the feed from the cameras at the hotels. With every day that passes, I fear Wade has moved on to a new location. That all of this is for nothing. I picture my husband stopping himself because with each night spent apart, the wall between us grows higher, just like the wall that now stands between me and my partner.

I can't worry about this now. I have to find Wade. So I listen to the floorboards and drink more coffee and stare at people and cars coming and going in a parking lot. And hope that the walls can be dismantled later. That it won't be too late.

The phone buzzes, and it takes me a moment to process the sound. I've grown distracted, consumed by my every move. Offensive moves and defensive moves. I've set up more security in the house. Told Mitch it makes me feel better even though Wade had gone quiet. He is still out there, I remind him. Door alarms and motion sensors. I've told the detail to be diligent about delivery trucks coming from either direction. To turn the car every hour or so to face the other way. They are confused by my alarm because they don't know that he got past them. That the messages continue even now that we've discovered his past.

Don't think you know me just because you know my name.

I see his unmistakable image through the steam, standing in my bedroom, and worry about ways he can get back inside, thinking he'll try again. I have my one lead. A plastic bag. But he's made a puzzle I can't solve, so I protect what matters most. My family.

I open the message and stare at the screen. There's an image with an arrow, a play button. I can't tell what this is. A video or a live feed.

I close my laptop and steady myself. The girls are asleep. Mitch is upstairs. No one's come or gone, and the image is somewhere outside.

I press play, and the feed streams.

In an instant I'm on my feet, walking in circles, staring. Wanting to scream.

I grab my keys and run to the front door. The alarm chirps, and I hear Mitch call out, but I can't stop. The door locks behind me as I bound to my car. The detail sees me and watches my car speed away, but remain guarding my house because that's the protocol.

My eyes shift from the road to the feed as I drive. Mitch calls, but I don't answer. He calls again and leaves a message. Then he stops. The cops on the detail call too. And I ignore them as well.

I drive the residential streets at twice the speed limit, looking from the phone to the road.

A man walks, the phone strapped to his chest. His hands are free. I can see one swinging with his gait. The other holds a baseball bat.

Then comes a voice as he narrates his show. "He never should have set me up at the diner," it says. *He* says.

I know that voice and hearing it again after so much has happened steals my breath. *Wade.*

"And look—now he's had a few too many."

In front of him another man walks on a street downtown. I recognize the buildings. A strip of bars and restaurants that fill up after the workday and thin out by ten, later on weekends. There are people between Wade and this man, but I know him as well. The other man in this new show.

I look back to the road and call out his name as though he can somehow hear me. "Rowan!"

I call his number, but he doesn't pick up.

"Rowan! Look back!" I scream again as I wait for his greeting to play. His messages are full, so I hang up and dial again. Rowan always answers. Always.

I catch myself before I swerve across the line. I'm ten minutes from downtown. From the street they're on.

I dial again. Hang up. Dial again. And again. And then I understand why he doesn't answer. The people walking between Wade and Rowan shift to the right, and I can see Rowan's hand by his head, holding the phone. He's on a call. His other hand waves in the air the way it does when he's arguing. Making his case about something. I imagine he's on with a woman, and it could be about anything. A woman he stopped seeing. A woman who stopped seeing him. Maybe someone he was just with at a bar where he drank too much and now isn't thinking the way he needs to be.

Complacency. Distraction. *Damn it!* He knows better.

"Rowan!" I scream. I dial. I watch the road. I watch the feed.

He's at his apartment. He stops at the entrance but doesn't go inside because he's still on his call. It's a walk-up, and he needs his keycard for the front door. He searches his pockets with his free hand.

Wade pauses. If he gets too close, Rowan will sense him.

I stop at a light and stare at this image. Wade taps the bat against the cement, softly, just enough for me to hear the sound and understand the message it conveys. Five steps, one swing, and Rowan will be dead.

"Rowan!" I look both ways and run the light. Then I step on the gas as my vision blurs with tears. I'm five blocks away, but Wade is five steps.

He's caught me off guard. This was supposed to be about *me*. Everything he did was to torment *me*. Wade came at me through my children and then Mitch. He'd been inside my home, watching me in the shower and leaving that package, which he knew would cause me to visit Clay's parents and suffer the pain of seeing what lived inside them.

Now he's turned to Rowan. Another move I should have seen

coming. I thought I'd protected him by keeping him in the dark. I thought Wade wanted to fuck with his head, make him compromise his work. Not this. Nothing like this.

Wade takes a step closer and ducks into an alcove. I dial Rowan again. Drive faster.

The lights are not syncing downtown, and each one turns red before I can get through it. I look back to the feed and see Rowan with his keycard. He swipes it and gets inside and the door closes behind him. Locking. It's over! This is over. The light turns green, and I drive through the intersection, wiping my eyes, finding my breath.

And then the voice comes again.

"Don't go anywhere," Wade says.

I look back to the feed and see him walking. He stops at Rowan's apartment building and rests the bat against his legs. He's on the security camera for the building now. He'll be recorded. Even if he wears a cap and looks down, he won't be able to run from this. Everything else— the stalking and the images—is nothing compared to what he'll face if he goes inside that building and carries out this threat.

I tell myself he won't do it. Just like the drive-by at the Ridgeway Shopping Center, this is an unforced error. The mistake he should have foreseen, thinking backward from the interrogation room where I picture him now. Because we will catch him. I will catch him.

The car behind me honks. The light is green, so I drive through it and stop at the next one. I look back to the feed and see Wade's hand reach out toward the lock. He's holding a keycard. He has a keycard for Rowan's building. *No!*

Now he's inside. He takes the stairs. Rowan lives on the third floor.

Another green light, another red light. I call Rowan again—and again it goes to voice mail.

Wade is up one flight. I drive. Another flight. I call.

"Hey, partner. What's going on?"

The sound of his voice takes over every sense, and I don't see the road. I don't see the light. I don't see the car coming through the intersection.

"Rowan!"

A horn blares, and I slam on my brakes. The other car swerves, missing me by mere feet. It stops, and a woman yells at me through an open window. She has a teenage girl with her. A daughter maybe. Her right arm stretches across her in the passenger seat.

"You almost killed us!" She catches her breath, then drives away, and I think, *Yes, I did. I almost ran right into you. I could have killed you, both of you.*

What am I doing? This has to stop. It has to stop!

I stare at the car as it disappears. Behind me are skid marks. The smell of burning rubber seeps through the vents.

More horns blare because I'm blocking traffic, but I can't move. I can't even answer as Rowan asks me what's happening. "Are you in your car?"

I look at the feed and see Wade back outside now, walking away from the building.

If he's speaking, I can't hear because I'm on the call with Rowan. But the feed ends, and a new message appears. A simple text. *Guess what comes next?* And then a still shot. It looks like an empty cafeteria.

"Elise? Are you there?"

I manage an answer. "Yeah. Hold on."

I pull over to the curb and put on my hazard lights. I expand the photo with my fingers until it grows larger, and then I see the small chairs and the gray speckled tables. It's at the school. He's been inside the girls' school.

"Elise . . ."

"I'm here," I say. I'm about to tell him what's happened. I want to get out of my car and run to his building and see his face and know he's all right. I want to see him look at me like I'm crazy and then fill with rage when I reveal what's happened so I won't be alone with mine. My rage and now a new fear because "what comes next" are the girls.

He's been inside their school. In spite of the security. He's worked his way in through the employees in the cafeteria, but now he'll switch it up, won't he? Employees come and go through all different entrances. There's always a way around. *Always.*

I reach for the door, but something stops me. I can't explain it, not even to myself. It's instinct. This is what Wade wants. This is what he's expecting me to do.

Of course he didn't hurt Rowan. He would be on the security footage. The waning local media coverage we had now would escalate into national news. Every cop everywhere would be looking for him. He wouldn't be able to stroll in and out of a Getaway Inn, rent cars and vans, buy food and cell phones. He would have to disappear, and then the fun would be over.

No, tonight was part of a larger plan. One move on the game board.

I'm supposed to tell Rowan. And Rowan is supposed to react. Wade has his profile, and he'll have done his research. Yes, Rowan is smart and brave and skilled in combat. But he has demons that need tending with a few beers down the street and drama with women who come and go and keep him occupied on the phone even as his partner tries to call him a dozen times. We are all human. We all make mistakes. But Wade knows what mistakes Rowan is likely to make, and he's calculated how to use them.

Rowan needs to be levelheaded. He needs to be careful and patient, so when we do come for Wade, he won't see us. The more personal this case becomes, the more mistakes both of us will make.

"Elise!" Rowan sounds concerned now.

"Sorry. False alarm. I thought I had something, but I was wrong." I ramble about a tip, someone who saw a blue truck and how I went out to find it. It wasn't Wade's, but that's why he heard the sounds from the street.

"You went out alone? On a tip from the call line?"

Now Rowan is the one who rambles—about how careless that was and how I should have waited until morning, and I argue that the truck might have been gone by then and why didn't he pick up? He says he had to finish his call and I always text him so he was waiting for that, for a text. He didn't think a few minutes would matter. I was home with Mitch, and the detail was outside my house. How could he have known I ditched them?

We stop arguing, and I tell him I'm sorry and that I'm heading home now. I'll have to deal with Mitch and the cops who stayed outside the house. They saw me leave and called and left messages and probably reported it back to the department. We get enough tips about blue trucks that I can cover myself there. No one will check. No one will ask which one and no one knows what street I was on or where I was heading.

I drive home slowly, thinking it all through. Rowan will never know, but Wade will assume he does. He will assume I've told him and that now my partner is filled with rage that will cloud his judgment. Make him volatile. Make him useless. Or perhaps vulnerable. This entire night was meant to compromise my backup, just like the stunt he pulled with Briana and Mitch had infiltrated my marriage. He is tearing down my life, one brick at a time.

But I haven't told Rowan. He hasn't been taken from me. I think that maybe, just maybe, I've shifted the scales again, made a move he didn't see coming, and now I have the advantage. I don't know how to use it. I need to get through what waits for me at home. I need sleep. I need the thoughts to settle and rest so they can find their right places in my mind.

Still, I know I'm right about this. The end is near.

CHAPTER TWENTY-EIGHT

The woman on the team still doesn't like the notes from the interview with Laurel Hayes's friend in Bridgeport. Her story doesn't add up.

The friend's name is Kendra, and she works as a nurse in a pediatrician's office. She and Laurel went to school together. Laurel was studying to be a social worker, which is what she did at Clear Horizons. The phone records for Laurel Hayes go back two years. They've already established a close connection through texts and calls—and later many more calls than texts. And the calls suddenly got longer. The woman on the team continues to be suspicious of this change of behavior. Something was going on that required conversations, either because it was serious or because Laurel didn't want to leave a written trail.

She's finally cleared to go to Bridgeport to speak with Kendra, which she does. One on one, at a coffee shop. Plain clothes, concern on her face. She is straight with Kendra but delivers the message "woman to woman."

She gets more of the same—nothing was wrong, Laurel was just upset about the shooting and having worked with Clay Lucas. Not depressed, but you know, sometimes friends need a little more hand-holding. This was one of those times. So on and so forth.

It goes on like that, with the investigator hiding her frustration, until she asks about the man with the red jacket. "Did she ever mention a man watching her at work from across the street—he sometimes wore a red jacket?"

It is so subtle, she thinks. The way Kendra's eyes widen and how a breath rushes in the way it might when you're taken by surprise, which she is. It happens in a split second. That magical moment when a cop knows they've found an opening and has the experience to work it.

Now, to be clear, they still aren't sure this man was watching Laurel Hayes at Clear Horizons. The young male investigator spotted the jacket on the surveillance feed and remembered the red jacket from the shelter, so it became a possible "thing." From there they focused on that bench and that man and saw him several other times, right up until the day Laurel disappeared. Then he disappeared as well. He didn't always wear the red jacket. Sometimes a button-down shirt. Sometimes a sweater. But the red jacket he did wear was the same style and color as the one at the shelter.

"He stopped watching the day Laurel Hayes disappeared," the investigator pushes gently. "We think he knew her and she knew him and that she told you about it during your conversations."

Now Kendra looks down into her latte, blushing. Both indications a witness is lying or hiding something.

"Kendra, this man is still out there. If he was watching her there, he could have been watching her anywhere, which means he could have followed her anywhere."

At this point, all Kendra presumably knows is that Laurel is missing. The shelter investigators have not told her about the remains or that they are waiting on dental records to determine if the victim is, indeed, Laurel Hayes. Which means Kendra is presumably still worried about her friend and, now, if this man with the red jacket might be after her. Still, she doesn't speak, though she seems confused and undecided, which means there is something she has to decide. Which means she knows something she's not saying.

The investigator gives it one last push. "When we got her phone records, the carrier told us someone had been accessing her account from a different device. They had the password and her social security number—they were able to see what we saw, which were the calls to your number, which means we aren't the only ones who might be paying you a visit looking for your friend."

This, of course, is a lie. But cops are allowed to do that. It's a useful perk.

And this time, it is used perfectly. Kendra is pushed right over the edge of her indecision.

"There was a guy," she begins. "They met at a coffee shop. He was handsome and polite. Not like the jerks she was meeting online. He said he worked in a building across the street, but Laurel later found out he was lying. He said his name was Fisher Brand."

That's a hard name to google, the friend and investigator both agree. Thousands of entries about the brand name *Fisher* blanket the screen.

He said he worked in insurance, and Laurel had no reason to doubt him. He was staying in a residence hotel because he'd just moved to town. She dated him for about two months before she got "weirded out." It was too much too fast. He was talking about their future like it was a done deal. He wanted to see her every night and all weekend. He never met her friends and didn't have any of his own.

He was obsessed with his own behavior and how he was being perceived by her. He would bring up conversations from days before, ask if he'd sounded stupid. Every time they were talking, he would study her words and thoughts and then always have a similar thought or feeling. His stories started to mirror hers.

She said she felt like she was dating a ghost. Not a real person. She couldn't find anything about his past and, finally, when she went to the place he said he worked, there was no one there by that name.

"He should have at least used the name of someone on the company directory," Kendra says. "She was bound to check sooner or later."

She broke it off that same day—about a month before the shooting at Nichols and her disappearance.

"How did he take it?"

Kendra shakes her head. "Not well." He begged and pleaded, which, both women agree, is not very attractive. He sent messages to her phone that swung wildly from desperate pleas to threats and vulgar name calling. *Bitch, whore, cunt.* Kendra says that's when Laurel started calling her, asking for advice, seeking comfort. "I told her this guy sounded dangerous. But she thought he would go away."

"Did he?"

"No. She started seeing him everywhere. Outside her apartment. In the grocery store. A few rows away in a parking lot. Just far enough that she felt she couldn't go to the police. He never approached her."

The investigator notes that he must have known that was enough— what he was doing. He knew he was causing her distress, and this made him feel powerful.

"He used to text her and tell her how pretty she looked that day or the night before at some bar. He made sure she knew he was always there, watching her. It was ruining her life."

Laurel Hayes never went to the police. She thought it would make things worse. Antagonize him. She figured he would move on when he met someone new.

"Did she ever admit what was happening? Did she understand?"

"Understand what?"

"That he was stalking her. That she was really in danger."

Kendra swears she tried to convince her. But Laurel kept hoping. She left town not because of this guy, but because she was terrified the police would link her to Clay Lucas and find out she'd been in touch with him. This man named Fisher Brand was far from her mind.

"Well, perhaps not," the investigator says. "Because now she's gone."

CHAPTER TWENTY-NINE

I go home and watch the feed from the hotels on my laptop in the kitchen. Wade had to have gone back to one of them after following Rowan. That would put his arrival anywhere between eleven and midnight. Unless he didn't want to risk being seen and slept in the truck. Then he would enter the hotel in the morning when foot traffic picked up.

I stare at the screen, but I can't focus. I can't shake the images from last night that linger in my mind.

Rowan walking, unaware of the danger right behind him. His need to escape hijacking his judgment. The green light. The sound of the horn behind me. The bat and the arm, swinging casually in and out of the frame. Then the screeching tires and the woman yelling. Terror on her face as she holds her arm across the body of her child, protecting her from me. From what I've almost done.

I could have died last night. I could have killed two innocent people.

I see the cafeteria at my girls' school and the view of the playground from the place where Wade stood, watching them. Filming them.

I know what I have to do. And now I have cover to do it.

I type a letter to Mitch on the laptop. I use words like *space* and *time to heal.* I say there's been a development, a change, and the girls will now be safer in Florida with his mother. Wade won't risk showing his face at an airport to follow Mitch and the girls there. I know this about him now. Mitch's mother lives in a gated community. And Mitch won't let them out of his sight.

I say just enough to scare him, God help me—about the man who's infiltrated our lives. I make sure to ask, not tell, to plead, and to do so with words like *desperate* and *terrified.* He has to keep our girls safe. And he has to give me some space.

I book tickets, email Mitch the itinerary. I print the boarding passes and the letter.

I leave them by the coffee maker.

I am wrecked as I creep up the stairs and look in on my daughters. My sleeping angels. I don't go to them and kiss them and pull up their covers because it's close to daybreak and they could wake easily now. Instead, I wipe the tears from my eyes and tell myself I have no choice.

I'm gone before the sun comes up. I only had time to watch the feed from three of the hotels last night. He didn't return to any of them after leaving Rowan's apartment building. I have to play the odds that he's staying at the fourth. And if he is, he could leave before I get there. So I just go.

I tell the detail I'm going to work early. I apologize again for ditching them last night, and they're over it—or maybe just tired. It doesn't matter as long as they stay put and watch my house until Mitch takes the girls and leaves for Florida.

Please make him listen, I think as I drive away.

When I turn the corner, I pull over and send Rowan a text. I tell him I need to take some time and can he please let Aaron know. I tell him this thing with Briana is too much and that Mitch is taking the girls on a trip and I'm going to find someplace safe to rest and think. I don't get specific, but I ask him not to tell Mitch and that I'll explain more when I see him. He knows how precarious this is, the situation with my marriage, and he won't do anything that could make it worse. He'll cover for me if Mitch calls. As far as the job is concerned, I'm on another leave. As far as Mitch knows, I'm at the job. I don't know how much time this has bought me, but it's the best I can do.

I get to the hotel in twenty minutes. It's still dark. I holster my gun, then leave my car behind a grocery store in the area where employees park and deliveries are made. I walk three blocks to the bench where I've chained the bike and remove the camera from beneath the seat. I replace the battery. Then I return the camera, make sure it's filming again and find a place where I can see the entrance to the hotel but also watch the recording from last night on my laptop. I choose the diner next door, a table with a window that faces the left side of the hotel parking lot. I order a cup of coffee and get to work.

I fast-forward the recording to the eleven-thirty mark. Wade was at Rowan's apartment not long before. I don't know exactly when he left, but I know when I got home so I can make a rough deduction. Today I don't speed up the replay because I also need to watch the hotel. If Wade is in there, I can't let him leave.

Guess what comes next?

The girls come next. My girls. My babies. He hasn't gotten what he wants, and this is his best leverage. The people I love. It makes sense now. Why he targeted Mitch and Rowan. And I still haven't satisfied his needs.

The waitress brings a refill, and I wave her off politely. My insides churn with nervous energy. I can barely finish what's in the cup beside me.

The sun is rising, and the sky changes quickly from black to orange. People begin to trickle out next door. I count the time as I watch the recording from last night. I don't let more than three seconds pass before turning back to the scene at the hotel. Three seconds, then I pause, watch the hotel, return to the screen.

Fifteen minutes in, I see something. It takes every ounce of self-restraint not to keep watching but I don't allow myself. I count to three. Watch the hotel. Return to the recording.

He's on foot. It's him! I know that walk. The gait and the swing of the arms. I know the slouch in his shoulders and the way his knees fold inward.

One. Two. Three. I look back to the entrance and watch a couple with rolling suitcases walk to their car. Back to the screen.

A sharp pain passes through my heart, which is not expecting the surge of excitement. But I can't control it. He's there! On the recording. He walks into the hotel and disappears. The camera doesn't film above the first floor so I don't bother watching for a light to come on in a room.

One. Two. Three. I force my eyes again to look at the hotel. No one comes or goes. Back to the screen.

I double the playback now to get through the hours between his arrival and the end of the recording. It takes several minutes. Count to three. Back to the hotel. Again to the playback. One. Two. Three. I force a breath all the way in, slow and steady. It struggles against what I so desperately want to do. Run out the door and across the parking lot and into that hotel where this man is holed up, plotting against everyone I love and, I have to assume, capable of anything now.

I get to the end of the recording. He hasn't left. He's still in there. I look again to the entrance, longer this time because the sky has turned blue. Morning is here. I think that Mitch will be up by now. That he's seen my note and started packing the girls and finding a way to tell them that sounds exciting. He'll have to deal with work and the school, but he'll figure it out. He's the boss. He hasn't called or texted, which means he's angry with me or indifferent or something in between. But I can't be distracted.

I go back to the image of Wade entering the building last night. I watch backward to see where he comes from. It's not the parking lot of the hotel. He comes from down the street, from the other direction, which means he's parked somewhere else. And that's where he'll go when he leaves again. To whatever vehicle he's driving.

The waitress returns. "You all set here?" she asks me.

"Yeah, just the check." I throw down some cash and pack the laptop into my bag.

And then I walk quickly out of the diner and across the street. I walk until I'm past the hotel, my eyes never leaving the entrance, then I cross back over and look for places Wade might park. Again, I remain disciplined, returning my eyes to the hotel every three seconds. I keep counting them in my head as I walk in the direction Wade came from and observe.

Next to the hotel on the right side is an office building. There's no parking in the back and the front lot is empty. Beside that is a car wash and then a strip mall. And just like the grocery store where I left my car, the strip mall will have parking behind it. Now comes the choice.

The camera is recording the entrance. It's barely seven, and the hotel is still quiet. I take a chance that Wade won't make a move yet. He chose the hotel closest to town, which means there's a greater chance someone will have seen the alerts from our department. It doesn't matter how hard he tries to mask his face. Every alert that we've released describes him as a tall man, six foot five—the one thing he can't hide.

I decide that he's still in his room, maybe watching the street from a window. Looking for me.

So I leave the camera and my view of the entrance and walk quickly past the office building and the car wash and finally to the strip mall. I go to the end before crossing over the front lot. I clear the side of the building and turn the corner and see it. It's unmistakable. The blue truck.

Okay. Okay . . . I force myself to breathe. This is harder than I imagined.

I check my surroundings. There are a few cars around it. None of these stores will open before nine or ten, so I don't expect much activity for at least another hour. The truck is in the very back row, which abuts a patch of trees and a small stream.

I walk quickly now, light-headed. It feels like years that this torment has been happening. It feels like a lifetime.

I reach the truck and stop. I see now what he's done. The plates are bright orange with dark blue letters. New York State. He's swapped out the originals because we've been looking for Connecticut blue and white or a sticker plate taped to the window like he had before. The orange plates stand out. Anyone looking for the blue truck with Connecticut plates would immediately dismiss it. They wouldn't bother to check the driver or anything else about it the way they might if the plates were more similar to Connecticut's.

And he's done something else—added a logo to the side, just like the one he used on the white van that was parked outside my house. He's found a place to have them made. This one says Anytime Repair. There's a website address and a phone number with a New York prefix. Everything ties together.

He's here. I've found him. It's happening, and I don't know if I'm ready.

I step closer and look inside the window. *This truck.* I think about how I leaned against it on that back road. Telling him just enough of my secrets. Giving him just enough to infiltrate my life. Laughing and crying and letting him in after I'd pushed away the others who tried to be there. Rowan. Mitch. Even my girls, though it kills me to remember. But seeing it now, everything rushes back relentlessly, until I drown in the memory of how it felt to be there with him. How I needed it.

Fuck, Elise. This is not the time.

I think through my plan and convince myself I can see it through. And then—

I sense someone behind me. I don't turn around.

An arm is around my chest. A hand pressed to my face, a cloth covering my mouth and nose. I know the smell that comes from it. Rowan and I had a case years ago. A woman was abducted in a parking lot. All that was left next to her car was a rag soaked in chloroform.

I try not to breathe, but of course this is impossible.

I try to move from his hold, but like before he overpowers me.

Did I even tell him about that case—with the missing woman and the rag? We found her eventually. Buried in the woods behind the killer's house. When he was arrested five years later for assault on another woman, his house was sold and the new owners wanted to put in a pool.

I remember the smell as I take a breath. The smell from the rag in the evidence box. The smell from the cloth pressed to my face.

Chloroform takes at least five minutes to render a person unconscious. In the case of our missing woman, the car was completely isolated. The killer had time. Wade won't take that chance.

He slips a loose plastic bag over my head to keep the chemicals in the air I'm forced to breathe into my oxygen-deprived lungs and from there into my blood. This frees up both of his arms so he can place me in the same choke hold he did the last time we met. I feel the pressure against my carotid arteries.

And I think, as my mind begins to go dark, that I was right. This is the day it will end.

CHAPTER THIRTY

I'm sick the moment I come to. My stomach is empty, and nothing is expelled when I heave. My head throbs. I open my eyes, and my first thought is that I'm still alive.

Panic rushes in next, and I try to free myself. My wrists pull against a plastic zip tie. I try to stand, but my feet are tied as well, together but also to something cold and hard. A metal pipe. I am forced in a prone position, lying on my stomach with my arms beneath me. I lift up onto my elbows, then tell myself to stop moving. I'm alone, which means I have time to figure out where I am and what holds me in place and, from there, how I can escape. Pushed from these thoughts is the fact that I have moved to the dreaded second crime scene, and that never ends well.

Light washes in through the closed panes of one window. I scan my surroundings and feel an eerie sense of familiarity. I haven't been here before, but this room reminds me of a case our department handled three years back—the execution of a drug dealer in one of the odd hunting structures in the backcountry.

There is no furniture. Just a sink with a small metal shelf on the wall beside it and a hand pump beneath it. I follow the pipe, which snakes across the wall to where I sit. This is why I can't move. My feet are tied to the plumbing that exits to the outside through a small opening. I can feel the cool air seeping in against my calves.

Across from me is a closed door. The floor is wood but covered with plastic. I can see the blood stains that lie beneath, having seeped into the grains over the years.

The detectives who worked that case called this the Kill Room. The place where the hunters field dress the deer they've shot. The place where that drug dealer was executed three years ago.

And then I remember.

Not only did I tell Wade about this case on that back road, I wrote about this case for the college. I uploaded it to the portal. Every detail I was free to disclose. How the hunters use these shelters and how the large one has a basement with a cremation oven for the deer carcasses. This was an unnecessary fact, but I knew the students would find it fascinating. Anything to keep them engaged. I even wrote about the room with the blood.

The Kill Room.

What have I done? I thought if I let him catch me, if I let him take me somewhere alone with no chance of being followed and captured, I could finally put an end to things. But he hasn't brought me to his hotel or on a long drive where we could talk. Where he could convince me we should be together. He didn't want to be alone with me so he could be with me.

What have I done?

I twist my head as far as it will go to look down at the pipe and the wall. I am less than two feet from the pump and the sink, and I know, if I have the time, I can disconnect the pipe and free my ankles. Then maybe I can find something sharp enough to cut through the plastic.

But there is no time. The door opens, and there he is. Wade.

He wears the same outfit as last night. Blue jeans, a red jacket, and a white baseball cap. And I remember that the couple leaving earlier that morning wore the same colors—red, white, and blue head to toe.

"It's a One America convention," Wade says with a smile. This is how he's been blending in. This is why he chose that hotel. "Two hundred patriots all in one place. Celebrating America and watching baseball."

Yes, I think. That explains the bat he carried last night.

I stare at him like an animal in a cage. I can see myself reflected in his eyes. The satisfaction runs deep. He is calm. Nonchalant. High on control.

I take a breath and fight to mask the fear in my eyes. I force myself to stop shaking. I have to change the narrative. Shift the balance of power.

"Do you know what's been so surprising?" he asks me.

I don't respond.

He leans against the doorframe and stares at my face, waiting. When he sees my defiance, he shrugs it off. "What's surprising is that it's so much easier to be the criminal once you learn the technique. Thinking backward. I needed you to come to me alone when you thought I wasn't expecting you. So I asked myself, how can I let her find me? The rented car. The plastic bag. The little cameras under the bike seats. You've been a busy girl, Elise."

I draw a deep breath and let it out slowly. *Change the narrative.* He has to question himself. He has to feel enough doubt to tap into that place inside him, the same one that made him follow Vera Pratt into the changing room. The damaged little boy.

"Now, a smart girl would have called for backup. The moment you saw me walk into the hotel after my stroll downtown. You should have been patient."

I see the opening and grab it.

"How do you know I didn't?" I ask him.

And for a split second, his face changes. I see a twitch as his confidence is shaken by the emotional fault lines that lie beneath the surface. He's thinking now what he should be. Maybe I baited him. Maybe I lured him out of the hotel where it would have been far too easy for him to hide and then escape. So many rooms. So many corners in the guts of the place. The basement where they prepare the food and wash the sheets. So many people coming and going.

His face changes back when he finishes this silent line of questioning. "*A* for effort," he says. "Except Rowan is at the station. I called there before we left. And no one followed us here. There's one way in and one way out. I removed the memory cards from the game cameras. There's no live feed. And I checked you for trackers, not that it would matter. There's no service up here."

He's right, of course. But from everything I know about him, the doubt will fester.

I shrug. "Looks like you've thought of everything." I give it a beat, let him study my expression. "So what's the plan? If you'd wanted to kill me, I'd be dead. I've already felt the fear, when you covered my face with the rag and then the plastic bag. And then—nice touch—another choke hold to remind me of the first time you did it. When you couldn't take the fact that I was going back to work. That I would find out what you did to Vera Pratt."

His expression is blank now. I haven't seen this one before—this neutral facade.

"It must be hard to be you, Wade."

The sound of that name causes another shift. He smiles and then reaches behind him, pulling out my gun. "Is this the same one you used to kill Clay Lucas?" he asks.

"No," I tell him. "Of course not. That one went to forensics. I was due anyway—you know, for an upgrade." My tone is defiant. Mocking.

He examines the firearm, turning it from side to side. He practices the release of the safety, aiming it at the wall with a squinted eye like he's homing in on a target. This is the first time he's held a gun. I can tell by how enamored he is with it. How he strokes it with curiosity and then puts it back inside the jacket pocket.

"I brought you a present," he says now. Then he leaves.

I let myself fall apart, just for second. A silent cry escapes as my breath becomes shallow and quick. Blood rushes to my head, and I have to drop it between my wrists to keep from passing out. Another dry heave. I need water. My throat is on fire.

I hear a door open and close. Then shuffling. Then the muted cries of a man. Wade yells at him to shut up. His voice is commanding and urgent. Like he's getting excited but also scared. Impatient for this to be over. Whatever he's planned, he can't get his head around it. He is not a psychopath. He is not devoid of empathy or emotion. Everything he's done has been a desperate attempt to be liked. To be loved. To feel accepted by us.

I settle myself again and get ready for what I am about to see. I imagine Rowan bound and gagged, being dragged across the floor. And then Mitch. These thoughts come and go in flashes, and before they ignite any more terror, the question is answered.

Wade enters, his back coming first through the door as he drags a young man by his underarms. The man writhes, twisting and turning, trying to scream through a strip of black duct tape. His hands are bound behind him with a zip tie. Wade drags him across the room and tosses him against the wall. His feet are also bound, and he fights hard to sit upward.

It's then I see his face. The face of the man from under the bridge. The one whose picture was circled in red and left in the package at my door. Left there by Wade after he slipped undetected into my home.

The man I told him I would kill. Because he deserved it.

CHAPTER THIRTY-ONE

The man he drags into the room is the one Clay Lucas knew from a rehab. The man Clay's parents recognized that horrible day I sat in their living room and felt their pain. Their hatred for me. Nix. Billy Brannicks.

Now it all makes sense. Wade has been hunting for this man. Taunting me in between as a distraction. But everything has been about this. This man and this moment in a place that I wrote in my post was perfect for killing.

"His name is Billy Brannicks. He goes by Nix," Wade tells me. "But you already know that. He met Clay at a program he was forced to go to as part of a plea deal for selling drugs to minors. A real piece of shit. And then, when Clay beat his mother with that shovel and ran away, he found this piece of shit because he knew where he hung out. Took him two days but he found him. He wasn't too crazy to do that, was he? Part of his brain was thinking straight. Sure, go off your meds, see all kinds of demons and monsters, and beat your mother to a bloody pulp, but when you need a place to crash, some food, some drugs, some booze—you know right where to go. And this piece of shit took him in."

I let him talk so I can think. I let him tell his story of how he found this man. How he took everything I told him about Clay and then asked the most important question—how did Clay Lucas know about the bridge to begin with? From there, he found out about Nix.

Billy Brannicks caused the shooting. Because, Wade tells me, it was his gun Clay took from a stash in his apartment. He was living with some guys who knew how to trade them. He was moving up in the world, Wade says sarcastically.

"It was painstaking work to find him. But I did, right?" Wade looks at the man and expects a nod. When he doesn't get it, he walks to him and kicks him on the side of his head, knocking him sideways until he falls over. He struggles again to sit up as Wade yells, "Didn't I?"

The man nods.

I notice then that Wade is wearing hunting boots—and that so am I. My sneakers are gone. He's changed my shoes. I wiggle my toes and can feel that they are at least four sizes too big. I could kick them off one at a time even though laces pull in the sides.

The man, too, wears boots. All of them are different makes. Different treads. And they look worn.

He's read my case about the man who killed his wife. How he wore a different size shoe to throw us off.

Shit, I think. This is the kill site. This is part of his plan.

Wade begins to pace. The excitement is too much for him now that the moment is here. It's one thing to fantasize. It's another to be living it and breathing it. Experiencing it.

Our brains react differently. They respond to the presence of other human beings. To our faces and our movements and our voices, muted as they may be, and even to our smells. The fear. Perspiration. Cologne. I smell it on the man. All of it.

Our brains react too, as our senses take in the surroundings. The room. The feel of the gun.

It's true of everything we dream about. A first date. A first kiss. Holding our baby for the first time. Skydiving. Reaching a summit. Jumping in a cold lake on a hot day. Watching the sun rise from a place we've only seen in a picture. Embracing a long-lost friend.

Dreams, fantasies, delusions—they generate from a different part of the brain than a present moment or even a memory. A memory can provoke a visceral response, good or bad. And by remembering we can grow less, or more, sensitive, depending on if the memory is of joy or trauma.

But a dream? A fantasy that's never happened? A delusion about something that is never going to happen? The emotional reaction is imaginary, so we don't recognize it when it becomes real. We can't plan for it no matter how hard we try.

Which is why every single person in Nichols that day was surprised. And why I was surprised at how my training took over in spite of everything else. The training had given me muscle memory so I knew what to do. But it could not simulate the emotions. The terror. Nothing ever can.

Wade is feeling it now. The same reaction he had when Clay Lucas stood before him with that gun and, even before that, when he heard the shots and froze while others ran for safety.

I watch him now, knowing he's surprised, and that his surprise was not part of the plan. This is an unstable situation. I watch carefully as it unfolds, and I see the wheels turning inside his head. He seems to get himself together. He takes out a zip tie and walks to the man. He drags him until he sits beside me, then locks him to the same pipe. It's the only one in the room. The only way to keep him from moving.

Then he takes out a knife and cuts me away from the pipe, pulling me to my feet. My wrists are still bound in front of me.

He grabs hold of my arm and leads me across the room and into the hallway and then the main part of the structure. It has a door, benches that line the walls, and a counter with stools. It has been cleared out entirely. The windows are all closed. The air is stagnant. Putrid, really, as the smell of sweaty men and dead animals lingers.

I hear Nix struggling to break free, pulling on the pipes, trying to scream with the gag in his mouth. He is now a captured animal, waiting for the slaughter. But I can't think about him. I have to stay focused.

"What's the plan?" I ask.

Wade lets go of my arm and steps away. I don't make a move. I can't overpower him. I can't open the door and try to run, and even if I could, I wouldn't get far. I have to find another escape.

He looks at me like he did on that back road. With adoration and longing. Only this time, he's nervous, sweating, so he removes his red jacket and hangs it on the back of the door where there are two empty hooks.

Then he wipes his brow with his hand and smiles. "Well, it's simple. I've brought you the gift. The man who put the gun in Clay Lucas's hand. The man who made you a killer."

He walks slowly backward to the jacket and pulls out a plastic baggie with small balloons inside. Only, they're not balloons. They're latex sacs filled with drugs. It's a common practice for mules, hiding drugs inside their bodies, coming across a border or through airport security. They also work well in drains and toilet basins because water and even human digestive chemicals won't erode them.

"Nice, huh? Found these on him. He's a real contributor to society. Oxy. Guns. You name it."

I think I know what's happening here. Do I? Yes. I convince myself.

I think about this structure. Things I can use. Things I learned three years ago on the case with the Kill Room.

"What am I supposed to do with this gift?" I buy time while I think. *Think!*

"Do you remember when we spoke about how much we hated them? The people who put that gun in Clay's hands? You even said you wanted them dead."

I remember thinking that many times, though I don't remember everything we said that day. Everything we've texted since. It doesn't matter. It's true, and he knows it.

"Well, there can't be justice here, Elise. Because the gun had no markings and this punk can't be tied to it, even though I have his confession. They'll say it was coerced. But how else are confessions made? You know that. Still, it won't hold up. And then what? He'll get a few years for something? Maybe they'll find more drugs at his place over the border, in New York? And they'll get jurisdiction, but those jurors won't give a shit about our little department store shooting. Do I need to go on?"

I shake my head.

"So there can't be justice. But there can be payback. Right here and right now." He takes my gun from his pocket and looks at it again like it's the key to the cage that imprisons him.

And while he does this, I remember the rifle under the counter from the case here, the execution three years before. I remember how the hunter from upstate left it on a mount—loaded perhaps, ready for the next season—because his wife wouldn't allow it in the house and because he thought no one knew about it, and the ones who did would never touch it because that's part of their code. Forensics removed it, cleared it, then returned the rifle to the owner. Our department issued a warning. But these guys do what they want. I pray that's still true—that the hunters are creatures of habit with no regard for authority.

I didn't write about the gun in my post to the students because it wasn't public information.

"It would have been so different if you hadn't turned on me that day we first met. But maybe all of this had to happen for you to finally understand."

I slowly sweep my arms against the underside of the counter. I stop when I feel something metal—the edge of the gun mount. I trace it with my fingers and search for the hunting rifle. I can make out the shape. I find the barrel and the trigger. It's there. The rifle is there!

I think now that zip ties can be broken. We learned this in our training because we use them in the field sometimes. We carry them because they're lighter than handcuffs and there could be, even for me and Rowan, a situation where we had to make an arrest during an interview. So we got the training, just like I was taught to fire my weapon even though I hadn't drawn it once in twelve years until that day that changed my life.

Wade tells me next about filming Rowan as he walked home last night. "If I'm being honest, your partner surprised me. He was so careless. I had underestimated the power of his dysfunction—the demons from the war. He lost himself so easily in those beers and that woman on the phone."

He walks to the other side of the counter so we can stand face-to-face.

I am now flush against the edge, and just beneath it is the gun with the mount. I sit on a stool and let my arms slowly drift beneath the counter. I feel for the metal, then for an edge.

"And the girls. I would like to tell you that I was sorry about that, but they never knew a thing. They were running around and playing. I wasn't going to hurt them. I was never going to do that. That would make me a monster. Did you think I would?"

I shake my head and say, "I didn't know, Wade. Honestly, I didn't know what you were up to. And then that drive-by at the diner. And Briana's tires, that word you carved into her car door . . ."

Wade nods and sighs, but it's from nerves releasing the tension that builds now as he finally gets to tell me the stories he's rehearsed for days. Weeks. And as he gets closer to the end of his plan, I still don't understand. Not entirely.

"I didn't make your husband go there. But I knew he would. I'm so sorry about that. Really. I know how painful that must have been. But aren't you glad you know?"

We cover his break-in at my house, which he says technically wasn't a break-in because I'd left the front door unlocked. And then the photos and, finally, my visit to the Lucas family.

I pretend to cough. Not once, but over and over. A spell from the chloroform. Wade gets up, looks around for a sink, but there isn't one in this room. While he's turned and my body is heaving, I break the zip tie with a quick, forceful motion against the metal of the gun mount. I feel it fall to the floor and kick it beneath the counter.

My hands are free when he turns around again.

"Sorry. No water."

I get ahold of myself and the fake coughing spell.

Wade continues with his story. "It got a little dicey there. I thought for sure you'd find me sooner. I didn't count on you watching all the hotels. I thought you'd pick the closest one right away. So I had to move things along. Make you think I'd go after your kids again."

"Yes," I say, interrupting him now. I feel for the hunting rifle with my fingers, finding the release of the mount. "I didn't know what was going on with you. I can see now that you haven't lost your mind. That you would never hurt any of us. I can see that this is about payback, like you said, for what Billy Brannicks did to us by putting that gun in Clay's hand."

He smiles widely. "Yes! Yes! Exactly. I knew you'd understand once I got you here. And this," he says, sweeping his arms around him, his eyes taking in the room. "You wrote about this place. And how it has a cremation oven. And you said in your class notes . . . do you remember what you said? About the perfect murder?"

"First, you burn the body," I tell him.

His face settles down, and he draws a breath. "Right. I signed up for a feminist studies course and got access to the entire portal. It was so easy to find your class and what you posted after. You said this was the perfect kill site. Don't you see? I did everything exactly right. The Kill Room. The cremation oven. You were just as excited writing about this place as I was to read it."

His face softens. Relaxes. We are back by the blue truck, out on that deserted road. I'm here with him, alone. The delusion is, right now, a reality. We are together, connected by our hatred for the man in the other room, who is the only one left to blame for what happened at Nichols who is still alive.

"So what now?" I ask. "Are you going to kill him and cremate the body?"

He walks closer and leans over the counter. I hold the rifle in the palms of my hands beneath it and pray he doesn't notice that I haven't moved since I sat down. That my arms remain hidden beneath the wood.

"My life is changed, Elise. I have nothing to go back to. I have to leave. And so do you. I've been waiting for you to see. To understand. Your life is changed after killing that poor sick young man. You know now about that woman in the dressing room. How I didn't see Clay Lucas fall. How I wasn't in the line of fire when you killed him. The guilt will never leave. There's nothing left for you."

I feel the hunting rifle with my hand, finding the safety and the trigger. Visualizing it in my mind. I don't let my eyes leave his. I don't let his words get inside my head.

"When you wrote, 'They don't deserve you'—that's what you meant, right? That I'm damaged now. That I can't be a wife and mother and partner. That they're better off without me."

He nods and smiles. "Do you know the expression—burn the boats?"

"Yes," I tell him. "When explorers discovered a new land and they knew it would be hard to stay, they would burn their boats so they had no choice. So their crew had no choice. There is no going back when you burn the boats."

"Precisely," he says.

I stop breathing when I hear him finish his thought.

"So I'm not the one who's going to kill Billy Brannicks. You are."

CHAPTER THIRTY-TWO

I am reeling now, fighting to hold my thoughts in place. Fighting even harder to find a response.

"You want me to kill this man? This young man—this boy? With my own gun?"

"Yes. And then you can never go back to your old life. You'll have to come with me and start over. It will be your bullet they find in the body. Your perfect murder, posted for the world to see." He waves his hands around the room like he's presenting his case. "It won't take long for them to figure it out, and then you will be prosecuted and sent to jail. Dishonored. Loathed by your children and your husband. Rowan will be ashamed. Or you can start over—the way I have to."

There it is—the reveal of his plan. How he deluded himself into believing he could have what he wanted. This connection with me. Some kind of future where we lived in mutual acknowledgment that we are one and the same. A way for him to feel accepted and to not be alone. Not for one more day.

"You've been trying to be someone you're not, and I'm going to save you. Don't you want to do it? Don't you want this man dead?" he asks me.

Yes. Of course I want that. Rage has been coursing through me since the Nichols shooting. It seeps out at every target it can find. The man who put the gun in Clay's hands. The woman who slept with my husband. The system that failed the Lucas family. Hospitals and schools. His mother who didn't make sure he took his meds. His father who didn't fight hard enough to have him committed. Who clung to the belief that they could care for him at home. Who didn't want to lose his child.

And then Mitch for showing me what I'm capable of, and Rowan for giving in to his demons, and even my girls for wanting pink towels. It's not rational, where it flows—this rage, after it's done feasting on the first course, which is always, always, myself.

Fuck, Elise. Pull yourself together! I wrap my hands around the rifle.

"Okay," I tell him. "I'll do it. But I can't leave my family. You can leave. Find another place to start over. You've gotten very good at hiding. I can see that. You've been masterful. Surpassing anything I could have taught you."

Wade is again taken aback by the change in my demeanor. He watches me now as I go on.

"The boots," I say. "Bought at different locations? The treads sanded down?"

He nods cautiously.

"And the zip ties, the chloroform, the plastic sheeting on the floor?"

He repeats the gesture.

"I presume you were careful picking up this Brannicks kid, however you managed that. He's not as small as I am. Was he high on something? Is that when you did it? He smells bad, like you've had him for a couple of days. He looks dehydrated."

"I told you, I was expecting you to find me sooner," he offers in defense. "I thought you'd be smarter. That you'd call the hotels and find out about the conference and know that would be the perfect location."

"I haven't been myself."

He looks remorseful, like he didn't mean to cause this fallout. But there is always fallout.

I continue, "The plastic will melt in the oven. The body will burn. I can do the kill so it's through and through. That way I won't have to worry about letting the body cool and searching for the bullet in a pile of ash and bone. I can't go with you. I can't burn the boats. But we will always be connected by this. You will always have this piece of me, and that has to be enough."

Wade is silent now, surprised by my proposed compromise.

"I will kill Brannicks, but not in a way that will prevent me from being with my family, from returning to my life," I continue. "I think you're right. I think this is what I need to find peace. Even if you and I are the only ones who will ever know. But how will we get out of here? How will we cover our tracks?"

He glances out the window, and I use this moment to release the rifle. I hide it behind my back.

Fantasy and reality are at war inside his head. He never believed it would be this simple. That I would leave my children. I see the wheels turning again.

"I planned it all out, Elise. How we'll leave together, where we'll go . . ."

"No—that can't happen, don't you see? You know that. I can never leave my children. If I told you I could, you would know I was lying. You would know I would always long to find my way back to them. This has to be enough. I will kill this monster, and we will be bound together forever. And then I can help you, see? I can help you stay hidden by pretending to look for you. You'll be able to live in peace, not looking over your shoulder. Find a nice girl. Maybe start a family . . ."

He moves slower now as he thinks about this new twist to his plan. It's better, and he knows it. But more than that, his delusion is morphing into something real, something tangible, and it is shifting the emotions inside him from an anxious high to a euphoric longing. He wants a normal life. He wants what he craved as a child, and I am showing him a way to have it, even after all he's done.

He looks disoriented, but the plan is taking hold. "I have the truck. I'll drive you to your car. And I brought a pull rake. Just like that man used in the case from Colorado. There won't be any tracks. And there will be too many boot prints to sort them out."

"Right," I tell him. "Too much evidence or not enough."

"Yes," he says as he settles into these new feelings. "Let's go."

I nod, tilt my head. Smile. The body language of reassurance. "Ok. How are we going to do this? Are you going to give me my gun?"

"Once we get inside the Kill Room. I'll stand behind you, then hand you the gun."

I take a breath and make my move.

I pull the rifle in front of me and aim it at his chest.

Wade is stunned—frozen the way he was that day at Nichols. But it doesn't last. Like me, he's now been here before, and he's not the same person. He has the memory of this emotion and can wrangle it under control. He lifts my gun and points it at my face.

"Oh, Elise! Why did you do that?"

"I'm sorry, Wade. I told you I'd kill Billy Brannicks, and I meant it. But not with my gun. I won't take that chance. What if the bullet gets lodged in a floorboard or the wall? What if it doesn't go through and it stays in the body? We have another weapon, and it belongs to someone else. And a dealer was shot here before. You already know that. And this way I make sure you don't hurt me when it's done."

A bead of sweat rolls down his cheek. I'm inside his head, confusing him.

"I want this to be over. I want this man dead so I can sleep at night and not fantasize about finding him and gathering evidence and watching him skip out on some technicality. So let's go in there and take care of business. Time is not our friend in this situation."

Wade's hand begins to shake as he holds my gun. "I don't believe you. There's a reason you came alone today after you knew where I was. After you saw me on the recording coming back last night. I was expecting Rowan to be with you. It was a test. If you came with Rowan or another team, I had a way out. If you came alone, that meant you wanted to take care of me your way. And that's what you did. You came alone, which means you aren't worried about justice for me either. You want me gone."

I can't argue with him. I did come alone when I could have brought an undercover team. I had most of the night to prepare. To bring in a large unit. This was the last hotel. The chances were damned good he was in it. They could have come in through the service entrance. Gotten his room number. Guarded every door. We're not as incompetent as Wade thinks. And he's not as smart as he's come to believe.

"Fine," I say. "You keep my gun. And I'll keep this one. You can hold it to my head until it's done. You can even drop me on the main road once we get clear of this place."

Wade thinks for a second and then waves his hand toward the Kill Room. I don't let him get behind me, so we walk side by side, guns drawn. It's only a few steps before we clear the entry and find Billy Brannicks huddled against the wall.

He's so young, this kid. Jeans and a hoodie. Clean shaven. Short hair. He could be one of the students I used to teach at the community college, except for the terror in his eyes.

I turn my gun from Wade and aim it at him instead. He lets out a muted scream and shakes his head back and forth. *No, no, no . . .*

"Yes," Wade says, mocking him. "Yes, yes, yes. You are going to pay for giving that gun to Clay Lucas. For being responsible for his death and for stealing something from every person in that store. You are a murderer and a thief, and this is your sentence."

Wade looks at me and nods. I release the safety on the rifle and take proper aim at the quivering young man on the floor. What I see in his eyes is different from what I saw in Clay Lucas's that day in Nichols and what I saw in Wade's just moments before. And I realize that in the moment before you take someone's life, what you really see is what's inside yourself.

I have the chance to rid the world of something dangerous. Even if all this man did was leave a gun in a place Clay Lucas could get his hands on it. The fact is that he had the gun and planned to sell it or use it and that killing him could spare a life—maybe more than one.

Now my hands shake because I know what I have to do. And that is to finish the plan I had made. The plan to lure Wade from that hotel, once I knew he was there. To walk where he could see me and find his truck, to walk and not run because that's what I would do if I were trying not to be seen. Of course, if I had not wanted to be seen,

I would have made damn sure he never saw me. I wanted him to see me coming for him. To find his truck. To give him the chance to take me and do whatever he needed to do. The reason he'd been taunting me with threats against the people I love. It was the only way to bring this story to an end.

Now, it seems, we're writing the first chapter of a new one.

I lower the gun. Billy Brannicks lets out a moan of relief, but it's short lived because Wade turns his gun now, the one he took from me, and aims at the kid on the floor.

"I knew you couldn't do it," he says.

And now comes the question I need answered. It's so desperate, this need, that I struggle to say the words. "Can you, Wade? Can you kill him? Is this really what you've become?"

Something passes through him, and I see the clarity on his face. The look of delight because, finally, he knows what he is capable of. I am the one who has given him a gift this day.

He aims my gun at the boy and pulls the trigger.

His eyes close as the gun fires because, even though he's found whatever it takes to kill another person, he doesn't have what it takes to watch him die. Still, it's enough for him. It's enough that he was able to squeeze his finger against the metal. A smile creeps over his face.

I study him carefully because I want to be sure. I have to be sure.

He opens his eyes and finds the boy sitting in the same spot—unharmed, whimpering.

His smile fades.

"Blanks," I tell him. "They're blanks. When I decided to make myself your victim this morning, I came prepared, just as you did with your chloroform and your plastic bag. I knew you'd take my gun. I didn't know what you had planned for me. I just knew that this had to end."

"You did this," he says. "You made me want to kill, and I would have done it! I would have killed him!"

"No," I tell him. "I didn't make you anything. I don't know how it happened. Whatever it is you've become—that's not on me. But this is."

I raise the rifle and point it at his chest, and I think I can do it. I think I have it in me and, *Christ*, how I've thought about this moment every second since that back road.

I hear the words inside my head. *Pull the trigger!*

But I can't. I don't. I hesitate.

Wade sees it on my face or in my eyes. Or maybe it's the split second that passes when I don't kill him. Like a missed beat in a song. He knows. And then he acts, raising my gun over his head, the metal handle facing down, ready to strike me.

Wade is a killer even though he has yet to take a life.

His hand comes down and my finger pulls and the rifle fires. Wade collapses onto me, and we fall to the floor. I feel the weight of him. The deadness of it.

And I know that this is, finally, over.

CHAPTER THIRTY-THREE

I roll Wade off of me and stand. Then I turn to Billy Brannicks who has gone silent. He'd been more afraid of Wade than me, but now all of that has changed.

I look at him and try to process what I'm feeling. I walk to him slowly. "Do not scream."

He nods.

I pull off the tape that covers his mouth. "Tell me how it happened."

"How what happened?" he asks.

I say simply, "The gun."

He's heard enough to understand what this is about. How I'm connected to Wade and why Wade brought him here to die at my hand. So he tells me about Clay Lucas. Where they met, how they became friendly. Clay was medicated, so to Brannicks, it was just killing time, talking to this semiconscious kid. But Clay remembered things he'd said. He knew where Brannicks hung out. Where he sold his drugs. And Clay found him.

Brannicks gave him shelter for a few nights. Clay had access to a small stash of guns Brannicks's roommate bought from a guy in New Jersey. It was done online, he tells me. They used code words. Transacted in cash. The drops were always remote. Nothing in person.

He tells me that Clay said some "crazy-ass shit about demons and zombies" and that he was obsessed with some "chick" from a place his parents sent him when they had to work.

I ask him if her name was Laurel Hayes, and he says, "Yeah, I think."

And then he tells me the strangest thing. "He said she was in trouble. That the devil was after her, and she was scared. He said he needed to kill the devil."

And right then, the last few missing pieces of the puzzle fall into place.

"How did he end up at Nichols that day?" I ask him.

Brannicks tells me without hesitation. He has no idea how unhinged I might be. "I told him he had to leave. I asked him where he wanted to go, and he directed me through the streets until we got to this parking lot on Elmford . . ."

"Elmford? That's adjacent to Clear Horizons. The adult care center."

Brannicks doesn't know the place. He let Clay out of his car in the parking lot, and he walked over to a blue truck—the same one that was sitting outside right now—and climbed in the open flatbed.

"Wait . . ." I stop him, thinking this through. "He climbed into the blue truck and hid in the back? With a gun he stole from your apartment?"

Brannicks shakes his head. "I didn't know he had the gun. He carried a backpack. And he was fucking crazy! I dropped him and left. Never wanted to see him again."

Wade and Laurel Hayes. Clay Lucas and Laurel Hayes. She must have confided in Clay about Wade's behavior. He knew where to find Wade. Where he parked his truck near Laurel's work. He got in Wade's truck, and they drove to Nichols. Then he followed him inside. Hunted him like an animal.

My God. That's why he didn't shoot anyone else. That's why he stopped when he found Wade in the men's department. The cameras outside the store recorded Clay walking in alone with the backpack. And the few blurred images we had of Wade show him walking casually, not running or looking behind him. He had no idea he was being followed. Hunted down. Not even when he stood frozen, Clay right in front of him pointing the gun. He had no idea everything that happened that day was because of him. No one did. Until right here and now as the pieces all come together.

The thought tears through me, nearly sending me to my knees. Clay Lucas was going to kill Wade. He wasn't there to draw fire on himself. He wasn't trying to get killed—suicide by cop. I don't know how this makes me feel. Now I've killed them both.

"I didn't know," Brannicks says again. "I mean, I thought he was just a weird dude on some weird shit."

"Give me a name," I tell him. "The guy in New Jersey." I have no idea where this comes from. The rage hasn't left me. Maybe it never will.

He shakes his head.

I raise the rifle and press it to his forehead. "Give me a name, and I'll let you live."

He doesn't know what to make of me. I've just killed a man in front of him. He has no idea what I'm capable of. He didn't see the hesitation. The missed beat. So he gives me a name. I've heard it before. He's a known dealer who comes from Newark to feed on our little reef. And it's enough. For now.

"Listen carefully to what's going to happen next. If you do everything right, everything I say, you can get out of this mess. You can start over."

CHAPTER THIRTY-FOUR

Laurel Hayes's friend—Kendra—is scared now, thinking that the man stalking Laurel hacked into her phone account and was tracing her calls and texts. Maybe even her location. She leaves the meeting with the woman on the team and doesn't notice that a young man follows her.

She goes back to her apartment. An hour passes. Then another woman comes out, wearing a hoodie and sunglasses and carrying a duffel bag. She's on the move, this woman.

The man follows her on foot. The woman investigator is close behind in an unmarked car. The woman they follow walks to a parking garage four blocks away and enters. She stops at a car and opens the trunk, tosses the duffel inside, closes the trunk, and proceeds to the driver's side.

"Do we have confirmation?" the man asks, watching her from two rows away.

The car is a dark gray Toyota with plates 275 TFG.

The woman in the unmarked car responds, "Yes—confirmed. The car is registered to Laurel Hayes."

"Should I pick her up?"

He walks and listens at the same time. She's about to close the door.

"Yes—confirmed. Pick her up."

He approaches with caution, badge in hand. He knocks on the window, presses the badge against the glass.

Laurel Hayes puts her hands in the air. It's a common reflex. She follows the instructions to exit the vehicle. She is trusting and compliant, not wanting to cause any trouble, and the woman who now watches from the unmarked car thinks that this is exactly the behavior that attracted her stalker—the man with the red jacket who sat across from her work at a bus station.

Laurel Hayes has been hiding at Kendra's. She told her parents as soon as she found out the police had called them, scared them half to death. That's when they flew back to Portland. When they learned about the man stalking her, they stopped helping with the effort to get her dental records. She'd left town because of her connection to Clay Lucas, but now she needed to stay gone. It was better if this psycho thought she was dead. They didn't have a plan beyond keeping her safe. They had heard enough stories over the years—true stories—to know that the police were ineffective when it came to situations like this.

It isn't until the investigators speak with me that they learn the identity of the stalker. When they show me their file and tell me the details of their investigation to this point, I see the photo of the man with the red jacket sitting on the bench across the street from Clear Horizons and recognize him in an instant. I do not tell them all that I know—how their investigation and ours have collided head-on or how deeply Elise is wrapped up in this case—but I assure them that Laurel Hayes is safe now because the man who's been stalking her is dead.

CHAPTER THIRTY-FIVE

Brannicks and I wrap Wade in the plastic. We carry him down to the basement, put him in the oven. I turn it on and let it run.

I am a machine. Fight-or-flight chemicals surging through my veins. Unlike the day of the shooting, I don't shake or tremble. What has to be done is crystal clear, and I feel no hesitation. Rowan would tell me these are the callouses.

I wipe down wherever our prints might be and leave the rest. I do the same with the rifle and return it to the mount under the counter. I retrieve the casing from the Kill Room. Brannicks watches and waits. I tell him the rest of the bullets in my gun are real, and he doesn't know it's a lie. I don't trust him, and he doesn't trust me. But we're in this together now.

I forget about the red jacket that hangs on the hook on the back of the door after I've removed the drugs. I forget because the door is open while I do a final check. I step outside and pull it closed and never even see it hanging there. I haven't slept for days, and I'm emotional as hell. I'm bound to make a mistake.

When I'm done with the shelter, I go out to the well. The dealers used to hide their stash here by connecting it to a rope and lowering it down. The rope is still attached, so I connect the Oxy balloons and let them fall. Now there will be something to find.

Next, I move around the side of the shelter to the truck where I told Brannicks to wait. Wade backed it up the hill, so it's not hard to drive out, the pull rake dragging behind us. When it gets stuck, Brannicks gets out, clears the brush from the blades, then gets back in. The leaves have started to fall, so those get picked up as well. It takes half an hour, but we reach the end of the road and make our escape leaving no tire tracks.

From there we drive to the parking lot where I'd left my car. I park the truck behind a semi to block us from any security cameras.

"There's money in the back," I tell him. Wade brought everything with him, including a duffel with his savings and 401(k) proceeds. "It's a lot of money. Enough for you to disappear, start a new life. Do you understand what I'm saying?"

He nods. There's been time to think. And for me to tell him about the situation he's in. Maybe I'm in one too, but who would believe a crazy-ass story from a punk kid trying to escape a murder charge? I tell him he's one phone call away from being wanted by the feds and another call away from being wanted by the guy known as Diesel, who sold his roommate the gun that was used in the Nichols shooting. The guy whose name he just gave up to me, a cop, making him a snitch.

"You are going to sink this truck in the river not far from here. Within twenty miles. You are going to wipe it down, every inch of it. Make sure the doors are open."

I go to my car and grab the keys hidden under the wheel well. I get a tracker from the trunk—the one I bought and registered online under Wade's real name, Brett Emory. I convince myself that the remains will not be found until next year when the hunters return. Maybe it's just a prayer. The criminals who come and go in the off-season don't have any use for the cremation oven.

Tomorrow, an anonymous tip will help them discover the tracker under Wade's real name and then see the last place the truck was online. This will lead them to the location along the river where Brannicks sinks it. Divers will discover the truck. A towing unit will pull it from the water, and all they'll find inside is a duffel bag with the clothes he brought with him from the Getaway Inn. He hadn't planned to return to that place after kidnapping me and bringing me to the shelter. His wallet will be in the console, but there will be no prints. And no bag of money. Brannicks will take that to start his new life.

When his body isn't found, they will assume he's dead, carried down the river to the ocean. The current is strong. The case of the 404 will be closed. By the time his body is found next season in the shelter, it will be unidentifiable—an unrelated mystery to solve.

I pop open a panel under the steering wheel of Wade's truck and place the tracker inside.

"Okay," I tell Brannicks. "Now I'll know where you are. I'll know if you do what I tell you. If the tracker isn't found in that truck when it sinks, everyone on the street will know you gave up your boss."

He stares at me like I really am crazy. Like I'm worse than any criminal he's ever dealt with before. Because I tell him all of this without a trace of emotion.

That will come later. After I've returned to my car. And opened the door. And climbed inside. And finished what I started.

CHAPTER THIRTY-SIX

The first thing I do is leave an envelope on the windshield of Rowan's car. Inside is the account information for the tracker I left in Wade's blue truck. Tomorrow, they'll find the truck in the river. They'll match the VIN number and know it's his, even though he changed the plates. They'll send divers to look for his body. The beginning of the end to the case of the 404.

The second thing I do is go home. It's late, and the house is empty.

I sit on the floor in my daughters' room, one small lamp turned on. I place the two phones on the floor. Mine and the burner Brett Emory used to torment me. I force myself to use his real name now, even inside my head, from this moment forward.

I feel no relief that this is over. The torment has stopped, but something else is just beginning.

Staring at the two phones, I lay out my thoughts like cards in a game of solitaire. One at a time, in a neat row, and then down into columns. Each one put in a place where I can see it. Make sense of it. Organize it in a way that I can live with. A narrative of what has happened to me and Clay Lucas and now Brett Emory.

I examine first the cards about Brett. I consider Dr. Landyn's analysis, and that gives me a context for what I learned when I watched him pull the trigger of my gun with his eyes closed, finally evolving into a man who could kill another man bound and gagged, whimpering on the floor.

Billy Brannicks was not a threat. Not in that moment. There was still a chance for him to change. To make a better life. It was not the same as the moment I pulled a trigger and killed Clay Lucas. This is not a lie I tell myself so I can find peace. It is the truth. Though peace, I fear, will remain elusive.

Next is the card with Vera Pratt and her unborn son in that dressing room. Then the coworker Brett assaulted in the elevator. After that, Laurel Hayes. I don't know the details yet, but he did something to her. Enough to make her confide in Clay Lucas. Enough to make Clay find a gun and hunt him down in Nichols that day. And now she's disappeared.

Finally, what he did to me on that back road and every day since. He was not going to stop.

I stare at these cards and repeat this over and over: *He was not going to stop.*

I think about justice and whether it has been served. Whether it is ever served. Billy Brannicks led Clay to a stash of guns—whether they were his or not didn't matter. He would never pay for that crime, but he'd given me a name—the dealer who calls himself Diesel—and with that name, maybe there would be a different kind of justice. Brannicks would have to stay gone to avoid retaliation. And we might stop another Clay Lucas from killing or being killed.

I stare at the cards, my thoughts, carefully laid out. More rush in, and I fight to keep up with them. I close my eyes, and they play like a silent movie.

Rowan walking down that street, Brett strolling behind him with a baseball bat. My girls on the playground, and Mitch kissing me goodbye at our front door. The shadow in my bedroom that I see through the steam in my shower. Brett pulling the trigger of my gun, aimed squarely at Billy Brannicks. Clay Lucas, his head turned, those eyes looking into mine as I pull the same trigger. And, finally, Brett's eyes as I fired the rifle into his gut and felt him fall into me.

What unsettles me now are the loose ends after every crime. Every loss. Every trauma that uproots the moral compass inside every one of us. Uproots it and then leaves it to roam freely until we can find it again. Reshape it. Make it square with our new reality. The things we feel and the things we know about ourselves that are new and disturbing. What unsettles me is what remains inside when a loved one is found, dead or alive, when it is learned that a child is never coming home, when the gunman is killed and the shooting has stopped, and we are still breathing.

What remains inside of us is uncertain. Unknown. Unfamiliar. Unruly.

What remains inside of me now I haven't even begun to investigate. I find refuge in one single moment. The hesitation as I held that rifle to Brett Emory's chest. The missed beat before my finger pulled the trigger.

If this is all there is, all that remains, I pray it will be enough.

CHAPTER THIRTY-SEVEN

The investigation into the shelter killing is just five days old when I first hear of it from Aaron. They have moved quickly.

He calls me into his office, not because of the remains that have been found, but because he can't find Elise. If anyone would know where she's gone, it would be me. Her partner.

"She's not answering her cell. She's not with her family in Florida. I sent a unit to her house and no one answered," he tells me.

I think carefully about how to respond. She's not ready to come back.

Aaron continues, "We tracked her phone to the house. There's been no activity since she called you. What exactly did she say when you told her the 404 was dead?"

I shrug. "Something about a retreat."

Aaron nods, thinks on this for a moment. "I'm sure it was a relief, having this whole thing over. But strange that she's not with her children, isn't it?"

I weigh my options. If I tell him about the problems she'd been having with Mitch over the Briana situation, this inquiry will be put to bed. Aaron won't press me for more details because he won't want to intrude on her personal business. Of course, he will never look at her the same knowing this about her marriage. I don't know exactly how he will look at her—whether he'll think more of her for sticking it out or less of her for sticking it out—but it will be different.

If I don't explain why, after Brett Emory's truck has been found in the river, an apparent accident having caused his truck to barrel down an embankment and plunge off the side of a ledge, she didn't run into the arms of her husband and little girls, he will also look at her differently. Isn't that the first thing any of us would do after living in fear for weeks? After being stalked and threatened? It was time for celebration. Or at least a return to normal life.

I make a decision and don't look back.

"Remember that woman whose car was vandalized?"

I don't give too many details. Just that her name was Briana and that Elise's husband had an affair with her four years ago and that we think Brett Emory is the one who keyed her car to cause trouble in their marriage.

Aaron hides his shock and disapproval that none of this was brought to his attention when it was happening. "Is that all in the report?" he asks.

"It will be. I'm pulling everything together now. Briana, the assault on the coworker, the truck registered to Brett Emory—"

"And the tracker that was inside the truck."

"Yes. That was a lucky break, finding that account."

Aaron wags his finger at me. "Not luck. That was hard work. How many companies did you have to call?"

It was a lot, but it was because I had to make it look good. The envelope containing the account information for the tracker was left on my windshield the day Elise said she was leaving town. I didn't want to know how she got it.

So I made the calls and eventually "stumbled" upon the account registered to Brett Emory. We found the truck later that day, pulled it out of the river. No way anyone survived that crash. Both doors had swung open. Brett Emory's body was long gone.

The tracker first placed the truck in a parking lot near a Getaway Inn.

Brett Emory was identified by the staff. Used the name Fisher Brand and paid in cash. He'd checked out the same day I woke up with a hangover and a message from Elise saying she was leaving town. Strange that the tracker wasn't turned on until later that afternoon.

Aaron suddenly remembers why he's asking about Elise. "They've found a body," he begins and tells me everything he knows. About the burned remains and the cremation oven, the drugs found in the well and residue in the pockets of a red jacket hanging on the back of the door, the pull rake used to clear the tracks on the road leading up to the shelter. "They think the killer accessed Elise's posts for that class she used to teach. Did you know she was doing that?"

And I think one word over and over: *Fuck.*

"Yeah," I tell him. "So—what are they thinking? That it was a student at the college?"

"It seems like a long shot to me, but they're looking into anyone who accessed all of her posts. Especially the one about the killing three years ago—that drug execution."

"Right," I tell him. But, really, I'm thinking that word. *Fuck.*

"They had two possible victims from missing persons reports. The first was Laurel Hayes, who, as you know, has just been found. Leaving one lead—a drug dealer named Billy Brannicks. Some CI reported him missing in New York."

"So a coincidence? With Elise's posts?"

"Has to be."

"And this Brannicks guy? What's the fixation there?"

Aaron tells me Brannicks was a dealer. They think the body was burned between five and seven days ago and likely killed there—at the shelter.

"In the Kill Room," I say.

"Yeah."

"So maybe drug related?"

Aaron agrees, but it's not our case. Not our problem. He just wants to make sure Elise is all right.

"I'll find her," I promise him. And I will. But first, I need answers. "Do you mind if I speak with them?"

"The state investigators?"

I tell him that yes, I might be able to help. After all, this is what I do. Solve impossible cases.

"Be my guest," Aaron says.

CHAPTER THIRTY-EIGHT

THE KILL ROOM

I use my key to go in through the back door. I smell coffee. Really shitty coffee.

"Elise?" I call out. I hear movement upstairs, which concerns me. She hasn't left the house since she put that envelope on my windshield. I found her here the next day.

She sleeps all day. Scours the file on the 404 all night, watching the footage from the cameras, fueled by the shitty coffee and the voice inside her head that's fighting to climb out of the depression. This is the next stage, Dr. Landyn has assured me. It's normal. It's progress. Don't I remember? Landyn has no idea how good I am at making myself forget.

"She couldn't let herself go there until the crisis was over," he explained.

The first trauma was the shooting in the men's department of Nichols Depot. The second was the assault. And the third, the stalking by Brett Emory. The ongoing threat has kept her in an elevated survival state. Now that it's over and she's come down from that high, the pain of each trauma has to be processed. So now we wait. Me. Mitch. The little wardens.

She carries a prepaid phone with her so she can call them, which she does throughout the day. Mitch wants to come home. The wardens are on the fence. They miss their mom, but not school and homework. Amy, though, has been doing her assignments online. Fourth grade can be a bitch. I check in with them after each call with their mom. They all know something isn't right, so it falls on me to reassure them.

Elise says she doesn't want anyone else to know she's here, holed up in her house. So she leaves her real phone off. But I think maybe she doesn't want to be reminded of the messages that used to come. The live feed of her girls at school. The warnings that he could get to them if he wanted to. I make a note to buy her a new phone. Erase the history.

Sometimes I sit with her in the dark while she stares out a window. I ramble about work, benign stuff. Nothing about wrapping up the 404 case or the ongoing search for the gun dealer. I tell her that when she gets back, I'll let her pick the oldest box in the basement, the worst dogshit case we've got. And I'll work it with her start to finish, no matter how tedious it becomes. Hell, I'd help her find a missing cat if she'd dig herself out of this hole.

Other times she tries to respond, talking about what the wardens did with their grandmother and Mitch that day. Now that the threat is gone, they'd been venturing out. Disney was on their agenda, and I got her to smile by talking about Mitch riding on "it's a small world." But that smile led to tears like the emotions were walking in lockstep. Joy and despair.

She says she'll never be the same, having killed Clay Lucas. She says she sees his eyes, his face, in her dreams at night. Twisted, dark dreams that replay that moment. It doesn't matter what I tell her. How many people I've killed. How it gets easier to live with. We all go to our graves covered in the scars from the things we've done and the things done to us. Nothing helps her.

There has to be more. I know there is. But now is not the time. Dr. Landyn says to be patient, so I am. But covering her ass on the job just got a hell of a lot harder.

"Elise? I'm coming up!"

I walk through a house that used to bustle with energy. Lights on, kids playing. Food in the oven or waiting in a takeout bag on the counter.

Mitch always had shit to talk about, guy shit because he was outnumbered here, his deep voice bellowing about the cost of lumber or some project in the garage. And Elise, quietly soaking it in, letting it fill her up and now there's, what? Dark. Quiet. This can't be helping.

I find her asleep in Amy's bed, a half-empty glass of scotch on the floor beside it. I kneel beside her and touch her shoulder.

"Hey. It's me. We need to talk."

Back in the kitchen, I make a fresh pot of coffee. She sits at the table and stares at nothing. The next stage is supposed to be acceptance, then hope. I'd settle for some caustic sarcasm.

I start out slowly. "They found a body, Elise. Remains."

This gets her attention. I thought it might.

I tell her everything, start to finish. The similarity to her posts. The drugs. The Kill Room.

"And Laurel Hayes—she's alive. They found her, which, frankly, makes us look like schmucks. They used our file to track her to her friend's house. It was all right there."

Finally, she speaks. "What did we miss?"

I see a spark of light and hold my breath, praying for another. "The camera outside Clear Horizons. We were looking for Clay Lucas. They were looking for anyone suspicious—a man, in particular." I tell her about the young investigator from the state team who spotted the guy at the bus stop day after day. "Sometimes he wore a red jacket—and they found a red jacket hanging on the back of the door inside the shelter."

It takes her a second, but then she draws a long breath. She's coming back to life. "It couldn't be seen when the door was open," she says, more to herself than to me.

"Right."

"Still . . ."

"I know. A serious fuckup. They found traces of drugs in the pockets. Then more of the same in the well outside."

I tell her I met Laurel Hayes this afternoon after I drove up to speak with the investigators. They had her in a safe house while they looked into this man who's been stalking her.

"The thing is, Elise, there were too many coincidences. Laurel Hayes knew Clay Lucas. She admitted that she kept in touch with him after he stopped coming to the day center. Mostly by text, but FaceTime as well. She told him about the man who wouldn't leave her alone. How he sat at the bus stop and watched her at work, and then followed her home and watched her there. He drove a blue truck."

I wait. Let that sink in. Elise drinks the coffee and sits up straighter.

"I showed her our photo of Brett Emory and sure as shit she confirmed what I already knew—it was the same guy."

She looks at me now, and I finish the story.

"Clay must have waited and watched that bus stop, looking for the man who was stalking Laurel. He followed Brett to Nichols that day. He was there to kill him."

Strangely, she doesn't flinch. Not a shred of emotion washes over her face.

I tell her next about the missing drug dealer the investigators now think was killed at the shelter. His name is Billy Brannicks, and he was seen under the bridge in our town.

She listens. And thinks.

I remind her that Clay was also seen under the bridge. "And when they found Brannicks's apartment, they also found guns, along with the usual stuff—drugs and cash and, get this, a litter of pit bull puppies pissing and shitting all over the place." I let her think this through before continuing. "So the missing link," I say, "is connecting Brannicks to Clay Lucas with more than proximity. We can put them both under the bridge, but not at the same time."

She looks away. Nods. She understands.

"Do you think we'll find the connection? The missing piece?" I ask.

"And if we do? What does that mean? I assume they can't confirm the remains belong to Brannicks."

"Right. No dental records, and that's all that's left of him. We'd have to speak to the Lucas family. Go back over Clay's life. Every inch of it.

Brannicks's roommates aren't talking. And no one's thought to match the gun Clay used at Nichols to the ones found in that apartment."

"Half the battle is knowing what questions to ask," she says. "And where to ask them."

We sit quietly for a long moment. I can see her making calculations—not in her head, but in her heart.

She reaches out and takes my hand. "Clay didn't follow Brett Emory to Nichols. He was hiding in the back of his truck."

I stare at my partner as the implications unfold. "Tell me . . ."

Her cheeks flush, her eyes well with tears. She can't catch her breath.

"Elise," I plead with her. "Let me help you."

She falls into me and lets go. This part I remember. When I fell, there was no one to catch me. That's not going to happen here.

EPILOGUE

Mitch finds me in the kitchen. I've made coffee and poured some for him in his travel mug. I feel his arms around me, his lips close to my ear. Warm breath.

"Good morning," he says. A kiss follows when I turn my head.

"Busy day?" I ask.

He's working on a new kitchen across town. The client is a pain in the ass, constantly changing his mind about fixtures and appliances. He doesn't understand that every time he does this, they have to take new measurements for the countertops and cabinets because everything has to fit together like a puzzle.

I understand puzzles.

"I'll be glad when this one's over."

I walk him to the door. We exchange another kiss. Nothing spectacular. Just normal. Like we've been doing this same kiss for sixteen years. Like it was never interrupted by an affair or a shooting at a department store. I watch him walk to his car, and in spite of myself, I look up and down the street, then lock the door behind me.

Next come the girls about an hour later. I've made the muffins for the afternoon snack because Kelly will meet them at the bus and I will be working a full day. It's going on a year now, and just like the kiss at the door, we've slipped back into this part of our routine as well. As if nothing has happened.

Fran comes first. Wild hair. Sleepy eyes. She sits at the table and moans. This is the start, I think. In another year, I'll have two girls to rouse from their sleep and no little bodies trying to sneak into our bed before the day pulls us away from one another.

"Hello, my sweet," I say, kissing her on the head.

I bring cereal and milk and a banana to the table.

"Are you working in that other place today?" she asks me.

"New Jersey?"

"Yeah."

"Will you be late?"

"Nope. Right on time."

She nods. "Good. Because last time you were late, Daddy cooked dinner, and he made us eat broccoli."

"What! That's horrible."

Amy is here now and joins the conversation. "It's child abuse," she says.

They are both at the table, and I sit with them for this moment—this wonderful, average moment—and feel grateful.

When the bus leaves, I drive to the station and meet Rowan. We gather our things, get in our SUV, stop for coffee. Then we drive to Newark.

We've been working there with a local narcotics team, trying to gather evidence on this man called Diesel, whose real name is Drew Garrison. Rowan told them about the connection to the presumed-dead drug dealer, Billy Brannicks, and said it came from a transient he'd talked to under the bridge. It was one of many lies he would tell to weave our story together.

When he held me in my kitchen that day that feels like a lifetime ago, he listened while I made my confession.

I started from the moment I began working on my own, in secret, to find Brett Emory. The phone he left in my living room and all of the messages he sent to it. The video of Mitch and Briana. The photos of our team at the Ridgeway, me asleep on my sofa, the cafeteria at my girls' school. I'd saved everything.

He stopped when he saw the screenshot of the night Brett followed him to his apartment. "Motherfucker . . ."

I didn't stop there. I told him about the break-in and the photo of Billy Brannicks and my visit to the Lucas family. How I'd hidden a camera at the Ridgeway Shopping Center and then found the car and zeroed in on the Getaway Inn.

He listened, holding back the urge to yell and scream because I had made myself bait, walking past the hotel until I found his truck and then keeping my back turned, allowing him to take me.

I needed it to end, I explained. This was what he wanted, and he wasn't going to stop until he had it, until he had me in a way that made him feel like he was in control.

I described the last scene in the Kill Room. My gun in Brett Emory's hand, aimed at Brannicks.

He pulled the trigger.

When I got to the last part, where I thought I could kill him, I got stuck on the words.

I couldn't do it. I hesitated.

Rowan already knew the rest because the body had been found, the red jacket hanging on the back of the door. Brett Emory's red jacket.

"He was going to kill you," Rowan said. "You had no choice. Just like Clay Lucas in that store."

"There's always a choice," I said.

We stayed there for a long time, in my kitchen. I cried until there was nothing left inside me. I cried for Clay Lucas and his family. For Vera Pratt and Laurel Hayes and the actuary named Georgina. I even cried for Brett Emory, whose life had been set off course when he was a child, never righting itself.

Something lifted then. It's hard to describe even now, a year later. I think it was the loneliness I had described to Dr. Landyn, the loneliness from not being known by the people I love.

Rowan told me that night in my house that he had his own scars.

That they don't ever leave but you learn to live with them. The next stage of recovery. *Acceptance.*

And that was enough.

He put me on a plane to Florida the next morning. I slept the whole way. I remember walking out of the airport into sunlight and warmth and the arms of my family. The girls wrapped themselves around my waist, but Mitch—he held my face, looked into my eyes, and said those three words that can mean everything or nothing, but then and there meant everything: "I love you."

I haven't looked back.

Now Rowan and I work the case to link the gun from the Nichols shooting to this dealer in Newark. We work with the team in Newark collecting information from sources and doing surveillance. It's dull most days. Far less exciting to me than pulling a dusty box from the basement and finding a piece of gold. Making magic by bringing peace to the bereaved and justice to the victims.

But it makes Rowan happy. I know we'll get him one of these days. And after we do, there will be another one like him. I suspect I will lose Rowan to this work. It's where he belongs. What remains inside of him after all that's happened, knowing he was stalked and taunted by Brett Emory, is a kind of reckoning with his past. His demons are being evicted by his pride.

We park outside a building—the last known location of Diesel's girlfriend—and if we see him, we might be able to follow him somewhere and get pictures and new names to investigate. We might even catch him at a drop, though that feels unlikely. So we settle in, drink our coffee, which has grown cold, and talk about his date last night and my plans for Amy's birthday party. She's turning ten.

We don't talk about the past, his or mine, because we can't get back the pieces that have changed or been lost completely. Instead, we look ahead, embracing whatever the hell it is we are now. Damaged and broken and scarred. Sometimes I barely recognize the woman I see in the mirror. But other times, I know exactly who she is. And I give her a forgiving smile.

ACKNOWLEDGMENTS

Being an author is a journey. It has taken me on highways, winding back roads, and bumpy dirt paths. Every book has been a new adventure. It is, at once, joyful and terrifying—which is why there are many people to thank for helping me succeed.

I am beyond grateful to my agent, Elisabeth Weed, and the team at Blackstone Publishing, for believing in this book from the very start. To Addi Wright and Celia Blue Johnson—your impeccable editing guided me toward the best version of Elise's story, uncovering my blind spots while honoring my passion for exploring the impact of trauma. With every book, I strive to learn and grow as a writer. Working with all of you has been an absolute dream.

To my team at CAA, Michelle Weiner and Olivia Blaustein, you have gone above and beyond in promoting my work. And to Jenny Meyer, thank you for bringing my books into the foreign markets with persistence, even in the most difficult of times.

To the writing community—I have no words to adequately express how crucial you are to my life as a writer. You never fail to lend advice, help promote my work, make me laugh, and pretty much do whatever I've needed to stave off self-doubt and the crazy-making isolation that is at the core of our profession. I love being a part of this world.

To Detective Christy F. Girard, thank you for inspiring many aspects of Elise, providing professional guidance, and answering every off-the-wall question that arrived in your inbox.

To my family and friends, because of you, I am never lacking for encouragement and support. I am deeply grateful.

And to my amazing sons who are now out in the world—you inspire me every day with your creativity, passion, and love. Being your mom will always be the best thing I've done in my life.

ABOUT THE AUTHOR

WENDY WALKER is the author of the psychological suspense novels *All Is Not Forgotten*, *Emma in the Night*, *The Night Before*, *Don't Look for Me*, and *American Girl*. Her novels have been translated into twenty-three foreign languages, topped bestseller lists both nationally and abroad, and have been optioned for both television and film. Wendy holds degrees from Brown University and Georgetown Law School. She is a former family law attorney with training in child advocacy, and has worked in finance and several areas of the law.